An Absence of Ethics

J.B. Millhollin

TouchPoint
Press

AN ABSENCE OF ETHICS by J.B. Millhollin
Published by TouchPoint Press
2075 Attala Road 1990
Kosciusko, MS 39090
www.touchpointpress.com

Copyright © 2014 J.B. Millhollin
All rights reserved.

ISBN-10: 0692249206
ISBN-13: 978-0-69224-920-8

This is a work of fiction. Names, places, characters, and events are fictitious. Any similarities to actual events and persons, living or dead, are purely coincidental. Any trademarks, service marks, product names, or named features are assumed to be the property of their respective owners and are used only for reference. If any of these terms are used, no endorsement is implied. Except for review purposes, the reproduction of this book, in whole or part, electronically or mechanically, constitutes a copyright violation. Address permissions and review inquiries to media@touchpointpress.com.

Editor: Taylor Bell
Cover Design: Colbie Myles, colbiemyles.com
Cover image © Scales of Justice, Image # 01-012, Lawyersites.net

Visit the author's website at www.jbmillhollin.com

First Edition

Printed in the United States of America.

10 9 8 7 6 5 4 3 2 1

J.B. Millhollin was born in Southwest Iowa and attended Law School at the University of Nebraska. He began practicing law in Corning, Iowa and remained in practice in that small farming community for 41 years. He left Corning with his wife of 42 years, in 2012 and now resides in Mt. Juliet, Tennessee. His current plans are to continue to write until he is too old to figure out how to use the computer.

Books by J.B. Millhollin

Brakus Series
Brakus
Everything He Touched

Prologue

Interstate 87, North of New York City

If his passenger had only known the purpose of this journey! Would he continue to insist on offering paltry, insignificant dialog or would the conversation suddenly turn meaningful? Would he be so quick to criticize the Family and its purpose as an integral part of society? If he knew, would he get down on his knees and beg for forgiveness or take his punishment like a man? These were all questions which would never be answered because at the precise moment Joey understood the purpose of the journey, he would die.

Tommie Thompson was driving up Interstate 87 about 60 miles north of New York City with an asshole, Joey Stringer, for a passenger and a dead body in the trunk. While Joey carried on a never-ending line of incessant bullshit, Tommie made certain he drove at precisely the speed limit. Being pulled over by a state dick at this moment would indeed complicate the trip.

As Joey continued his crusade to attempt to set a record for the longest one-man conversation needing absolutely no fucking response, he thought back on the events of the past week which brought them near their journey's conclusion.

Tommie had been told a week ago that Danny Blackstone needed to be removed—as in eliminated—as in murdered. Blackstone was the Family's attorney and had been employed in that capacity for years. But recently the Family had learned he had been telling tales out of school. They determined one night, after he had had too much scotch while socializing within a very public location, that he had bragged about representing the Family and had, in fact, told the group about an incident or two which should have never been revealed.

With the Family you soon find out once is once too much—there are no second chances. Word of the disclosure passed quickly and the decision was made to eradicate the source.

Originally, Tommie had been told to do the job himself. So he started to follow Blackstone to determine the most advantageous time and location to start the elimination process. He knew Blackstone well. He had attended many meetings with Blackstone involving Family business and had been his driver on many other occasions. To say they were friends was a reach—Blackstone was loud, obnoxious and overbearing. But, on the other hand, they did know each other well enough to be on a first-name basis. So when Blackstone was called by one of the Family members and told he would be picked up by Tommie and driven to a Family meeting, it did not seem out of the ordinary.

But Blackstone never reached the meeting. Along the way, a .45 with a silencer found its mark repeatedly. The end result was both favorable and unfavorable for Blackstone; he was dead, but then again, he would never need to worry about another monthly alimony payment to the "bitch." Tommie had placed the body of Blackstone in the trunk. It had been there a couple of days and the smell of rotting flesh was just starting to make its short, inevitable journey to the front seat.

The complicating factor was during the week it had been determined that a longtime Family employee, Joey Stringer, was banging one of the Family's bosses wives, and that it had become necessary to conclude his employment status immediately.

Initially, there was talk of simply beating the shit out of him but letting him remain in the employment of the Family. However, the husband of the woman he was banging quickly vetoed that notion, and it was decided he needed to be completely eliminated.

Since, in the near future, the Family would have to dispose of Blackstone's body anyway, they determined Tommy should simply dispose of two bodies, thus making maximum use of his effort and resolving the "Stringer" matter at the same time.

Tommie really felt the pricks could have consulted him concerning whether this double murder business was acceptable to him, but that wasn't the way it worked. He was never, ever *asked* to do anything. He was *told*. And, if he didn't want to end up at the same destination to which he was now headed, it would be prudent to complete the task successfully and without comment.

Joey again interrupted the sanctity of silence when he said, "Hey Tommie, what do you think of them Jets? Pretty fucking awful aren't they? Dirty bastards. I remember when…"

Tommie knew the entire trip would be like this. The son of a bitch never stopped talking. There would have probably been plenty of support within the Family to terminate him based strictly upon his continuous line of bullshit without even considering the fact he was screwing one of the bosses' wives.

The Family had a small burial site west of Interstate 87 outside of Kingston, New York. It was located deep within the trees and used infrequently. This was where the attorney would be laid to rest. They would need to dig a shallow grave for him once they arrived, but the two of them would make short work of that project.

Hey, what about this weather Tommie? Isn't it the most fucked up weather you ever seen for this time of year? What do think about that Tommie? Really screwy weather isn't it? You know, I remember back in '09…"

Goddammit doesn't this guy ever stop! The vehicle smelled of rotting flesh. His bum leg was killing him. The end of this trip could not come soon enough. They slowed down as Tommie pulled off onto the access road approaching Kingston to the east with their destination to the west. About an hour later, the two men reached the burial site.

"Tommie did you hear the one about the prostitute and the donkey? Did you hear that one Tommie?"

Tommie looked at him, said nothing, and opened his driver's side door. He then opened the back seat door and pulled out two shovels. As Joey exited the vehicle, Tommie threw a shovel at him and using the lights of the vehicle and a small amount of moonlight, they dug the hole—a little deeper than normal because it would ultimately house two bodies, not one.

They worked in silence until the hole was deep enough for its dual purpose when Joey said, "Hey Tommie, did you hear about that man that was doing a rabbit…or something like that…maybe it was a ferret…I can't remember. Did you hear about that?"

Tommie laid his shovel down and walked behind him.

Without ever turning around, Joey, still shoveling, said, "Hey, Tommie did you hear the story about that guy that got his dick caught in a lawnmower or something like that? He…"

Tommie drew his pistol and with a sound barely discernable shot Joey Stringer in the back of the head three times in rapped succession.

Joey never got an answer to either question and never knew what hit him. He dropped to the bottom of the hole without Tommie lifting a finger.

Tommie replaced the weapon in its holster near the small of his back and walked over to the trunk. He knew opening the truck lid was going to release an odor that would surely gag him, but he had no choice. He was initially going to let Joey help him remove the lawyer's body and *then* shoot him, but he was so fucking tired of Joey's continuous line of bullshit he couldn't take him one more second.

He held his breathe, opened the lid, and pulled the stiff body out of the trunk of the car. He laid it on the ground and pulled it by the legs to the hole, shoving the lawyer over the edge and watching as his body settled in neatly on top of Joey.

Tommie put his hand over his heart, mumbled a couple of words about God taking care of these two misguided soles, and grabbed his shovel to cover them up.

***

About an hour later he found himself on Interstate 87 about 20 miles south of Kingston headed for home. Once he had finished covering the grave, he had smoothed out the area and packed it down the best he could. He knew no one would ever find it, but he wanted to properly finish what he had started. The Family had been assured long ago the area would never be disturbed or used by anyone but Family Members, and he had no doubt that promise would be honored well into the future. He needed some sleep. He hadn't had a good night's sleep since this job had started a week ago. He wanted to sleep late in the morning, but he had an appointment with one of the bosses at 1:00 pm and he knew he couldn't be late. He had always been well paid for what he did for them, but you just couldn't piss them off. You had to do what you were told. You had to be where you were supposed to be on time. You had to finish the job they gave you to do, or you simply paid the piper.

He was somewhat concerned about the meeting. Apparently, there was an "out of town" issue that needed attention. He wasn't good with "out of town." He liked New York. He liked everything about it. He hated leaving and learning a new area. They had mentioned something about Nashville. Where the hell was that? He had never been west of Detroit or south of Michigan. He only hoped that when he arrived at the meeting, they had changed their minds about him going there or had sent someone else. *Because if they hadn't found someone else by now, he figured he had probably better buy a pair of fricken cowboy boots and learn how to yoddle.*

Chapter 1

Davidson County Courthouse
Nashville, Tennessee

She was an interesting combination—tall and leggy with an attitude. When you first met her, you noticed the legs. But it didn't take long until you noticed the attitude. Not necessarily an attitude to an extreme. But well enough defined that you could always feel it when you were with her. Especially if you confronted her—as was the situation at this very moment. As was the situation every time she set foot in the Courtroom.

She was dressed in one of the many business suits she had finally been able to purchase once the firm had hired her. And as her reputation grew, she was able to afford whatever color she wished.

Her blouse was cut low. She didn't know this judge at all; and the cut of her blouse was always consistent with the difficulty of the issues and the level of competency of her competition. The more difficult the issue—the more competent her adversary—the lower the top of her blouse. And there was plenty to view if you were so inclined. If her adversary was a woman, most of the time it didn't matter. But if it was a man, the cut of the blouse normally became a visual issue. She had learned these seemingly insignificant tricks over the years and after many, many confrontational hearings with her male adversaries. They all tried in so many ways—married or not—to get her attention. There were many times she had to redirect their eyes to her eyes—to move them up to where she could look in their eyes and try to determine what they were really thinking. Physical appearance in the courtroom, as part of the overall picture, didn't amount to much. But sometimes it could distract her adversary just enough to produce a small advantage for her, and every advantage, no matter how small, was important.

"Miss Norway, are you ready to proceed?"

Why did she know so little about this judge—this Judge John T. Hampton. She did know he was just appointed to the bench, but the firm should have had some information on him, something to give her some indication on how he might rule on motions of this nature.

"Rosa...is it Rosa...Miss Norway? Are you ready to proceed? This is your motion to suppress. I see the testimony you refer to has been stipulated to by the prosecution. But it's still your motion, so proceed. What you are waiting for? One side or the other needs to present additional evidence or you need to express your position in more detail—one way or the other."

She was representing Jake McKay, who had been charged with voluntary manslaughter. He should have been charged with murder, but they had trouble with motive. The cops had, during the course of their investigation, tried to determine whether he intended to kill her or whether it was accidental. Both the victim and McKay had been covered with bruises and blood, but while he came out with only scratches, she had died.

Her client had no wife and no children. Somewhere along the way, he had developed a substantial amount of wealth. Apparently, as he tells the story, he employed a hooker and agreed to meet her in a downtown hotel in Nashville. She got the room and he arrived after she was already there.

Not long after he arrived, according to the timeline provided by witness statements, people heard a considerable amount of noise emanating from the room. Security was called. The voices were both male and female. People walking outside the door could hear the sounds of a scuffle and some of the guests started gathering outside the room. Shortly thereafter, McKay opened the door in just his underwear with blood all over his hands. He did not appear excited or upset. He looked at the crowd gathered and simply said, "She deserved what she got." He said nothing more.

Of course, everyone assumed he meant his victim needed to die, but the statement was certainly open to discussion as to its true intent and meaning, depending upon which side you cared to support.

His bond was initially set at five hundred thousand by the magistrate who first saw him, but Rosa was able to convince the magistrate to reduce it to 10 percent of that amount. After all, she said, there appeared to be no motive. In addition, he lived in Nashville, owned a home there, had no passport, had absolutely no prior record, and was obviously not a flight risk. The magistrate agreed and reduced the bond to 10 percent of the total, which McKay immediately posted.

This was just the start of the motions she was filing in this case. Other than the statements he had made to others and the statements he had made to the police, there wasn't an abundance of additional evidence. This motion was to suppress the statements he had made to the people standing outside his door that night. If she could get these statements suppressed along with statements he had made to the officers, she might be able to work out a bargain with the prosecutor, Arthur Walling, and perhaps plead to involuntary manslaughter, which would most likely not carry a prison term.

She knew her motion was a long shot, but she also knew it was worth a try.

"Judge, the motion pretty much speaks for itself. Mr. McKay did make some statements right after this happened, but we don't feel they should be allowed into evidence. They are obviously hearsay. They don't fall within a clear exception to the hearsay rule, and they should be excluded from evidence altogether."

"I've read your motion Miss Norway. But it appears to me *maybe* the exceptions *do* apply. I realize they are out of court statements and are used to prove the accuracy of the statement itself. That's the very definition of hearsay. But wasn't it an admission against interest? Wasn't it an excited utterance? Didn't it establish a state of mind? What do you have to say Mr. Walling?"

Arthur Walling was basically a good guy, as far as good guys go. He hadn't been a prosecutor very long, but he was good at his job. He was a little short in intellect, but he was compassionate and fair.

"Judge, I agree with you. These statements may be hearsay, but all those exceptions apply and I referred to all of them in my resistance to Miss Norway's motion."

Walling looked at her and then slowly looked down at her breasts.

Men—they are all the same, she thought. *So fricken predictable.*

In addition, Art had a little "tell." Like every time a particular poker player gets a good hand his eye twitches—a "tell." Art would always stutter just a little when he was uncertain about the outcome, and she knew this was the exact moment he became somewhat concerned about the possible outcome of a hearing or a trial.

Even though she felt she was really on weak ground, she also knew she had absolutely nothing to lose by filing the motion.

"Judge we just don't believe the exceptions apply. They were *not* admissions against interest. They did *not* indicate the defendant's state of mind concerning the commission of a crime nor do we believe any other exception to the hearsay rule applies in any respect."

"Anything else Miss Norway?"

"No, you're Honor. That's about all we have concerning this particular motion."

"I assume, by making that last statement, you are intending on filing additional motions in this case."

He said it with a smile and she could tell he did not intend on punishing her while considering this motion just because she did plan on filing additional motions.

"Correct. I do plan on filing additional motions in this case."

This Judge was good looking. He had a good smile. He didn't talk down to her and he left his eyes where they were supposed to be.

"Mr. Walling, anything else?"

"No, Your Honor. We believe the pleadings speak for themselves and that, along with the arguments of council, we feel is enough for the Court to make an informed ruling."

"Thank you Mr. Walling. Well, I have read the motion and the resistance filed by the State. I've had a chance to review the file and look at a few cases in this area. And while I realize the State did the appropriate thing in including these statements as part of their evidence, after listening to arguments of council, it is clear these statements *are* hearsay. And my research leads me to the conclusion that the exceptions do *not* apply. As a result, I am concluding these statements should be excluded from the testimony at trial. Now Mr. Walling, I want you to refile a new county attorney's information setting out all the essential elements of the crime as you originally did, but when you present the testimony of the witnesses, I want these statements excluded, not only in the paperwork you file with the court, but when the witnesses testify on the stand. I do *not* want these statements mentioned at any point during the trial of this case. Do I make myself clear Mr. Walling?

"Bbbut Juddge. That justtt doesn't ssseem consistent with exisssting case law."

"Mr. Walling, that is my ruling. You know what you can do if you don't like it."

He smiled at Rosa, got up, and walked off the bench. She couldn't believe what had just transpired, and neither could Walling.

"What the heeell just hhhappened here?" he asked.

"Didn't work out for you that's for sure. Want to bargain?"

"*NO.*"

"See you next time around. Maybe you'll be ready to deal then."

"WWWe'll see."

She walked off. She had clearly won round one. But she was a little concerned. She probably shouldn't have won this round. Who was this guy—this Judge Hampton? What was his story? She needed to know more about him, not only professionally but personally. As a judge, his ruling may have been wrong. But putting that aside, she definitely wanted to know more about him as a man—that did tend to interest her.

Chapter 2

They were just plain dirt poor. Her father worked as hard as he could all the time, but his pay as a low level mechanic amounted to nothing. Her mother could only find part-time work as a housekeeper, and feeding three growing children who were hungry all the time was difficult to say the least.

This was the atmosphere Rosa came to accept, not enjoy, but accept. They were broke—not just at the time she was born, but all the while she was in school. They had nothing. New clothes were hard to come by. Spending money of any kind was hard to come by. They got by the best they could, but nothing came easy.

School was difficult for her. Whether it was grade school, high school, or college, it was always an effort. Because money was tight, she had a job from the time she was old enough to work, all the way through law school. She never knew the freedom of only attending school. She was always saddled with the responsibility of earning income for herself and her family *and* trying to attain good enough grades to get through—a tough task for most people, and Rosa was no exception. But she was determined she was not going to end up in the financial predicament her parents were in and continued to be in all of their lives. She was going to find a way to get out of her financial hole one way or the other.

She had learned at an early age if you worked your ass off, most of the time good things would come. Not always, but most of the time. Because she was only average as a student, she had to work harder to achieve a good grade point average. The results of her labor were commensurate with the amount of work she put in. She was successful at every level of education within which she participated.

But the extra time she spent compensating for her inadequacies constantly affected her socially, and she basically had no social life whatsoever. But she didn't care. She was goal oriented and was prepared to do whatever was necessary to achieve her dreams.

At an early age, she was noticed for her beauty. She was a stunning child, and as she grew older, she transformed into a beautiful young lady. Her physical attributes made for an appealing but apparently untouchable picture, as she had absolutely no time to waste with the opposite sex.

While she was attending college, she decided to apply for law school. She studied all the appropriate primers endlessly, hoping they would do the job, and they did. She was accepted.

Her family was overjoyed. Both of her brothers were proud of her and because they were younger than she, it was the general idea in the family that she would be able to help them as each brother made his own effort to apply for and be accepted into college. Neither ever made the effort. Even though she continued to try to maintain contact, she was hardly ever in touch with them. They both found jobs directly out of high school, and even though she tried to maintain a consistent relationship, the effort was not returned. They just didn't seem to care.

Law school was also an effort. Her grades were initially low, but as she moved into the swing of things, her average inched higher with each semester until her senior year when she excelled.

It was because of her senior year and her accomplishments, especially that second semester, when she was first noticed. And when she graduated she was offered a position with one of the most prestigious law firms in Nashville. She specialized in criminal law and fortunately, the firm needed someone to handle that area of expertise. She was given a tremendous amount of responsibility from day one and she did not disappoint. She worked hard and she learned how to work the system quickly. Once again, her social life suffered, but it didn't matter. Nothing mattered but success and the paycheck. And as the former grew, so did the latter.

She quickly became one of the higher paid associates in the firm, and she knew before long she would be offered a partnership. With it would come a huge increase in pay. She was more than ready for both.

She lived in a townhouse in West Nashville. It was large enough for her to avoid feeling claustrophobic, but small enough to remain cozy. The morning traffic into downtown Nashville often caused her fits, as it did many others, but it was worth it. She basically lived in a small town in a large city, which was perfect for her.

While her social life was not active, by choice, she did on occasion go out with a guy or two, but they always eventually wanted the same thing…sex. There was never talk about the future or how much love he had for her. It always just came down to sex. That was not the way she wanted it to work. She was a romantic and she wanted the romance to work first—before the sex— before the talk of a long-term commitment. Besides that, she was having too much fun with her newfound success to be interested in men. She figured that would come around but later—not now. This law firm and her practice meant too much to her to let a man screw it up.

Rosa was tough and she knew it. She had survived a difficult childhood and had learned how to survive as an adult using her intellect and a little common sense. She was serious about the practice of law and at this point in her life, it meant everything to her.

But this Judge—this Judge John Hampton—he had a way about him. In addition, he was attractive and had a great smile. While his ruling in her favor may have been wrong, she needed to know more about this guy—the man—not the judge. She decided to seek out her mentor within the firm, Gene Wakefield, and see if he knew anything about him. She would most likely deal with him again in this case and she wanted to know a little more about him—in more ways than one.

Chapter 3

Gene Wakefield was an icon in the legal profession. He had been around forever. He had been in practice for years and while practicing, his firm had grown and prospered. Eventually, he just decided to manage the firm and give up an active practice. He knew there would be headaches associated with handling management, but he was tired of litigation and felt it was time to move into another area within the practice of law.

He managed an office consisting of nine other attorneys and had a good relationship with everyone in the office. They were all veterans and specialized in their own areas of law.

Rosa was the youngest of the attorneys and one of only three women in the office. She had thought to herself many times that anyone who thought it wasn't a man's world was nuts. And many, many times in the last few years she had thought how difficult it was to continue to fight the system in that respect. She had to be continually watchful to make sure she was never an outsider in the games some of the men would play while involved in the litigation wars. She had to always be vigilant that they weren't making deals at the bar the night before trial and leaving her out, especially if the case was a civil action involving multiple defendants.

Her relationship with the other attorneys within the firm was acceptable. She was, however, not the best team player in the firm and she, along with most of the other attorneys in the firm, were well aware that she had a weakness in that area—which is probably why she hadn't made partner before now. But she couldn't change who she was. They would need to deal with her 'as is' and she had made them aware of that many times.

Gene walked into Rosa's office after she had asked him if he had a moment to discuss the McKay case. He was always well dressed as was the case today. His gray hair was combed but looked like he had used some type of tire grease to slick it back. All in all he looked like your typical slippery lawyer. But she couldn't complain—he had been good to her.

She noticed he looked thinner than ever. He was a tall man and always slender in build, but today he looked like he could just blow away in the wind.

Her office was bare. She was all business and her office reflected that approach to her practice.

While most of the lawyers in the firm would small talk with their clients involving irrelevant trivia, when one walked in Rosa's office, the lack of décor kept the focus solely on business and the reason for the meeting. That was the way Rosa wanted it. If that approach didn't work for you, then neither did Rosa.

"Morning Rosa, how is everything? How's the McKay case coming? How did the judge rule on your motion?"

"Hi Gene. Actually, it went well. We prevailed, but I'm not really sure we should have. It was a strange hearing. Art didn't push hard enough, and the judge ended up ruling in our favor. I'm not really sure it was the right ruling. I just filed the motion as an afterthought."

"Well, you know that happens," he said with a smile.

She had seen that smile before. It was the smile he always used when he already knew the answer to the question he had just asked. Had he heard from someone else or did he know the result before the hearing even started?

"I know that happens, but not very often and not in cases like this. This case is fairly high profile and the result surprised me. What do you know about this judge? It was Judge Hampton…John T. Hampton. I know he was just appointed, but I really know nothing about him. What's his story?"

"Well, he went to high school in a small town in the northeast corner of Tennessee. He went to law school at U of T and practiced with a small firm, as you probably know, in Knoxville. He was and is pretty well connected. He was correct politically and when he applied for Judge Gourds' open position after he retired during his term, he was the logical choice. What were your conclusions about his ruling? It sounds like you don't agree."

"I don't. But on the other hand, I liked it. You filled me in on his legal background, but what about his personal issues? For instance, does he have children?"

"Why don't you just cut to the chase Rosa—just ask the question. *No,* he isn't married. He was but he isn't now and he's has been divorced long enough that he is over her. They had no children. He's not well off financially, but one day I can assure you he will be. The judgeship, as you know, pays well and he is, as I hear tell, frugal with his money. He's a good catch Rosa and someone you may want to take a second look at after this trial is over."

Without hesitating, she said, "Thanks Gene, not interested."

"This case is important Rosa. This McKay is a wealthy man and could potentially be a good client for us. He has already paid us a large retainer, as you know. We need to win this case. Not so much outright, but at least to the point where he is satisfied with the result. This is a big case for you Rosa. We are all looking at making you a partner in the firm and the results of this particular case could impact that decision. I'm not trying to put the pressure on but I do want you to understand."

"Oh, I understand. I get it. I really need to win this case. *Sure*. No pressure there at all Gene."

She took a deep breath. Everyone in firms of this nature understood how much it meant to become a partner. It was huge and something she had been waiting on for some time.

"Now don't let becoming a partner affect your judgment Rosa. You have always had good judgment when it came to sorting out the relevant and the irrelevant in this type of case and coming to the correct conclusion. This case is important to this firm, but please continue to use your good common sense while you are representing this guy."

"Oh I will, I will," she assured him. But, it was obvious this case had become important to her future with this firm—a win could finally mean partnership status.

"By the way, I want another client to come visit with you about his case—a man by the name of Tommie Thompson. I assume you know nothing about the case. He is charged with operating while intoxicated. I don't really know much about the specifics. I do know someone put up his bond. He's out."

"Has someone from the firm already talked to him?"

"Yes. Jerry did but you are the expert in this area and I want you to visit with him too. He apparently has some backing because someone put up his bond, in cash, and paid us a hell of a retainer for a case of this nature. I can visit with you later about the case but there seems to be a push to work this case hard and try to obtain an acquittal for him. For some reason, there is more talk about this guy and his case than is normal for a simple OWI."

"Ok. I'll set down with him sometime next week."

She sat alone after he left still thinking about their conversion. Big stakes for her concerning the McKay case and now she was involved in another case that seemed to be more important than a normal OWI. Feast or famine. It had been that way all her life.

Time to roll up her sleeves and get to work. This time, though, the stakes were as high as they had ever been in her life.

Chapter 4

He walked in shadows, literally and figuratively, as he had done for as long as he could remember.

He was born Paul McKay, but from the time he could remember, he had been called Jake.

He was born into more trouble than one could imagine. His Family was in it deep. They were Brooklyn, New York born and bred. The whole Family resided in the New York/New Jersey area and from the moment Great Grandpa decided numbers and illegal booze were the correct and proper ways to make a living that was all the Family knew.

Jake was small. He was small as a child and just never grew up, either physically or mentally. He had three siblings—all brothers and they were all born and bred to do whatever was the easiest and quickest way to make a buck. Their grandfather had run numbers and provided illegal booze. Their father had also been involved with numbers, but by the time Jake became well involved in the illegality of the Families activities, booze was legal. It was time to move the Family in a new direction and they decided to move into prostitution, and, to a small degree, into this new world of drugs.

Jake was born into this world of shadows, deception, and illegal activity. He never knew what it was to have a legitimate job or an hourly wage. Nor did any of his siblings. They worked for their father, they respected what he taught them, and they did what he told them to do. They knew no other way.

It made no difference what they were told to do. They were told to simply handle whatever it was that needed to be done. More than once they were told to transport someone to the landfill and finish him off. They never hesitated. Most of the time all the brothers went along. They never asked questions and they never looked back.

The money was incredible and Jake received his share. For years he bankrolled almost everything he made. While the others were spending it as fast as they made it and living the good life, Jake saved. By the time he was 40, he had had enough of this type of lawlessness and was ready to move on. But it wasn't so easy getting out.

His mother was gone—his father had killed her off long ago—not so much with a weapon, but with a lifestyle. Jake watched as she grew old long before her time, until she finally never woke up one morning. His father, who was alive but in failing health, threatened him about leaving the Family. His brothers did the same.

Jake would listen to their threats and intimidation in response to his statements about leaving, but they went in one ear and out the other. He knew, once he was ready to leave, they would never take the time to find him. He knew if he moved far enough away, it really wouldn't matter to them. They had their hands full in Brooklyn and didn't have time to go chase a "dumb fuck" brother, as he was so often called.

Jake was small as a child and just never grew up, neither mentally nor physically. He remained about five-feet-eight from the time he was twelve until adulthood. He was unattractive and always slicked his hair straight back. He talked slow, considering each word before speaking. He was never well liked, but once he had reached his goal of putting away a couple of mill in cash, none of that mattered to him.

He walked in one day and told his father he was leaving. His father asked him for how long and Jake replied he wasn't sure. His father, realizing he had been unsuccessful in changing Jake's mind about leaving, simply said, "We'll see you when you get home." But Jake never went back. He cut off all contact with his father and his brothers relocating to Nashville.

He had lived in Nashville a number of years alone and in obscurity. He belonged to no organizations, never went to a church of any kind, and never tried to meet new people or socialize in any manner. He lived a singular life bothering no one and being bothered by no one. He had no life with the opposite sex. He really never wanted any type of relationship with anyone—man or woman.

He had purchased a nice, but unobtrusive home and lived a quiet life within the four walls. Neighbors would try and be social, but he never bought into the "block party" mentality and they finally left him alone, noting that he was "a little strange but seemed like a nice man."

His sexual release involved an occasional prostitute, which had resulted in his arrest. He had gone about the process the same way he always had. He knew the man to call to line up the best in town. They were expensive but good, and he figured since it was his only pleasure, why not spend the money.

He had never had an issue with any of the women. They were always good at what they did and they did what he wanted.

But the night he was arrested was different. She was different. …..he had never been with her before. She smelled of booze and mentioned she had only recently started working with this particular boss. She was mouthy. She hesitated to do what he wanted and he told her two or three times to shut up and just do her job. *She wouldn't do either.*

They argued. He gave her one last chance, but when she went down on him, she used her teeth. That was the last straw. He gave her a shove that put her on her back and cut her mouth. She was bleeding all over. She came after him and struck him repeatedly all the while screaming at the top of her lungs. She cut him with her fingernails while he was simply trying to get her away from him. He finally gave her one good punch to the left side of the face. The punch didn't do her in, but striking her temple against the corner of the end table did. He had seen enough death to know she was gone when she hit the floor.

He could hear people outside his door demanding that he open it immediately. He pulled his underwear on and opened the door drenched in her blood and scratched up from one end to the other.

They looked at him in disbelief, and finally he said, "She deserved what she got."

Law enforcement arrived shortly and carted him off. He was arraigned and bond was initially set at $500,000.

However, Rosa, whom he had retained immediately, asked for a bond reduction hearing and at the hearing the magistrate reduced the bond to 10 percent of the original amount. Jake was able to provide cash for the bond and he was released pending further hearings. He knew from the outset he was in a substantial amount of trouble, even though the circumstances were really not as they appeared. But, regardless, he simply wasn't going to prison under any circumstances, and he hoped it wouldn't come down to a jury trial. He didn't figure he could take a chance with 12 red-necked backcountry boys from central Tennessee.

He needed to evaluate his situation and figure this out. This problem was going to turn out the way *he* wanted it to. He wasn't going to end up, after all the trouble he had successfully walked away from in New York, in some goddamn Tennessee prison for the next 10 years on a charge as stupid as this—no way in hell.

Chapter 5

Rosa concluded her meeting with Gene and after finishing up a number of small items of work that needed completing, it was time to close up shop. Her day normally ended around 5:30, but many of her days went well into the evening depending on her schedule. There were nights she ended up sleeping on the couch in the conference room. She had purchased double cosmetics and kept one set at the office. She also kept a couple of changes of clean clothing in her office just in case she stayed there overnight.

Her job paid well but was extremely challenging. She was tested and challenged every day of the week in some manner or another. She was driven. She knew it and, as a result, let it work for her instead of fighting it. As much as anything, she was driven by fear— fear of ending up like her family. She was always concerned about ending up broke—not a penny to her name—just hoping to survive another week. Fear was a major factor in her formula for success. And if it took working all day and all night to achieve her definition of success, she was willing to do that. Helping that along was her love of the work she performed. The intrigue associated with her profession made it interesting enough. But add to that the income it produced, along with the pride generated with a job well done, and there was no better occupation in the world. Every aspect suited her.

Even down to the examination of each and every activity by the Bar Association. They followed nearly every move attorneys made in their practice as thoroughly as they could, and she had no problem with that. She knew there were thieves in this area of life as there were in every other aspect of life, and she had no issue with the Bar Association sticking their noses into her professional life and making sure she was living by their rules.

She followed every rule—each and every one. She always made sure she checked their conflict records and that the new clients she agreed to represent didn't create a conflict of interest with another client employing a different attorney in her firm. Every retainer fee was deposited in the office's trust account and accounted for as provided by the Rules. Her trust accounts had been audited on numerous occasions by the Bar Association accountant and always checked out to the absolute penny. She had nothing to fear when it came to the Bar Association, nor was she about to place herself in any type of situation that would create an issue with them.

She was, in fact, considering a possible client conflict within the office when her cellphone rang.

"Hey *dumbshit*…what's up?"

It was Amy Glass. She was Rosa's closest friend and had been for years.

"I was just walking out the door. Did you want something or are we about to small talk our way through another useless conversation?"

"You know one of these days I'm going to become fed up with that holier-than-thou attitude you seem to use with me and tell you to go to hell you asshole."

Amy used the term asshole way too frequently and whether you knew her or not, she got your full attention when she used it.

"I suppose you want to meet somewhere and have a drink before I head home."

"Why not? I'm right around the corner anyway."

"Ok. Let's meet at Tootsies in about five."

"You got it."

***

They walked in the door virtually together. Neither was ever late for anything. Growing up they had both been raised to be on time, and both remained that way when they reached adulthood.

Amy was slightly overweight, and Rosa had been on her and on her about exercising and losing some of her baby fat. Amy always swore she would, but she always had an excuse for not working out.

Other than that small issue, she was not unattractive, but also not nearly as striking in appearance as Rosa.

Amy had jet-black hair and blue eyes that sparkled when she laughed or when she got pissed off for any of the many reasons she did. She became more attractive the better you got to know her. First impressions never worked much for Amy. She took knowing. The more you were around her, the more you liked her. And in Rosa's case, all the years they had been friends had resulted in a relationship that was stronger than sisters. It had stood the test of time and circumstance on many occasions.

They had known each other since grade school. Amy knew all about Rosa's family. She had visited their home once while they were both in grade school but never cared to return. They had shared it all—the childhood dreams, the boys, the stupid teachers in high school.

When the boyfriend issue raised its ugly head, they ran to each other and no one else. They were totally inseparable from the time they were in first grade. Even when planning their advanced education, they made sure they remained close geographically. On a couple of occasions, Rosa, as she had done with so many others, tried to shove Amy out of her life. But Amy would never allow that to happen. As a result, Rosa finally accepted the fact that Amy was one of best things that ever happened to her, and never again questioned the fact that they would always remain the best of friends.

When they arrived at Tootsies, both ordered a glass of Merlot—the house was always good and there was no need to search the menu.

"So what about today?"

"Not so bad. I really got a good ruling from a judge which I didn't expect, but other than that, it was an average day I guess. What about you?"

Amy worked for a local real estate office as a saleswoman. She was good at her trade. While her first impression normally didn't help, as people dealt with her while looking for a home, before their business was over she normally had new clients and friends all out of the same transaction. She was as dedicated to her job as Rosa and many times found herself working as late or later than Rosa.

"Slow day. I hate these kinds of days. Days when those assholes come in, wonder around, ask a few questions, and then walk out the door. It makes for a really long day. So was this ruling important or not?"

"Yes, it was. But, in addition to the success with the motion, I met a new judge today. He was good looking and seemed competent. He was overly fair to me, I know that."

"You know, very seldom do you compliment a judge. Normally you are telling me they are all pompous assholes."

"You know you use that word way to much don't you?"

"Only use it when it applies." She smiled that great smile—the one she normally used when she was pulling Rosa's leg about something. That was how well they knew each other—there wasn't a look Amy had that Rosa couldn't identify.

"I'm trying to find out about him. I know he's divorced and has no kids. He interests me."

Whoa. That's the first time in a long time you have said that."

"I know. It's the first time I have felt this way in a while. I'm going to do a little more checking into this guy before I go much further, but I like what I've seen so far."

Amy, like Rosa, had neither husband nor children. She had been serious a couple of times, but nothing had materialized. They were both single and had the world to choose from, and they had both decided it was going to be perfect before they settled.

Amy thought for a minute before she commented.

"Maybe you'll be the first of us to go. Maybe this is the guy you've been waiting for."

"Oh, I doubt that. But I must admit he does interest me just a little."

Amy smiled.

"And then again he could just be another *asshole*."

And with that, they ordered one more glass of Merlot before they walked out into the cool Nashville evening and headed to their respective homes, once again, each of them realizing how lucky they were to have someone they could discuss absolutely everything with at the end of a long day.

Chapter 6

She found it difficult to like this man—this short, seedy little man who "murdered" a prostitute. He really wasn't a bad guy to visit with, but he seemed greasy, somehow dirty to her. It was nothing she could put her finger on, but he made her uncomfortable.

This was the time they had set aside to discuss, again, the details of the problem that brought him to her in the first place. They had gone through the facts before, but it was not unusual for her to go through them with her clients half a dozen times, if not more, prior to trial.

"Ok, now Jake, you know we have been through this a number of times, but we need to go through it all again, and particularly the time you spent with the cops. Do you understand what I mean when I tell you the judge sustained our motion to throw out the statement you made to those people standing outside your hotel room door? You understand that element of the evidence can now never be used against you—that we won that little battle?"

"Yes. I think I understand the significance of that."

He was very slow and deliberate in his speech. He thought about all his words, one at a time, as they slowly tumbled from his lips. He had told Rosa that he had never had any significant involvement with the legal process so she was very careful to keep him totally informed concerning each element of the proceedings.

"Let's talk specifically about the time period that night when the cops arrived, until the time you were actually placed in a cell. Let's only talk about that portion of it today."

"Might I ask why you just want to focus on that portion?"

"Because based on our earlier conversations, I have a feeling the statements you made to the officers might have all been before you were given your Miranda rights and if that was the case, we may be able to suppress those statements also. The idea here is to pick away at their case a little at a time with the thought in mind that we may be able to pick away enough to either have it dismissed or at least convince the State to reduce the charge to something you can live with and remove the possibility of prison. Later, as the trial date approaches, we will focus on witnesses and testimony but, for now, we need to somewhat narrow the issues. Do you understand?"

"Yes, I understand what you are trying to do. You know prison won't work for me. I cannot, under any circumstances, risk going to prison. I'll do whatever I need to do to avoid going there. Now, do you understand what I'm saying?"

"Yes, I do. But right now, go through the facts with me from the time you were confronted by law enforcement until you were placed in a cell."

"Ok. Let me think this through. First, there I was at the door in my underwear and all those people were standing there, and I really was embarrassed. But, then again, I guess I shouldn't have been. I got myself into the mess in the first place didn't I?"

"We got those statements made to those people tossed so that is no longer a problem. What happened then?"

"Well the cops showed up and took all kinds of pictures of everything and me. They made me sit there in my underwear until they were finished taking all their blood samples from around the room and taking all their pictures. That was pretty embarrassing."

"After all their pictures were taken, what happened then? What did they do? What did you do?"

"Well, I didn't do anything other than put my clothes on. But after a while, they started asking me questions. And I guess I just answered them the best I could until I saw you and you said don't answer one more question. Then I quit answering anything they were asking. And you remember they got a little upset about that and I hated to make them mad, but that was your advice."

"I remember. But let's back up. Let's talk specifically about their questions and your answers. Can we focus on that?"

"Sure if that's what you want to do. Well, that one bigger cop—you know the one who looked like he didn't have all his teeth—that one. He asked me if I did this. And I told him 'yes, me and that woman did all this. I guess I knocked her down but she scratched and bit me.'"

"What happened next?"

Good God this was like pulling teeth, Rosa thought.

"Well then he said 'why did you do this to her?' And I just said 'because she deserved it.' And then he said 'so you killed her because she deserved it.' And I said 'yes, I guess so.' And then you came in and that was all the questions he asked me because you told him to stop."

"Did he ever read you any of your rights? Did he ever tell you that you had the right to remain silent? That you did not have to say a word? Do you remember him or any other cop ever saying that to you?"

"No. No one ever told me that. If they would have I wouldn't have said anything. I didn't know I could do that. What can we do about it now though?"

"I need to do some additional research on the issue. But they knew what happened immediately upon arrival. They had you in custody at that moment. Someone screwed up. They should have informed you of your rights and as a result, I really think we can get those statements tossed out. I need to file a motion, as we did before, and it certainly doesn't mean we are going to win the war. But in my opinion, we should win this battle. You know, from what you have admitted to me, you are clearly responsible for this woman's death. Is that a fair statement?"

"Yes. I caused her death. But she *deserved* it. No man deserves to be treated that way."

"I understand that. But what I am saying is that you may need to accept some responsibility for what happened here. I'm not saying we should admit anything that sends you to the pen, but along the way we may get an opportunity to plead this out, and if we do you need to take advantage of that situation. Do you understand what I'm saying?"

"Yes. But, I'm not going to prison. I couldn't under any circumstances handle it, and I'm not going to try. I'll work with you on a plea, but I'm not putting myself in a situation where I may go to prison."

"My plan is to file another motion to suppress and try to have those statements you just told me about thrown out too. If we can get that done, we may have a good chance of bargaining this case out and keeping you out of jail."

"So what are our chances of getting my statements tossed? Talk to me in percentages. I understand those."

"I would say about 50/50—maybe somewhat better."

"And if they aren't thrown out? Then what do we do?"

"Take our chances with a jury if we can't get the prosecutor to bargain with us. And he just told me, based on the where we are in the case right now, that he wouldn't bargain. I assume nothing will change if we lose on our motion."

"Ok. Thank you. Now I understand. But we should come out good with this motion you are going to file" he said with a slight smile.

"Oh, really? You have that much confidence in me?" Rosa smiled back, she hoped with more appeal than the smile he had just shown her.

"Yes. I have confidence in you. But even beyond that, we should come out fine."

Rosa had absolutely no idea what that was supposed to mean, and as strange as this little guy was she wasn't sure she wanted to know.

The conference ended shortly thereafter and he left. But long after he left, the conversation they had near the end of their interview lingered with her. What did he mean? Was she missing something?

She thought about it as she lay in bed that night and finally came to the conclusion she could think about it all night but she would come no closer to an answer than she was right now. She would need to remember to ask him how the hell he was so sure about her motion the next time she was with him. Time to knock off the thought process and fall asleep. She needed to prepare a motion to suppress tomorrow that hopefully would result in some type of plea bargain in this case, and end her involvement with this strange little man.

Chapter 7

He was alone—again. Even though there were at least 50 people in the seats, another 12 in the jury box, and the attorneys with their clients all scattered out in front of him, he still felt alone. He had driven to the Davidson County Courthouse early this morning—by himself. He hadn't really felt like walking inside yet, so he took a walk to the river—the Cumberland—only about four blocks. He walked it alone. And as he stood there in silence, watching the sun start to rise and reflect off the river, he was, as was normal now days, once again, alone.

The sound of a loud "*objection!*" from one of the attorneys trying the case before him terminated his wandering thoughts in a hurry.

"Reason?"

"Why judge, that's clearly hearsay. The guy may have been dying when he made it, but it's still hearsay."

"Really? Overruled."

He needed to get his head back in the game. No time to let his mind wander. There was way too much at stake.

It seemed he had always been alone in some respect or another. His family had nothing. He had adequate grades in both high school and college to be accepted into law school, but no money. So rather than going straight into law school from college, he sat out a year and put together enough to at least pay a portion of the tuition out of his own pocket the first year.

His parents were never able to help. He was an only child but when it came to them, they just never seemed to have enough to put food on the table, let alone help him. He knew of his mother's spending problems. Everyone knew of it. No one discussed it but everyone knew about it. They all knew how she drained their checking account on a regular basis. But no one ever had the nerve to stop her—including his father—and as a result, they never had anything. Her mother had clothes she had never worn. There were appliances she never used. But the rest of the family had nothing. And his parents certainly were not in a financial position to send him on to law school, even though they both knew that was where he belonged.

He retook the bar exam after he had waited a year and again was accepted. But during his second year of law school, he had to find a job to at least help with some of the out-of-pocket expenses. That made remaining in law school extremely difficult for him, but he not only made it, he graduated with honors.

"Judge, would you please instruct the witness to answer the questions asked and not ramble like he is doing?"

"Ok Mr. James, just confine your answer to the questions he asks you. Can you do that?"

"Oh I guess so but he isn't getting the full story if I do that."

"That's fine Mr. James. Let the attorney determine what the full story might be. Please answer the questions he asks you and nothing more."

Again his mind wandered—this time to his graduation from law school. He was offered a number of very good positions and ended up taking a job with Werner and Werner, a small firm in Knoxville started by a couple of brothers.

From day one he specialized in Corporate Law and after a few years even local attorneys were calling him for advice in his field of expertise. He would, on occasion, represent people in other areas of law, but he basically tried to restrict his practice to corporations and corporate law.

He met Jayne during his second year in practice. He had dated other girls while in law school, but none of them particularly excited him. However, once he started practicing with the Werner firm, even though he worked his ass off every day of the week, he also started taking a little more time to smell the roses. And that's when he met her.

An Absence of Ethics

He knew the moment he met her that she was the one. She was beautiful in every way you could imagine. Together they made a striking couple as both were physically appealing. They dated for almost six months and one day he just popped the question. She accepted and six months later they were married. She worked in the Knox County Clerk's office. She had never been married and wanted no children. Nor did he. Certainly prior to the marriage, there seemed to be many areas of life upon which both agreed.

"Judge, may this witness be excused?"

"Mr. Johnson, do you have any objection to excusing this witness, or do you think you may need to recall him as a witness for rebuttal?"

"No your honor. He can go."

"Next witness."

But a few months into the marriage, he could see some issues needed ironing out. She seemed to be gone from work and from their home more than was necessary. He would stop in to see her in the clerk's office and she had "stepped out." He would come home from the office early, and she would arrive sometimes hours after he did. When he would ask her where she was she would say "out with the girls."

It took a little time, mostly because he just plain didn't want to believe it, but he finally caught on. She was doing one of the judges he practiced before. He attempted to confront the judge in his office, but could never get past his secretary. He tried twice, and both times failed. He talked to her about the issue, and she said she would stop seeing him, but she never did.

After a year of arguing, he decided he had had enough. He filed for dissolution of the marriage and the marriage was dissolved. But financially, the whole situation was a complete disaster. He wasn't about to represent himself, so he had his attorney fees to pay, and because she had no money and her income was considerably less than his, he also had to pay a good portion of her attorney fees. Then there were all those court costs. And she was awarded alimony for five years—and half of everything they had left—which by then, was very little.

Once all the legal proceedings were concluded, he was deeply in debt. He tried to look at it optimistically; at least the mental abuse stopped when the marriage was dissolved. And even though he was broke, he figured now he had a second chance—a chance to at last start paying off his student loans, which were significant, to pay his marital debts off, and to start putting some money away. They had little money when the marriage started and after the dissolution, he was a financial disaster.

"Judge that is the last of our witnesses. Unless the State has rebuttal witnesses, I think we are finished and ready to close."

"Mr. Johnston, do you have any rebuttal witnesses?"

Shortly after the divorce, he applied for and was eventually appointed criminal court judge for Judicial District 20 to sit in Davidson County. That, of course, was a huge step for him and resulted in a guaranteed wage each month, which he could depend on and use as was appropriate for each of his many debts. It would necessitate a move to Nashville, but getting out of town and away from his ex, who still worked in the clerk's office, was a welcome change.

His debt troubled him on a daily basis, and he worried about when he would ever be able to get over the hump and finally find some economic security. The pressure with finances had never changed. It was an issue when he was ten years old and it remained an issue today.

He had a few things in mind, though, that might somewhat help cut his debt. He had a second meeting later tonight with a man who might be able to alleviate his problem. He wasn't sure of all the particulars yet, or if he would even want to complete the deal. This was a big step and one he wasn't sure he wanted to take, but he would at least visit with him one more time before coming to a conclusion.

Tommie Thompson was the man's name. Tonight, he would meet with him, listen to his story, and then decide what to do. He was so tired of his continuing financial problems that he had reached the point, short of robbing a bank, where he would do about anything. And he had a feeling that was probably what Mr. Thompson would indeed ask him to do…*about anything.*

Chapter 8

Rosa was busy with a number of small jobs that needed to be completed, but, she really needed to see this guy—this Thompson. He was about to be arraigned for operating while intoxicated, and she needed to know the facts before he made his initial appearance before the judge. Apparently, someone had referred him to her, although no one ever said who it was. There obviously was money backing him because someone put up his bond in cash and paid a substantial retainer for their firm to represent him.

He was waiting for her in the office lobby and she escorted him back to her office.

"Good morning Mr. Thompson. Other than the reason you are here, how are you getting along?"

He was tall and balding. Although only average in looks, he clearly worked out or was involved in some type of work that kept him physically fit. But he had a limp. His right leg appeared to be locked into a straight line. He drug it into its next position as he walked.

"Everything is fine, except for this criminal charge. I'm somewhat concerned about it. I've never had a ticket or been charged with anything and I can't afford to lose my license. I really need to be able to drive."

"Tell me about yourself Mr. Thompson, about you, your family, your background."

"Well, I graduated from high school and never went to college. I was raised on the East Coast and moved here this year. I do a lot of driving for a living and I need my license. I have a wife and a couple of children who aren't with me right now. I can't afford a conviction on this charge. I need to be able to drive. You need to fix this for me."

"Are you now driving on a temporary permit?"

"Yes, but you know if I plead guilty or am found guilty that will end and I really need to drive to make a living."

He had a funny way of looking at her. As if this was not a question and answer session at all. He was *telling* her to get this fixed. It was not a request or a plea for help, it was a demand.

"I understand. Let's just start from the beginning. How did this all come about?"

"That's what's so confusing to me. I was driving down the street, minding my own business, alone, and the officer pulled me over. He said I was speeding. *I wasn't.* There was absolutely no question about that. I was under the posted limit. I'm so very, very careful about that anyway. I had had a drink or two, and I told him that but he had no reason to stop me in the first place."

"Have you had prior issues with this officer in the past?"

"Never met him. I have never had any issue with law enforcement anywhere let alone in Nashville."

"Ok. Let's talk some about the procedure from here on out."

She tried to evaluate what type of witness he would make. He didn't appear to have any particular drawback as far as testifying was concerned. He appeared fairly believable and honest. He had the right type of family to present a good picture and absolutely no prior issues with the law, which was certainly an advantage.

"The county attorney's office will be filing what is called a county attorney's information, which will contain all the evidence they feel they have against you. We can review that together and determine where we want to go from there. We might be able to bargain this out, but if we can't, you are looking at going to trial. Can we talk about your line of business again?"

"Well, I drive people around. I have a list of cliental and if they want to go somewhere, they pay me to pick them up and to drive them wherever they need to go. Obviously, they were upset when I was picked up and I need to get this problem resolved."

"Could I have a list of the people who employ you on a regular basis?"

"That's not really important is it? I mean I suppose I could provide it to you, but why is that important?"

"Well, I guess it's not that important. It doesn't really affect the factual issues involving the case, but I just wanted to have an idea about whom you might work for. Are you prepared to take this all the way to trial if we need to?"

"Yes. I don't want to plead to this charge. I don't want a record of any kind. I've been very particular with my life and have worked to remain out of the system. I want that to continue. Do you understand what I'm saying? Can we make this go away?"

"What do you mean?"

"Beyond trying the case, is there anything you could do to just make it go away?"

"Nothing beyond working through the system. Do you mean like paying someone off or something along those lines?"

"That's exactly what I meant."

"No. That isn't the way we do business here. If that's something you want to pursue, you will need to find a different firm."

"Ok. I understand." He paused briefly before continuing. "Just keep doing what you are doing. If we have to go to trial to get rid of this, I'm prepared to do so."

"We may want to depose the officer that was involved. Maybe that way we can figure out the real reason he stopped you. Or at least determine why there is such a discrepancy with the story you give and the one he is obviously going to provide."

"Do whatever you need to do to resolve this favorably. The money is in your trust account and if you need more it's available."

"Might I ask about the source of these funds? Do they come from you, your employment, or someone else?"

"That's no concern of yours. The money will be there if you need more."

"Fine. One more thing. The presiding judge is Judge Hampton. Do you have any prior knowledge or have you ever had any contact with him. Would he be a problem for you?"

He thought for a moment, while carefully choosing his words. "Let's just say I have heard of him and no he won't be a problem."

She ended the interview shortly thereafter. But she thought about their conversation long after he walked out her door. Something didn't seem quite right with him. Maybe she needed to screen her clients a little better from now on. This was the second one in a row that concerned her.

Chapter 9

Rosa had worked on the second McKay motion to suppress well into the night. It was not that difficult to prepare as she had forms from prior motions to follow. She had gone over the facts with Jake a number of times since her initial interview just to make sure there were no factual "mistakes." She was just trying to chip away at the State's case one small piece at a time, hoping to come up with some type of plea bargain that would suit everyone.

The presiding judge would again be Judge Hampton. She was a little giddy when it came to thinking about being in his court again. There was definitely something about him that affected her. Although she realized she only had contact with him on one other occasion, that didn't seem to matter. There was definitely something she felt when she was near him that kept her attention long after the last hearing had ended.

Prior to this morning's hearing, the attorneys were to meet in chambers to discuss the issues. Judge Hampton waived them both in and motioned for them to be seated.

"You both understand the ground rules here, correct? The State is obligated to go forward and establish what happened at the time the defendant made his statements and why they should not be suppressed."

She felt a little weak in the knees when he spoke. Art responded first, simply nodding affirmatively.

Walling looked fairly professional on this particular day, except for his silly bowtie he always wore to court. How could he possibly think that looked good? She noted he must have felt pretty secure though, as he hadn't started stammering yet.

"Yes, Your Honor. Both Mr. Walling and I have discussed procedure and we are ready to go."

Walling was up and off like a shot. She figured he wanted to brow beat his witness one more time before he took the stand. She stood to leave.

As she did, the judge said, "You really look nice today Rosa."

He caught her completely off guard. He was speaking to her! She could feel herself turning a dull shade of red. This was worse than the hearing. What should she say?

Finally she said, "*So do you,*" and she turned around and walked out the door.

"*So do you*" she thought? What the shit did that mean? I am such an idiot. Get yourself under control here Rosa. But he did speak to her—and it was something personal. Did he mean anything by it, or was he just being social? What could she draw from that?

As she took a seat at the council table, his gavel brought her back to reality.

"Everyone ready to proceed?"

Both attorneys nodded affirmatively.

"Then please do so. Mr. Walling the burden is on you. Present your first witness."

"Officer Carnov, please come forward."

After he was sworn in, Walling started with his direct examination. He dispensed with the basic information with haste. It was as if he needed to be somewhere else.

"Ok, Officer Carnov, tell us what happened after you took the defendant to the station.

"Well, we sat him down and asked him what happened and he told us. He said he had done it and she got what she deserved. He pretty much admitted it all and that's what I put in my statement."

"Was he under arrest at the time?"

"No."

"Could he have left if he wanted to?"

"I never thought about it I guess. He didn't try to leave, but then again at that time he wasn't really under arrest either."

"Was he read his Miranda rights at any point up to that time?"

"No. I read them to him then."

"Why did you wait?"

"It was really hectic in the station, and I didn't get around to it. To be perfectly honest, I was still involved in the investigation. He wasn't under arrest, I didn't consider him in custody, and until he told me what he told me, I really had no idea what had happened."

"So you didn't consider it necessary to inform him at that point?"

"Absolutely not."

"Your witness."

"Thank you Mr. Walling. Now sir, you knew he was in that hotel room when this happened didn't you?"

"Yes."

"You knew you had a dead body in that room didn't you?"

"Yes."

"Did you know if anyone else was in the room with them?"

"No, not at that point."

"But you still knew he was a suspect didn't you?"

"No. I really didn't feel I had enough facts to determine whether he was actually a suspect. That's exactly why he hadn't been charged."

"But you had him at the station. You're saying he wasn't in custody?"

"Correct."

"And you would have let him walk if he had asked to?"

"As I said it never came up but yes, if he would have asked, I certainly would have considered it. He was not under arrest at that point. He had not been charged at that point. And all I was trying to do was gather the facts when he made those voluntary statements."

Rosa could tell he had been well prepped. She could also tell she was going nowhere with this line of questioning. She felt she was just going to have to let the judge rule. If he ruled against them, which at this point she thought he probably would, they would have an appealable issue. She was not going to let McKay take the stand under any circumstances.

"Nothing further judge."

"Anything further, Mr. Walling?"

"No, Your Honor."

He didn't stutter. He thought he had this in the bag, and he probably did.

"Well folks, I'll make this sweet and simple. I *do* believe this man was in custody. I *do* believe he was under arrest, but I *do not* believe he could have walked out of the station if he had wanted to. I understand that is contrary to what the officer just testified to, in some respects, but the facts that are not in dispute tip the scales here. The defendant was the only one in the room other than the woman and they knew or should have known that when they took him from the scene. He had blood on him, he was near the body for some reason, he was obviously a suspect and in my opinion, the officer should have given him his Miranda warning at that time. These statements are also excluded as testimony in this case. And Mr. Walling, as a suggestion to you, I would think it's time to give your officers a little refresher course concerning Miranda before you let them do much more work in the law enforcement area. *Do we understand each other*?"

"YYYes sssir. I understand."

He was as red as his bowtie.

Rosa was shocked again. She knew it might be a close call, but she really figured if it were close, the judge would edge toward the State's position rather than the defendant's. Once again, he had surprised her. And was that just a little smile he gave her as he walked off the bench? What the hell was going on here?

She turned to her client and said "Well, we are pretty lucky aren't we?"

"Maybe" he said. He winked at her—*he winked at her*. Now that didn't make sense on any level.

"What do you mean—what are you implying here."

"Nothing. You did a really good job. I thought it came out just as it was supposed to."

And with that, he got up and walked out of the courtroom. That was it. Walling was watching what was going on between she and her client. She walked over to talk with him briefly before he left.

"Nice tie."

"Whatevvver. What the helll happened here?"

"It came out like it was supposed to Art."

"Oh sure it did" he said sarcastically.

"Would you like to discuss a plea deal for a minute?"

"Ggo to hell. I am not bbbargaining this down. See you at ttrial."

He walked out, leaving her alone in the courtroom. As she turned to leave, she knew she would need more than one glass of wine at the end of this day. She won; she was in the driver's seat. But why did she feel she had lost all semblance of control—that she had no clue what the hell was going on? She needed to meet up with Amy and have them bring the whole damn bottle to the table tonight.

Chapter 10

Walling walked back to his office so pissed off he couldn't see straight. He had not had much luck with this case before today and now this. It made no sense. Neither of his rulings in this case was consistent with current case law. *And what the hell was wrong with his tie?*

He turned around quickly. *Was that someone following him?* There was some guy behind him wearing a dark suit and sunglasses. He walked another 50 yards and quickly turned around. The guy was gone, but now there was a woman with a trench coat immediately behind him. Who the hell was she? Was she following him? He ducked into a doorway of a small shop just to see what she would do. She walked right on by. No problem with her, but he had the feeling he was being tailed. Ever since he turned 22 and entered law school, he had felt the eyes on the back of his neck. He had never caught anyone, but there was no doubt in his mind something sinister was going on. He walked out of the doorway and looked both ways before he started down the sidewalk.

He had gone to school in Tennessee at some level all his life. For the most part, school had been a tolerable experience for him but at some point early on in law school, he became aware of the fact that people really did not like him. He could hear them whisper as he walked by, but it really didn't matter at the time. He finished law school and he knew once he graduated, the people following him would stop too. He just figured it was other law students who had issues with him.

He was mostly alone. He had a considerable amount of trouble even engaging a partner for the law school mock trials that were conducted, as a requirement, with groups of two. He finally ended up with someone no one else wanted.

He made it through law school as an average student, and it was only because his father, who was an attorney, pulled a few strings that he was able to obtain a job as an assistant Davidson County Attorney.

He had an idea his father did whatever he had to do to get him the job, so he could avoid some type of partnership with him when he could find nowhere else to practice. He had no family, and probably never would. He was totally inept when it came to the opposite sex and didn't care. He never socialized with his coworkers or anyone else for that matter.

But one thing he did take very seriously was his job. He didn't care if he ate well, or how his parents were, or what the weather might be. But his occupation was a serious issue for him. And when he lost a hearing of this nature, it was like a part of him eroded away. He had lost *both* hearings concerning this case. His record in Court wasn't great, but it actually wasn't that bad either. To lose two hearings in a row, especially involving issues of this nature, not only hurt, but it also confused him.

This judge was new to him. He hadn't dealt with him before, and for a new judge to be this liberal and to set a precedent like this in his rulings just seemed a little strange. Clearly, the judge was not pro law enforcement. He had made that very obvious. Did the judge know him? Did the judge's prior knowledge of him somehow affect his ruling? A few more rulings like that in his court and he would start filing motions to have the judge recuse himself in any hearing he had before him.

He finally reached the office at 2:30. His walk wouldn't have taken near as long, but he had walked out of his way, ducking inside the doorways of businesses, continuing to ascertain whether he was being followed.

Once inside his office, he shrunk down behind his desk, which was situated so no one could come up behind him or observe him from behind.

The Davidson County attorney, Cal Jackson, walked through his door almost as soon as Art had sat down.

"Well, what happened?"

Art hesitated for a moment and then said softly, "He ruled against us."

"You have to be kidding. Why?"

"He said he felt when McKay was taken from the scene to the police station, he was in custody. At that point the process had passed beyond questioning and the investigation stage. As a result, since he was, in essence, under arrest, they should have read him his rights."

"You know, we discussed this hearing for a long time before you left for the court house and we had come to the conclusion we were on the right side of the facts. Did the officer testify appropriately?"

"Yes. He was well prepared and handled himself perfectly. Do you know anything about this judge?"

"Not as concerns his legal abilities. I knew him when he was in private practice and he seemed like an all right guy, but he has only just been appointed and none of us know what his position concerning any of these matters might be. Did you know him prior to his appointment?"

"No. But as you know, he ruled against us in a prior hearing involving this case. One doesn't surprise me. But two hearings that we felt we should have won surprises me a little."

"You sure you got the testimony into the record correctly?"

He knew it would come to this. He knew because his boss didn't like him. He could tell that from the day he had gone to work in his office.

"Yes. It went in the way it was supposed to. Have the court reporter transcribe her notes if you don't believe me. Do you want to take charge of this case yourself? You can if you want to. It won't bother me."

"No. You got it. See it through to the end. You know, Rosa is a good attorney. You have your hands full with her."

"We still should have won both those hearings in my opinion. Do you want someone else in the office to handle it?"

"No, goddamn it, I want you to handle it and handle it correctly!"

"Ok. I understand. I think it's ready for trial and I guess we'll just try it without any of the defendant's statements. I don't think we'll have a problem with a conviction anyway."

"That's what you said about these two hearings—that we shouldn't have a problem with either of them."

"I remember what I said. All I can do is try the case and give it the best I have."

"Hopefully that's enough. What are your thoughts about a plea bargain?"

"Rosa discussed it with me. Over my dead body! This case is going to trial and we will either convict him or they can cut him loose. I'm not backing off unless you tell me to."

"There has already been more publicity concerning this case than I had expected. I think you're right. Get the conviction. *And I mean— get the conviction.*"

"As in, 'my job is on the line.' You don't really mean that do you?"

"Just get him convicted so we don't need to worry about that."

He walked out. It was turning out exactly as he expected. The son of a bitch has it in for him. He knew he did. He walked outside his office door. Some guy in sunglasses was standing at the end of the hall looking his way. *Who the hell was he?* Why did he have sunglasses on in the building? And why was he looking at him—

Chapter 11

Rosa's calendar was unambiguous. It was clearly time to start preparing for the McKay trial. She had changed her approach concerning the trial date and had asked that the trial be scheduled as soon as possible. The State had no resistance, so everything would be fast tracked toward an early date. She had filed all the motions she could. And they had all been sustained, thanks to Judge Hampton. There was nothing left to do but prepare for the actual trial.

The State's witnesses would be limited. Cause of death would need to be established by the medical examiner, and that should work into her case very well.

The main issue that needed to be determined at this point was whether to call McKay as a witness. It appeared to her as though he would have to be called to substantiate the fact that his actions that night were in self-defense. There simply was no other way to establish that issue. She had raised the issue of self-defense as an affirmative defense and it apparently had raised no red flag for the prosecution. The prosecutor had asked no questions about their position that her death had been an issue involving self-defense. That was somewhat unusual. She figured Walling would at least inquire as to some of the specifics once he became aware the defense would use that type of defense. But he had asked no questions whatsoever.

If he *had* taken that extra step to determine exactly what position McKay was taking, resolution of the case might have become somewhat easier. At this point, Walling was apparently not interested in a compromise plea of any kind. He appeared completely disinterested in the defendant's position, which was very unusual for him. Normally he made at least a half-hearted effort to settle every case he tried.

The cops at the scene would testify as to what they saw, but, other than the medical examiner, there were no other witnesses. It appeared without a doubt, based on the information she now had, McKay would have to testify.

She needed to break the news to him and then would need to go through his past to determine if there was anything she needed to keep out of the record. Together, they needed to thoroughly review his history because she knew Walling. He was pretty good in the courtroom. He would apparently never lose that "tell," but other than that, he was pretty good.

Jury selection would be crucial. When McKay got up on the stand and started testifying the victim bit him while involved in a sex act, that testimony, in and of itself, would certainly turn a number of people off. She knew she needed to be very selective concerning the jury and make sure each and every one of them promised to listen to *all* the evidence before they came to a conclusion concerning the defendant's guilt or innocence. She had been down this road enough to know how very important selecting the correct jury would be, especially in a case of this nature.

While going through her mental evaluation of the case, she occasionally thought of him—of that tall, good looking judge who gave her that smile as he left the bench that day. A smile that appeared to be more than a pleasantry.

She had been working on potential questions for the jury panel for about an hour, when her secretary buzzed her.

"Rosa you have a call on line 2."

"Who is it?"

She hesitated a couple of seconds before she replied "Judge Hampton."

"Did he give you any indication what he wants?"

"No. He just said he needed to visit with you."

"Ok. Thanks."

A thousand thoughts raced through her mind in a matter of seconds. This has to be case related—*doesn't it*? She needed to hit the button, to connect the call, to be calm.

"Hi Judge. How are you?"

"Good Rosa. I'm good. How's the day going?"

Ok, enough with the small talk. Get on with it Judge, she thought.

"Fine. I'm just preparing for the McKay trial. Not to talk business here, but your rulings have really defined the issues and evidence in the case. I don't know if you knew, but we asked for a speedy trial and the State concurred, so it will all be resolved one way or the other fairly quickly."

"I would have thought both those rulings would have resulted in a plea bargain, but apparently not."

"No, there doesn't seem to be any desire on the part of the State to resolve it. They want it tried. So be it, I guess. I can certainly accommodate them on that."

"I saw where the case was being scheduled for an early trial date, and I told the Court Administrator's office to assign it to me. I already know a great deal about the case and I felt it would be easier for me to hear it than bring another Judge up to date."

"I didn't know that. I hadn't received any notification from Court Administration yet. That was probably a good idea."

"Enough about business, that really isn't why I called."

"Really? Why did you call then?" She held her breathe waiting for a response.

"Let's have lunch together. We can call it a 'business lunch' if you wish, but I would like to get to know you better. Are you ok with that?"

She almost dropped the phone. There was a long pause until she could think this all through. He waited.

Rosa looked to make sure her door to the outer office was closed, which it was. She wanted no one to hear this conversation other than the two people involved.

"You know Judge, that's probably not a good idea. Isn't that a rules violation? We're in the middle of a proceeding you are handling. Don't get me wrong, I would love to have lunch with you, but the timing seems wrong."

"I know it might be an issue, but I don't want to wait. I know a place in Antioch that serves killer sandwiches and I want to take you there. It's out of the way and the booths are fairly private. I want to get to know you better. But I don't want to wait until this trial is over. That's too far away. I know we'll need to be careful but I think we can do that—and it is, after all, only lunch."

She needed to think, to do some research. How much of an issue could this be? And she didn't want to upset him, personally or professionally.

"Would you give me a few minutes to think about this? Can I call you back?"

"Sure. You have my number. Give me a call. I know this is a little unusual, but I don't want to wait. If you do, that's fine, I understand. I won't like it, but I certainly will understand. It's entirely up to you."

And with that, he hung up.

She pulled out every book on Tennessee ethics she could find. She looked at ethics issues for both attorneys and judges. After about thirty minutes of review, she knew she was just wasting her time. She already knew the answer. This was wrong, just plain wrong. They needed to wait. He too, knew that was the correct answer. Why was he doing this?

As she looked out into space trying to come to a different conclusion, Gene Wakefield walked in her office.

He glanced down and saw all the books on her desk opened to issues involving ethics.

"Do we have an issue here?"

Rosa thought for a moment and then laughed.

"No, no, no, I have an old law school colleague who has a problem and he wanted my opinion." She started closing the books one by one. "This really isn't my problem. Now Gene, what's going on?"

"I was just on my way down to talk to Jack Mason concerning his pending trial and I thought I would stop in and see how you are doing with the McKay issues. Everything ok there?"

"Yes. I'm just finishing up preparations for trial. No problem so far."

"I understand Judge Hampton is trying it. That should be ok shouldn't it? How do you feel about that?"

She wondered how word about this relatively simple manslaughter trial got around so fast.

"Yes. That should be fine for us."

"Ok. I wanted to make sure."

He smiled, looked at all the books one more time, then turned and walked out.

J.B. Millhollin

Rosa swiveled around in her chair and looked out her window for a few moments. She then reached over and picked up her phone.

"Judge, it's Rosa. I just have three questions for you. Where is this place, what day works for you, and what time do we meet?"

Chapter 12

The plane started its long, slow descent into Nashville.

"Tray tables in the upright position. Seatbacks up. All electrical devices turned off."

Standard language he had heard a thousand times.

He could just start to make out the green surrounding Nashville. The hills and valleys were in perfect condition after all the rains of the previous weeks. The lake east of Nashville sparkled in the sunlight and it was obvious the recent drought they had experienced was over—the lake was bank full.

Gene Wakefield was returning from a trip to Las Vegas. This time he had gone alone. He normally took his wife Margie, but this time he had wanted to go by himself and gamble all the time he was there. When he was with her, she constantly wanted to dine at one of the many expensive restaurants now located on the Strip and spend five hundred a meal, or go to one of those stupid expensive shows—do something other than gambling. But, gambling was the only reason he went in the first place. Nashville was a great place to live, but the only gambling available involved the Power Ball—fun on Saturday and Wednesday nights, but a true bore during the rest of the week. He needed continual action to quiet the savage beast inside, and Las Vegas provided it.

Most of his trips to Vegas turned out the same, and he normally lost all the cash he took. But that never deterred him in any respect. He would come up with a new system for playing craps, roulette or any of the other forms of gambling that were available, and off he would go again.

This time it had been horses. He knew there was a way to beat those horses. So he would sit in his room for hours going over the racing form and any other data he could acquire. Finally, he would make his way to the racing book, believing he could, this time, be successful at a new form of gaming.

He seldom won at anything, and this trip was no exception. However, he had to try it and he was glad he had. Now, some $5,000 later, he knew he needed to try some other form of gambling, as his system with the horses wasn't worth a shit.

As the wheels touched down and made their short, high pitched squeal, he thought back about the many trips he had made to Vegas. During the past ten years as his habit had become more intense, he had been there at least three times a year, and each time he was unsuccessful. There had never been a time he had come home with more money than he left with.

Living in Nashville, he had found no outlet to quench his need for day to day gambling other than online, where he would continually bet poker and sports, but once again his success was minimal.

He had tried betting through a local bookie. With him he could bet on credit. He didn't need to put the money up when he made a bet on the Titans or any other sports team. But, as he lost, the debt became unmanageable. His obligation continued to grow until one day he opened his door and came face to face with a gentleman that wanted to break a leg or arm if he didn't come up with the balance he owed in a couple of days. He borrowed the money, paid him off, and that concluded betting with a bookie. He found himself trying to answer numerous questions his wife asked him after the visit from the "enforcer," and it just wasn't worth it.

As he took the shuttle to his car, he wondered what he would tell Margie this time. Their checking account was perilously low. There were many times recently that it had been so low he had had to take out a house equity loan to replenish it. That had worked five or six times, but he knew they would start denying him before long—the equity was almost depleted.

"Hi honey, how was the trip?"

He had walked in the back door and was rummaging through the kitchen for something to eat. She was always there waiting for him.

An Absence of Ethics

After work, after Vegas, she was always there.

"Good. It went good. I made a little money and had fun. It was a much needed break for me. Thanks for letting me go."

He held her in his arms and kissed her.

"You needed that. Glad it went well. By the way, we are a little short in our checking account. I need to buy a few things for the house and groceries and whatever. Can you move some over from savings?"

Savings had been depleted long ago. She just didn't know it.

"Sure, sure. I will take care of that first thing in the morning."

He had really banked on this trip to produce a positive return on investment so he could replenish both the checking and savings accounts. So much for that. He needed to think this through. He needed money. Gambling had not worked so far. He needed a new theory—a new system. He would work on that this evening.

And while figuring that out, he needed to determine how much it would take the first year of college for the twins. They were both graduating and both going to college. He wanted them to attend Vanderbilt, but the cost was incredible. They were both leaning in that direction and had the grades necessary for admission. The cost would be overwhelming. But to start them off in life after graduating from college with tens of thousands of dollars of student loans wasn't fair either. He had put off figuring out their future long enough.

***

He walked in his office door early the next morning. It had been another sleepless night. He had tried to work through all of the financial issues but had not come to a conclusion that was in the least bit satisfactory. One issue was crystal clear. He needed money now, and he needed it badly.

He looked around making sure no one was near as he pulled out the office checkbook. He had authority to write checks and normally wrote them to pay for most office expenses. He started to write one out which was not for a legitimate business purpose—at least a legitimate purpose for the law office.

He had done this once before, and it had not been discovered but it couldn't continue. He knew before long it would need to be replaced or he would eventually be caught. If he did get caught, he only hoped they would give him time to repay it and let him keep his job, just relieve him from his duties of having charge of the office finances.

But the real solution to all this would be to find a method of gambling that took care of all his financial woes. He had started working on a plan last night that had some merit. He would fine-tune it tonight and then test it out during the next week. And if it worked, he would be on a plane to Vegas the first of next month.

Of course, he may need to borrow a little more working capital from the office, but he would face that when it became necessary.

He wrote the check out and put it in his pocket. He would walk down at noon and deposit it. He had another idea for a possible infusion of cash into his personal coffers. It had started with a simple phone call, but had turned into potentially a considerable amount of cash very quickly.

He had already finished part of his job and needed to meet with his people in a couple of days to tie down his final responsibilities. Once finished, they had indicated a very, very large payday would be in order. The problem was the job wasn't quite legal but at this point, as long as no one found out, did it really matter? If it was profitable, no one got hurt, and it would dig him out of a very deep hole, what difference would it make. Everyone was a winner!

But if that was the case, why did he sweat every time he thought about it? He knew himself. He knew how good he was at justifying his actions when they were clearly wrong. But this time, he thought he might have gone just a little too far in what he was doing and what he was about to do. He would work on his gambling system and modify it until it was perfect. He was sure it was only a step or two away. And when perfected, he prayed all his financial worries would end—finally.

Chapter 13

He wasn't a big man by any means, but neither was he small. He wasn't unattractive, but then again, he wasn't attractive. He wasn't bald, but he was balding. All in all, Tommie Thompson was about as average as one could be.

He wasn't a talker; he just did what the Family asked of him—most of the time with little or no conversation at all.

He had just turned 50 with no fanfare of any kind. He had no family—at least a family that he had started. Oh yes, he had family, but it all involved family emanating from his grandfather and great grandfather—he had never been married and had never fathered a child, regardless of what he had previously told his attorney, Rosa Norway. Nor would he ever have a family. Those sorts of things amounted to nothing to him. Women were also a useless commodity. Perhaps an occasional hooker would fit into his schedule but again, with his life style, they to, were unimportant.

His work, now that was important. Work was his life and it was the only facet of his life that made a difference. He did it and did it well. He had lived on the East Coast most of his childhood, but during his middle teens his family had moved to Detroit. They needed to make additional inroads in that area and it was his family that they decided could do that best. Graduating from high school was difficult to say the least, and college was never even considered. He was making money without higher education and his family needed him anyway. He seemed to excel at cleaning up a distasteful situation, in whatever fashion was most appropriate. And that was what he was doing here—trying to determine how to clean up a distasteful situation.

He had completed his previous job about three months prior and then had been told he was needed in Nashville. Pursuant to orders, he had moved to the Nashville area shortly thereafter, renting a home north of Nashville on a month-to-month basis. The previous tenant had moved out in the middle of the night and the home had then become available for him. The house was spotless and that was all that mattered to him.

He had been up for hours, and yet it was only 7:00 am. Generally, no matter where he was, he slept little. His body didn't demand an excess of sleep. He had just completed breakfast consisting of a high fiber cereal and prune juice, and he would not eat again until midafternoon.

Now he waited, sitting in a big overstuffed chair in his living room. He hadn't dressed yet, as there was no need. He sat by his cellphone waiting for the call he knew would eventually come yet this morning. It would be the most important event of the day for him, and he would wait until it was over before he planned the rest of his day's events.

He wore nothing but a T-shirt and boxers. He had made a pot of coffee and had a cup on the stand next to him. There he sat with no TV, no radio, no newspaper—just him and his cellphone.

Finally, it rang.

"Hi boss. How are things back there?"

"'Things,' as you put it are fine back here. You got me on speaker phone? There better not be one fucking sole within a mile of that thing. If I find out somebody heard this conversation, your ass is grass."

"I figured this conversation might take some time and since the phone has a speakerphone function, I just figured I would use it. I don't have a neighbor within two miles of this place boss. And you know I wouldn't jeopardize our conversation that way anyway. You know that boss."

"Ok, ok whatever. Everything proceeding alright out there? You all set up by now?"

"Yes, everything is proceeding fine. I rented a small home north of Nashville."

"What about money? Should we wire you more money, or are you ok?"

"Yes, I'm fine as far as money is concerned. I have enough for a few more months and hopefully that's all the time I'll need to be here. This place sucks. I hate it here."

"Listen you fuck. You're staying there as long as there is work to do. Don't even think about leaving that shithole of a town before your job is finished."

Tommie took a deep breath and calmed his emotions.

"Don't worry boss. I'll stay as long as I'm supposed to, but not one day longer, if that's ok with you."

"Ya whatever. I don't want you running out of the money you need to complete the job. You sure you don't need more money?"

"Yes, I brought enough money. I have what I need to clean up whatever might happen here."

"Have you been able to follow along with everything that is going on with him?"

"Yes. I've read the newspaper accounts and been in court the few times he has been there."

"Does he know you are there and the purpose for which you were sent? Now God dammit, you know what I told you about that. We don't want him to know anything about this."

"No, boss, no, he doesn't know who I am yet and he has no idea why I'm here. He saw me once but never recognized me. We're only distant cousins anyway. Of course, with me living in Detroit and not moving back east until he left to come out here, he doesn't have any idea who I am. We're going to reunite shortly though. I want to know for myself what's going on, and the best way to do that is to spend time with him. I have no doubt when I tell him who I am he will recognize our relationship."

"Have you been able to uncover whether he has any other issues in his life that might have come up before this shit came up? Does he have any other problems we need to address?"

"No, like I told you, boss, up until about a couple of months ago, when all this came up, he had been living a very uneventful life. There was no indication anywhere of any issue or any problem. He was living the perfect life."

"So, do I understand now that *you* are dealing with your own problem? What the hell have you gotten into?"

"Well, yes, I do have a small issue. But that too is going to be resolved."

"Who represents you? Did you go to that same woman lawyer Jake did? Or did you hire someone else?"

"I went to the same lawyer. I didn't figure that would hurt, and we have already determined she is good at what she does. Is there a problem with that?"

"I don't give a fuck who represents you. Just get rid of the charge however you need to. What about that other lawyer we are dealing with? Have you talked to him?"

"Yes, he and I have made contact and everything looks fine. We're to meet again before long and that should solidify the deal. We really need to take this one step at a time. I think I already mentioned that to you, and I still believe that's the way this matter should be handled. It's become somewhat complicated and I really think we need to be careful and approach this slowly until I have everything completely under control."

"How much longer you gonna be there?"

"I'm thinking it will probably be another month or so. It's really hard to tell. I don't want to hurry things. The attorney files a lot of motions and I'm thinking if she files one more or so, the case will be so depleted and absent of evidence, they will have to bargain it out. And then he will again be lost in obscurity and we should be fine. Just let me handle this will you? This will all work out fine."

"You already know how important this is to me, to the Family. You can't screw this up. This has to be done correctly. That's why we sent you, because we felt you were the best one for this job. You understand what I'm saying don't you?"

"Yes boss, I know it's important. And I know you won't be happy if this doesn't turn out the way you want it to. I understand what happens when things don't turn out the way you want them to. But so far, all is going according to plan."

"Take whatever time you need. Just get it done right. Understand?"

"Yes, I understand. Will you be calling back?"

"Why don't you contact us when something happens of which we should be aware."

"Ok, that will be fine. Guess that's all I have for now. Thanks for the call."

An Absence of Ethics

He heard the disconnect at the other end and terminated the connection at his end. Never a "goodbye." Never a "job well done, keep up the good work." Always the same: success was expected, failure was an unacceptable option.

After a few minutes, he got up and made his way to the kitchen. He needed a drink. His leg hurt as he dragged it across the floor. He couldn't help but think of Johnny McDougal. That son of a bitch! Every time he pulled his leg he thought of him—the one that put a bullet in his knee.

The mental and physical pain that memory would bring back was exceeded only by the joy of knowing that right after that happened, he had blown Johnny McDougal's fucking head off with a shotgun. Literally—he had blown the fuckers head off.....there was nothing left but small pieces of a head and a body with a neck at the top.

His leg hurt every day, and today was no exception. Nothing helped ease the pain. Booze would get him through the day and dull it some, but nothing completely alleviated the pain.

"Bastard wanted to know if I had enough money. Why didn't he ask me that before I left? He waits until now, the dumb fuck."

He had always lived alone. He never had anyone to talk to and, as a result, he found himself talking to himself on a regular basis. He thought nothing of it. Sometimes it simply broke up the quiet of a long day, and today was no exception.

"The son of a bitch wants to question my actions does he? He sends me out here to do a job and do it well, which I've done all my life wherever they have sent me, and then has the balls to question my methods. I've had enough of this shit and enough of traveling all over hell to handle jobs like this for these sons a bitches. I'll finish what I was sent here to do and that's it."

He became more agitated the more he considered his situation.

"The son of a bitch questions my actions after all the successful jobs I've done for them. I'm getting to old for this anyway. Once this job is done I'm done. I'll find something else to do and somewhere else to live. I'm not going to deal with these people no more."

But later that evening, as he sat in his chair, in his underwear, half drunk, he wondered who the hell would hire an ex-killer with no experience at anything else. That could be a hard sell. Maybe he would have to reconsider quitting.

Chapter 14

The judge seemed almost as excited about being with her as she was about being with him. He had called her a couple of times just to tell her he was really looking forward to having lunch with her and nothing else. No business conversation of any kind—only that he was excited. He seemed easy to talk to, at least on the telephone. Time would sort this all out. Just a little time.

They had decided to meet at 1:00. The judge felt meeting at that time would mean all the regular lunch patrons would have finished lunch and left the bar, hopefully leaving them virtually alone.

She wasn't sure what to wear. She knew that issue shouldn't be an important factor, and it wasn't as an attorney, but it was as a woman. Everything about this lunch was important, on more than one level. Even if the relationship didn't really work out on a personal basis, she wanted him to respect her on a professional level.

She had given considerable thought about how to approach their meeting—or whatever it was. Was it a lunch date or a business meeting? That in and of itself was the issue. If this went badly, what would the repercussions be in the courtroom? She needed to tread lightly here. She needed to move slowly and figure the situation out as it progressed. This was going to be a work in progress. Until she was sure it would work personally, she would approach it somewhat as a working lunch and move into the personal issues very, very slowly. At least that was her plan as she thought about their "meeting" before she left her office.

She continued to consider her apparel options. What about seductive low cut? Nope. She wasn't going there. She would cover up. She didn't want to bait him. If this were to work, it would work because of the people involved, and not because of his desire to rip off her blouse and grab what was available. All the right reasons this time—nothing more nothing less.

She left the office at 12:30. It would take her half an hour to get there, especially with noon hour traffic.

She arrived right on time—shortly before 1:00.

The bar was dimly lit with traditional electronic games scattered around the room. A layer of peanut shells covered the floors, which were old and wooden. She had to look around for a moment letting her eyes become accustomed to the darkness before she spotted him. He was in the very back booth with his back to the door, but he had been watching for her and was waiving when she noticed him.

He stood as she arrived at the table and sat opposite him.

While grinning from ear to ear he commented, "You look great."

"Thank you. And thanks for inviting me."

That led to a continuing number of pleasantries all during which Rosa was responsive but cautious.

Finally she just blurted out, "Ok, Judge, what are we doing here? Do you know how risky this is? Let me rephrase. I *know* you know how dangerous this is and what type of repercussions could result if we are seen by the wrong people. So what the hell are we doing here, together, in the middle of court proceedings involving us both? Are we nuts?"

She took a deep breath. He just smiled that beautiful smile.

"Ok. First of all, call me John. No more judge. You can use that when you have to, when we are in the courtroom. Now, secondly, I like you. I like everything I have seen about you. I just didn't want to wait until the trial was over to be with you. Who knows how long all that will take, and I didn't want to wait. I realize how risky it is, but I was ready to take the risk to get to know you. And that's what I did. I took a chance and luckily you said 'yes.' Really that's all there is to it."

"But I have always, always been so careful about following the rules. I have never violated one of the Canons of Ethics. I've been so careful. My life is my practice. I don't know what I would do if I couldn't practice law."

"Tell you what, when we leave here today, if the time with me wasn't worth it, then we just had a good sandwich and talked as friends. No looking back. If you feel you enjoyed our time together, then we will figure out where we might go from her. No strings attached one way or the other. And I promise you, whatever happens here today will never affect what happens in the courtroom. If it does, you can request that I recuse myself concerning hearings in which you are involved. Lord knows I have enough courtroom matters to attend to anyway. Is it a deal?"

She thought for a moment.

"That's fair enough. Can we order, I'm starved."

He laughed.

"Absolutely."

He signaled for one of the waiters.

The conversation seemed endless. He was easy to talk to. He had experienced quite a lot in his few years and he wanted to share it all with her. He seemed thoughtful and the conversation involving both of their personal lives, flowed easily between the two of them. Business was never mentioned.

However, about an hour into lunch and after the plates had been removed, leaving both of them with only their refilled coffee cups, he did surprise her with a comment on the McKay case.

"By the way, it doesn't look like there is much evidence left in that McKay case. From my review of the file, it appears as though most of the testimony from the State's witnesses has been stricken. Do they still have a case?"

"Not much. I'm not really sure there is enough left to survive a motion to dismiss. But I can't get Walling to even consider a plea bargain. He seems hell bent for leather on trying the case."

"I have seen him that way before…with other cases. Why don't you file your motion to dismiss now and maybe that will resolve it."

"Ok, sure, I can do that."

"Did I also see where you were representing a man by the name of Thompson on a DWI?"

She looked at him for a second before she answered. How did he know that?

"Yes, I do. How did you know?"

She felt this conversation was heading in a bad direction, but, regardless, she needed to know how and why he knew about this particular case.

"I was assigned the case, along with about 50 others, and I was looking through all of them, as I always do once I'm assigned cases. I just happened to notice your name on the Thompson case. Nothing out of the ordinary, I simply noticed your name."

She studied him for a second. That sounded like a logical explanation.

"Yes, I do represent him. I really don't know a lot about the facts yet but he has retained us to handle the case."

"I was looking at the minutes of testimony, and you may want to look carefully at that one. The officers proposed testimony may be lacking in probable cause. I know that officer. He is, shall we say, sometimes a little short on the truth. And of course, if he had no probable cause to stop, the whole arrest and charge goes out the window. You may want to thoroughly review the evidence and this cop's background. I would think you may want to take his deposition and file an appropriate motion based on what he says. Just a thought."

He gave her that big smile that made her melt every time he did it.

"Sure. I'll look at that as soon as I get back to the office. Any other thoughts about my practice while we are here?"

She smiled to just make sure he knew she was joking.

"No, I guess that's about it. Never hurts to get a second opinion though. At least that was how it worked with me when I was in practice."

The conversation involving work ended. But the conversation about their lives, their ideas and personal thoughts went on long after and well into a third and fourth cup of coffee.

She looked at her watch.

"Lord, it's after 3:00. I need to leave. I told the office I would be taking a long lunch, but I know I have at least one appointment yet this afternoon. Who knows what else she might have penciled in for me that I don't even know about? I need to go."

He took her hand in his.

"When can I see you again? And don't tell me after these two trials are over with, please."

She never moved her hand.

"I don't know...I haven't thought about it I guess."

"Don't think, just react. Do you want to see me again? I guess that's the first question."

She hesitated. She thought again, about the issues involved.

"Yes, I do. Let's have lunch again next week. How does that sound?"

"Let's have supper. I want a little more time this time and I don't want you worrying about your schedule. What about next Tuesday at about 7:00? What do you think?"

"That sounds fine. Just give me a call Tuesday and let me know where and when."

He took her hand in both of his.

"I have really, really enjoyed this. I was a little worried, as I know you were, about whether we should do this. But now I have no doubt. It was the right thing to do. Take care and I will look forward to next Tuesday until it's here."

Rosa smiled, stood up, and walked toward the door.

As she got there, she turned around. He was watching her, which she hoped he was. She waved goodbye and walked out into the warm Nashville sun.

As she walked toward her car, she felt almost giddy. The sky seemed a little bluer, the people she passed seemed a little friendlier, and she felt just a little younger. He seemed like a good man. And that smile—that smile was almost more than she could take. Was he the real deal? What had just happened?

She needed to talk to someone about this, if nothing more than just to verbalize all that had occurred. Without much thought, she knew Amy was the one she needed to tell. Amy would tell her if she should or shouldn't be going down this road.

Hopefully, she would give her the answer she wanted to hear. Because she was afraid if she didn't, for the first time in her life, she might have to follow her heart and leave common sense and sound reasoning behind. Unfortunately, that smile trumped the Canons of Ethics all to hell.

But, about half way back to the office, the personal warmth of the conversation between the two wore off. She started considering the other side of the coin—the business side. His comments about the possibility of a dismissal concerning McKay intrigued her. There certainly appeared to her to be enough evidence left to at least try the case, but who was she to second guess the conclusion he had apparently already reached. He had reviewed the file, he was the one that needed to make the final decision, and obviously he felt there might not be enough evidence left to submit the case to a jury. She would file the motion immediately.

Chapter 15

It was almost noon. She was meeting Amy for lunch and she didn't want to be late.

She had way, way too much office work to do. Yesterday she had extended her lunch hour beyond what she should have when she met with John, or the judge, or whatever the hell she should call him. She didn't want to press it today. She felt comfortable with a 90-minute lunch today but no more.

She hadn't slept last night. All she could think about was him. It had been a long time since she had been literally swept away by someone, but he got the job done, and she was smitten. Was that still a word? In any event, he was all she thought about most of the night.

She and Amy always met at the same location for lunch: Puckett's on Church Street. It was noisy but if they got there a little early, they could always find a back booth that was fairly quiet.

Rosa found a small booth near the back wall that would suit both of them. Amy arrived right after she had found the booth and, in her own energetic way, moved at the speed of light through the patrons of the restaurant as if she was on a mission she had little time to accomplish.

"Hi. Wow do you look nice today. Something special going on or just feel like having a dress up day?"

Rosa took a second look at herself before she responded.

"I never thought about it I guess. But now that you mention it, I do look put together today, don't I?"

"Yes you do. How is today going for you? Anything going on or just another day?"

"No, today is just another day—nothing special. I will admit I didn't sleep much last night though. I'm tired so if I lay my head down on the table and fall asleep just wake me before you leave."

"Why no sleep? What was on your mind?"

"Did I tell you I had a lunch date with Judge Hampton? It was yesterday."

Amy just stared at her, as her mouth dropped wide open.

"Back up. Go through that again."

"Guess I didn't. I had a lunch date with Judge or rather, John Hampton yesterday. I met him about noon and got back to the office about 3:30."

"Aren't you in his court for something or rather? Can you do that? You aren't supposed to do that are you? Was it just for work? Or is he interested in you? If he is interested in you, isn't there some rule against that? What the hell are you doing? Do you know? Does *he* know?"

"Just stop. Yes, he is interested in me. And yes, there is a rule against it. I could get in all kinds of trouble, as could he. We discussed that and met anyway. You can't say anything to anyone Amy. This has to be kept quiet. But, oh my God Amy, we had such a good time. We're going to meet again soon, and it will be before my hearings are over. So we need to be extremely careful."

"Have you gone fucking nuts? You can't put your career on the line for this guy. Again, you have told me from day one, most judges were assholes. What makes this one any different? How could you even consider meeting this guy? You've gone off the deep end Rosa. You need to stop this and at least wait until your hearings in his courtroom are over with."

"Lower your voice just a notch. I thought it might bother you. I get it. It bothered me too, but not enough to stay home. I went and I'm glad I did. And I'll probably meet him again—at least that's the plan. Everything you say is accurate Amy, but this guy is special. And I'm not going to put everything on hold because of a couple of cases I have pending in his courtroom. This is the way he wants to handle it."

Amy looked away trying to process all she had been told. Finally, she looked at Rosa and smiled.

"I guess it's your life. But don't forget I told you so."

"Hopefully it won't come to that. Hopefully both the cases I have pending with him will be resolved prior to trial. Although I don't know, the prosecuting attorney is really being, to use your descriptive term, an asshole, at least with one of them. You know Amy, I am taking this hour by hour. I don't know what the hell I'm doing seeing him. I just know I like this guy. He's smart, good looking, and treats me like royalty. And I know he's interested in me. He started this and when we were done the other day, he set up another time for us to get together."

"I know, I know. I have heard all this 'he likes me, he really likes me' shit before. That's fine. If it's what you want, and if you're fully aware of all the consequences, I guess it's your call. But personally, I think you're nuts. I really think you're nuts."

"I get it Amy. But do you know how long it's been since I let myself go—since I let myself feel anything. I've been so wrapped up in my own life and my own career, the rest of the world has passed right on by. I'm ready to have a relationship. I'm ready to slow my professional life down and to fall in love. This guy, from what I can figure out, is what I'm looking for. And I'm not going to let a couple of idiots that I represent stop this from happening. The timing is not perfect, I know that. But the man seems like the right man, and I'm not going to put that in jeopardy because of my career. I've done that since I graduated from high school, and I'm not doing it again."

Amy took another deep breath.

"Ok. It's your career. Just don't forget I told you so. Now, tell me about this guy. This John Judge or whatever it is you call him. Tell me about him."

The conversation lasted well over an hour until Rosa looked at her watch, tapped it a couple of times, and told Amy she needed to go. They got up together and paid their respective bills.

As they both walked back to work, Amy said, "Tell me about these two cases you have. Are they interesting at all?"

"Actually, the one involving a man by the name of McKay is fairly interesting. He's the guy that allegedly killed that prostitute a couple of months ago. I suppose you read about it in the paper. Obviously, I don't feel at ease in discussing the specific issues, but that one is coming to trial first."

"You just told me you are having a relationship with a judge that you are trying a case before but you can't discuss the facts of the case with me? Ok, sure whatever. But, yes I remember reading about that in the paper. Can anyone sit in on those trials?"

Rosa was quiet for a moment before responding.

"Yes, you're right. There is a bit of a double standard there, but I'm still not going to discuss the facts with you. Sure. It's open to the public. Why?"

"I may come and watch. I've never seen you in action. The case sounds interesting and now with the extra added dimension of knowing the judge and the defense attorney are romantically involved, I just might take the time to watch this all unfold. Sounds like a good day to me."

Rosa laughed.

"Sure, I would love to have you sit in. It's a couple of weeks away. I'll let you know."

"Great. Should be fun watching the banter between you and your lover/judge."

"It obviously hasn't gone that far Amy. And I'm not really sure it ever will. But I am not taking a chance and waiting either."

"Just don't forget." Amy had started walking in her own direction toward her office.

"I told you so."

Chapter 16

Rosa had completed her pre-depo checklist and was as prepared as she was ever going to be. She had arranged to have her client meet her at the courthouse and was ready to walk out her office door. But, just as she got up to leave, Wakefield walked in.

"I understand you have the Thompson depo this morning."

"Yes, I do. In fact, I was just ready to walk out the door."

"What are your thoughts about the case?"

"It's really a little early to come to any conclusion. I'm going to take the officer's depo this morning to see if he can establish a factual basis for stopping him. According to Thompson, he wasn't speeding and hadn't broken any traffic laws. The cop just stopped him."

"That's what I understand. Of course, that's what they all say, but it will be interesting to see what the cop says. It could be your only defense. Thomson certainly tested above the limit, so there won't be much you can do about that element of the offense. Have you talked to the judge? Does he have any thoughts about the case?"

"You know I don't normally talk to any judge about a case pending in his Court. But, I did happen to have an opportunity to briefly talk to Judge Hampton about this particular case. And he was the one who thought I should take the cops depo."

She squirmed a little. Why would Wakefield ask that?

"Has a trial date been set yet?"

"No. There is a pre-trial hearing next week and we'll set it then. I wanted a little more information from this cop before we set a trial date. And I really want to hear him tell me why he stopped him. Do you have a particular interest in this case?"

"No, no, not at all. Our client comes from a little money, and I thought I would keep track of how it was going that's all. No particular interest. Good luck today."

"Thanks."

She walked out the door wondering how he knew so much about this case.

They had set off a special conference room in the courthouse to take the cops deposition. Once she arrived she had to run down Walling— he wasn't in the room. The cop and the court reporter were both waiting, but Walling was nowhere to be found. She finally found him in the clerk's office.

"You ready. Let's get this going. I have other things to do today."

"Yes, yes I'll be right there. Go ahead and I'll be right there."

She walked back to the conference room deep in thought. Thompson had arrived and was seated near the back wall. She motioned for him to come up to the conference table and sit with her. The cop was seated and she figured Walling had him well prepared.

The room smelled musty. It smelled of poor defendants and troubled people. The sooner she could get this over with and left this room, the better off she would be.

Walling arrived shortly. After the cop was sworn in, and the formalities concerning use of his testimony were completed on the record she was ready to delve into the specifics of the traffic stop.

"Now, Officer Miller, do you remember the evening of January 13th of this year?"

"Yes."

"Do you remember stopping the defendant Mr. Thompson?"

"Yes."

"Do you remember why you stopped him?"

"Yes."

"Can you tell us why?"

"Yes."

Walling had prepared him well. Short answers and to the point with nothing offered voluntarily.

"Then please do so."

"I was driving up West End Avenue with the radar unit activated, and as he approached me, I noticed he was running about 10 miles per hour above the limit. I turned around and stopped him."

"Did you exit your vehicle?"

"Yes."

"Did he?"

"No."

"What happened next?"

"I walked up to the driver's side and told him, through the open window, he was speeding, and I immediately smelled alcohol on his breath. I asked him to exit the vehicle, which he did. I asked him to perform tests to determine if he was intoxicated, which he did. He failed them all."

"Let's go back to the stop. What was the speed limit in that area?"

"40."

"And he was 10 miles per hour over that?"

"Yes. Actually a little more. I wrote it down to 10 over to give him a little break."

"Would you consider writing it back up to the actual speed and giving him a break on the DWI?" she asked with a smile.

The officer actually returned the smile.

"Sorry. Can't do that."

"Did you allow the defendant to view the speed displayed on your unit?"

"No."

"Why?"

"He never asked. If he would have asked, I would let him."

"From the time you observed his speed on your unit until the time you stopped him did you ever lose sight of the vehicle."

"No. Traffic was very light. And when he drove by me I was able to identify him as the driver and as the same person driving the vehicle when I stopped him, so there was never any question about the drivers identity."

"You say you had the defendant perform some physical tests to determine sobriety and that he failed all of them. Would the fact he had one leg that is not fully functional have affected his ability to perform those test, in your opinion?"

He thought a moment.

"No, I don't think so. In my opinion, he would have failed those tests if he would have had three good legs. He was intoxicated. End of story."

By then, Thompson was tugging at her sleeve nonstop.

"We need to take a short break. My client and I need to talk for just a second."

She got up and walked toward the door. Thompson walked slowly behind her, dragging his leg as he moved.

She shut the conference room door behind him and walked down the hall a few feet.

"That dirty son of a bitch is lying. I'll break that bastard's leg—I'll break both of them. I'll bury that lying fucker."

"Now, Mr. Thompson, hold on. He's just doing his job. Be more specific. What's he lying about? Be specific so I can question him further. Do you mean about stopping you in the first place?"

"Yes, I wasn't speeding, the lying asshole."

She thought of Amy.

"Ok, let me get into that with him again."

They walked back into the conference room. Walling and the officer were laughing about something. She paid no attention.

"Just a few more questions. Officer, had you had a chance to check the accuracy of your radar unit that day?"

"Yes. I checked it, pursuant to the manual, both before I came on duty and as I was getting off. It checked out both times, and I noted that in my manual."

"Do you have those records with you?"

"No."

"Will you provide those records to Mr. Walling so he can provide them to me?"

"Sure. But, I can tell you, you will find nothing. The tests all came out properly."

"You let me determine that. You provide the records."

She felt she had gone about as far as she could. She would need to figure out another approach. The officer had most of his bases covered, but at least she knew what he would testify to when called, and she could try to counter that the best she could.

It appeared as though probable cause, at least for now, would not be easily attacked. There were no other witnesses. She would need to attack his credibility. She didn't want to alert either Walling or the officer as to how she would do that. Questioning him about other cases in which it had been shown he had not been telling the truth would alert them to one of her main strategies and she didn't want to do that. She would be ready to use it when she was in front of a jury. That would be the appropriate time to raise that issue, not now.

"That's all I have. Thank you."

She got up to leave the room with her client close behind.

Once they were in the hallway, Thompson said, "Is that it? Is that all you're going to do? What the hell did we accomplish?"

"Now Mr. Thompson, let me handle this. It accomplished just what it was supposed to. It established the fact that we may need to try a different approach other than using the stop as a defense. Let me do my job. The depo went fine."

He turned around without saying a word, mumbled something under his breath, and walked away.

She walked out the other door of the courthouse so as not to come in contact with Thompson again and walked back to the office. As she did, she realized this was not going to be easy. She had a cop that stretched the truth and an ill-tempered client. Not a good combination. The judge may have been correct; the cop may be a liar. But that wasn't established today, and it was clear that she would need much more than what she had to work with so far to get this guy off. And if he was convicted, knowing what she knew about Thompson, she was a little concerned about his reaction. *The guy appeared to be a fricken ticking time bomb.*

Chapter 17

"Little man" had just had a seat. She needed to begin preparing him for trial. It would take a number of sessions, depending on how long it took him to actually comprehend what she meant when she compared a jury trial to "the circus."

The jury process was controlled chaos. Each presiding judge would do all they could to control the process, but with so many diverse people and all that human emotion in one room, there were always unanticipated issues. It would eventually settle down once the final 12 jurors were selected, but until then it really was a circus.

Rosa would try to clear her mind of everything other than this man's case, but it would be difficult. She had agreed to meet John for supper tonight, and the prospect of being close to him again was almost overwhelming. She couldn't concentrate. She had trouble generating enough interest to eat breakfast. She was uncertain what to wear. She would work a little later than normal and then drive to the restaurant from her office. So she needed to wear the clothes that she would wear "for him" to work. She really, really needed to settle in and concentrate on preparing McKay for trial and simply let the rest of the day take care of itself. But she was afraid that would be easier said than done.

"I am going to need to know about your background Mr. McKay. I anticipate you will need to testify and if you do I have no doubt the prosecutor will want to interrogate you about your personal history. First of all, are you ok with testifying?"

"Why do I have to?"

"Because there is no other way we can present your side of this case. We had all the verbal statements you made thrown out, but they still have witnesses who will testify as to what they saw, and what they saw is enough to convict you unless someone tells the jury what happened in that room. The only one left alive that can tell them it was a matter of self-defense is you. Now do you have issues with that? Is there some reason you wouldn't want to testify that you haven't already discussed with me?"

"No, not that I can think of."

Rosa wondered if she had worn the right clothes. Maybe she should have worn the dress, not this outfit. She wondered if she should go home and change before she met him.

He was staring at her. She was staring into space. She suddenly released what she was supposed to be doing.

"Sorry, sorry Mr. McKay. I was contemplating what you said. Can you tell me what you did in life before moving to Nashville."

"Family business. Import/export. Nothing of any consequence. I finally got tired of it and had a little money saved up so I moved here. Since I have been here, I have basically done nothing."

"And I assume you would have no trouble testifying to that then?"

McKay looked away as he thought. Normally, that was not a good sign. Looking away was normally an indication there was an issue or two lurking around somewhere.

"Mr. McKay, are you ok with testifying to that or not? I need to know now. The worst thing that could possibly happen is for you to throw a surprise at me in the middle of this trial. I need to know if you have problems in your background that the prosecutor could present to the jury that might affect our case. Is there a problem here?"

"No. There are no problems. It's as I told you, and I'll testify to that."

"Ok, good. Now do you understand the basic jury process? I know we have discussed it before, but I want to make sure you understand how it works. I know you made some notes on what I told you. Have you had a chance to review those notes?"

"Yes."

"So do you think you understand how a jury is selected—how we end up with twelve people who have no knowledge of your case and who can render a fair and impartial verdict? Do you think you understand that process well enough now that I don't have to go through it again with you today, or would you like me to review all that with you again?"

"No. There is no need for you to do that. But when do I get my chance to tell them what happened, to tell them my side. When do I get to do that?"

"When the State rests. When the prosecutor tells the judge that he is done presenting his evidence, you will be able to tell your side of it. But I am telling you right now, Mr. Walling is pretty good at cross-examination. And the next time you come in we will need to go over how that all works. It's not a pleasant thing for the individual being cross-examined, but I'll have you ready, and you should be able to handle it with no problem. As long as there are no secrets we are fine. I can't prepare for something I know nothing about. Do we understand each other Mr. McKay?"

"Yes, yes we understand each other. Now what about my testimony? What do you want me to say?"

She again thought about supper with the judge. She should order something that didn't generate a lot of gas. Fish. That would be good. Nothing spicy.

"Miss Norway, what should I say?"

The voice of "little man" brought her back to reality quickly.

She reviewed the facts with him—again. They were all consistent with the story he told her the first time she interviewed him. Nothing had changed and she was glad his story was the same each and every time they discussed it. The essential facts had never changed indicating to her he was remembering it as it actually happened and not trying to insert facts that favored him. She had seen that happen on more than one occasion, and when it did happen, it normally resulted in disaster.

When the facts weren't consistent, maybe even only a change in a small detail here and there, there were always problems. And after interviewing as many people as she had over the past few years, most of the time you could tell they were making it up as they went along, and so could a jury. They were smarter than most defendants gave them credit for. Most of the time, they could smell a liar, and most of the time they rewarded them accordingly.

Her conversation and prep lasted another long hour, and she had many other items to complete before she met up with the judge. But, regardless of the item she was handling, her thoughts would continue to return to the date she had with him later in the day.

***

Rosa finally walked out the office door at 6:30 having completed most all of the tasks she had scheduled for the day. As she drove down Interstate 65 south of Nashville, her thoughts returned to McKay. She was a pretty good judge of character. Not great, but pretty darn good. And something was wrong. She couldn't put her finger on it. She wasn't sure if it was the facts of the case, or it was McKay as a man, but something didn't feel right. She only hoped she figured it all out before the trial. She had a week to become more comfortable with him and his facts. Otherwise, she would carry this feeling all the way to the courtroom, and she didn't need that on her mind too. It was tough enough handling what you knew was accurate, rather than continually looking over your shoulder and worrying when the other shoe would drop.

Enough about the "little man." She had arrived. She walked inside and approached the hostess.

"I'm Rosa…"

Before she said anything else, the hostess said, "Gotcha covered. Come with me."

She took Rosa to a small table in the far corner of the restaurant, where the judge was waiting.

He stood.

"You look amazing." He covered every inch of her body starting at the top and moving to her shoes.

"Thank you."

During the next couple of hours, their conversation ran the gauntlet of subjects, avoiding only their mutual interests in work. The McKay case and the Thompson case were never discussed. Conversation concerning their past, their present, and their future went on for over two hours, during which they consumed tomatoes with mozzarella cheese and olive oil, a small dinner salad and grilled Grouper over a bed of cheese grits. The food was as good as the conversation.

Finally, it was time to call it a night.

He looked at her and said, "Do you want to go home alone or

come with me?"

She looked in his eyes and with an obvious degree of reluctance said "I need to go to my home. I'm just not yet committed John. Give me some time. I love being with you, but I'm not to that point yet."

He took her hand.

"You take all the time you want. This has been one of the most enjoyable evenings I've had for a long time. I don't want to screw this up. You take as much or as little time as you wish, Rosa."

The corner was dark. Most patrons had long since left. The few tables that remained occupied involved people deep in their own discussions. The judge made sure of that before he moved toward her and kissed her. Just once. Lightly on the lips. And she responded.

He walked her to her car and kissed her again before she got in. This time he put his arms around her and held her. She could tell this kiss was one that meant business.

"When can we get together again?" he asked as she slid behind the wheel.

"Just give me a call." She said with a smile. "I love being with you, John. Just let me know when you're ready."

"Oh I will. And it will be soon. I'll call you."

She left the parking lot and angled down the entrance ramp towards Interstate 65. She had been with him for more than two hours and it had seemed like two minutes. She knew what he had in mind—what he wanted from her—but she just wasn't ready. Well, maybe she was ready but just didn't want to give in quite yet. She needed to think this all through for a few more days. Let it simmer.

But she felt pretty certain, the next time they were together, they wouldn't be leaving the restaurant for separate destinations. She only hoped they would be as compatible in bed as they were around the supper table..

Chapter 18

Art Walling sat staring out his office window. He was trying his best to prepare for the McKay trial, but all he could think about was that this case appeared to be a complete disaster. The judge clearly didn't like him. He had twice ruled against the State, both rulings clearly intended to establish how much he disliked him, or maybe even hated him. The rulings weren't based on the law that was for sure. They were based on the fact that the judge just clearly hated him.

In addition, his boss was on his ass. He figured even if he won this case *and* the Thompson case, he was toast. They were going to fire him. And the officers in the case were pissed off at him for losing both motions to suppress filed by Rosa. On top of everything else, it was clear to him he was being followed.

And, of course, in the Thompson case, he had the added dimension of an officer that had lied on the stand in the past. He knew what he was dealing with when it came to Officer Miller. He had been down the road with him before. Sure, Rosa didn't bring that up at the depos. She didn't need to. He knew all about it and also knew he had to find some way to offset it. The officer's integrity and credibility would be an issue at the time of trial and he needed to be ready to deal with it.

He had handled multiple issues in his life before but not very well. He had always needed to take them one at a time and try to determine what to do about each one separately.

Concerning the judge, there was really nothing he could do except be aware—especially as concerned upcoming cases. He knew now this judge was very liberal and he had concluded he would need to adjust his approach accordingly, whenever he had to appear before him.

As concerned his boss, again there was little he could do. He just needed to be prepared and do the best he could with these two cases. That was it. Nothing more, nothing less.

And the officers would fall into line if he won both of these cases. All they wanted was to be validated as officers. Of course, that meant getting convictions.

Speak of the devil.

"Hi Art. How are things going?"

Cal Jackson, Art's boss, had just walked in his office.

"Great. Just couldn't be better. What do you need?"

"You all ready for McKay? Not much time left."

"Sure. Ready as I'll ever be. Just waiting for the officers to get here and go over their testimony one more time. Is there something we need to discuss about the case?"

"What do you know about this McKay? Has he lived here long?"

"He's been here for more than ten years, I do know that. We did a criminal background check and nothing came up. He hasn't had any contact with the law at all. What are you getting at? Is there something I don't know or should know about this guy?"

"No, not that I know of. It just seems strange he just shows up in Nashville for no particular purpose. And that he is so squeaky clean. I just wondered if you had had a chance to run a background check on him other than just a criminal check. Are the officers prepared to testify?"

"Yes. They're fine. They were disappointed with losing those two motions, but they are fine."

Cal walked over and looked out Art's window standing silent for a moment before speaking.

"I didn't mention this to you Art, but I had the court reporter transcribe both of those hearings concerning McKay. I needed to know why we lost."

Art held his breath, waiting for his next sentence.

"I read every word of both hearings and you know what? You were correct. You did everything you needed to do to win those hearings and in fact, you should have won both of them. Losing one would have been strange, but to lose both of those hearings when the evidence came in as it did, was more than strange. Do you think maybe Rosa and the judge have something going here?"

Art considered his answer.

"No, no I don't Cal. I would trust Rosa with my life. Ethically, she is above reproach. I don't think she would ever become involved with a judge she is trying a case before."

"Something doesn't smell right Art. Certainly you and the officers involved did your job. But something isn't quite right here. I think you may need to extend your research a little further concerning the judge and this defendant."

"I have no doubt the Bar Association did a thorough job researching the judge's background, at least up until the time he was appointed. But, based on his rulings in this case, we may need to look into his background and his current situation a little further. But for now, I think we need to concentrate on McKay—where he came from and what his background was prior to coming here. I don't feel comfortable with this case at all. Something smells and we need to figure it out. But, I did want to tell you Art, you did a good job on both those hearings. The result did not appear to me to be based on anything you did or didn't do."

"Thanks Cal, that's good to hear. I'm having our intern do some checking on McKay's background, but as of yesterday he hadn't come up with anything."

"Good, good. Ok, carry on Art. Let's see what happens."

He left Art's office with a wave of his hand.

Well, Art thought, that vote of confidence helped. As he considered what Cal had just said, he threw out any idea of Rosa and the judge somehow being involved. There was simply no way in hell she would ever do anything like that. So that left the other issue—that there may be more to this McKay than he knew. And if there was, how might it impact this case?

He got up and walked to his office door, carefully peering out both ways before walking into the hallway. There was no one in the hallway either way, so he walked out and headed toward Mike John's small corner of the floor. Mike was a second-year intern and a second-year law student at Vanderbilt. He was a smart kid, and there was nothing he couldn't figure out on a computer. As he approached

Mike's small cubbyhole, Mike turned around to greet him.

"Morning Art. I was just getting ready to come see you. I've found some interesting information on your man McKay. It's taken me two days to wind my way through it all, but I think you should see this. I'm not sure this is what you are looking for, but it appears to be information you should know."

Art started looking at the different pages Mike had accumulated while trying to uncover information about McKay. As he read the research, his heart started to race. There was page after page of references to McKay and his involvement with the McKay Family back east.

This man is, or at least was, connected. It might have been a few years ago, but the fact remained—he was connected. This case just kept getting better and better. He figured Rosa knew nothing about this. Or maybe she did. But, at least for now, she didn't know he knew, and he would leave it that way. He would read every word he could find and be fully prepared concerning this issue at the time of trial. He knew McKay would need to testify. And once he was on the stand, cross-examination would be like shooting ducks in a barrel. *Now if he could just figure out who the hell was following him.*

Chapter 19

They sat alone in an empty courtroom. Bill Stone sat at one table and his wife Carol at another. Their attorneys had walked out of the courtroom through a door behind the bench to conference with the judge concerning some procedural matter or another. Neither of them had any idea what was going on. They thought they had the issues all worked out. They thought they had finally come to a conclusion concerning support, visitation, and property settlement. But now there seemed to be a procedural issue that necessitated a conference without either of them present.

The marriage had been on the rocks for a couple of years. They had both tried to make it work for the sake of the kids, but it hadn't worked out, and both of them had reached the point where they were tired—tired of trying to make it work and tired of each other.

So they sat down one night and put together a plan to amicably separate their assets, establish a support figure, and determine visitation.

Bill knew Carol would never agree to any custodial arraignment other than for the children to live with her. Jack was only eight and Jenny just six. Bill admitted they should live with her but with liberal visitation, and she agreed.

The details were ironed out by their attorneys and here they were. After eight long years of marriage, this was it. Judge Jefferson Hagan, a general sessions court judge, responsible for handling civil matters of this nature, had scheduled today for a pretrial conference. But

An Absence of Ethics

since they had come to an agreement, and the paperwork was finished, they had decided to sign everything and use the day to finalize the paperwork with the judge and terminate their marriage.

Judge Hagan could not have been more accommodating. He was extremely helpful in assisting both parties, but apparently there was a small problem which needed to be resolved before the marriage was actually dissolved.

While waiting, Bill had time to reflect. It had been a long haul for both parties. They had been childhood sweethearts. They grew up together. They lived together in college. They had graduated together from U. of T. and had married not long after graduation. She was pregnant when they married, and Jack was born seven months later. They had no time to enjoy their new formal relationship before Jack arrived. Bill always figured that had been one of their problems. The relationship did change once they became legally bound, and they had no opportunity to really become accustomed to that extra layer of relationship once Jack was born. Neither of them would have had it any other way, as Jack was a special child and meant the world to both of them. But unfortunately, Bill had always felt his birth probably hurt their marriage.

They struggled month after month to make the marriage work once Jack was born. Carol became pregnant again almost immediately before either of them had a chance to acknowledge the marriage was in trouble. Jack and Jenny were born just a little more than a year apart. Once Jenny was born, the pressure upon both of them mounted to an even greater level.

During the coming years, they would seek marriage counseling on a regular basis. He would move out for a period of time and then back in. They tried everything to make the marriage work and keep the family together.

Of course, when he took a job as a beat cop with the Nashville Police Department, the extra pressure involving his safety didn't help either. He knew he wouldn't be a beat cop for long, and he was correct. Shortly after he was hired, he was promoted to homicide detective, which helped relieve the day to day pressure concerning his occupation, but the marriage was so far gone there was nothing that could be done to save it.

There were also financial issues that plagued the marriage from day one. Their money problems were nothing different than what most couples seemed to endure, but it did create one more area of pressure. Carol didn't work. She was a stay at home mom, which is what both of them wanted. But the lack of a second income did create financial pressure neither of them could ignore.

Bill's short trip down memory lane quickly returned to today's stark reality as both attorneys and the judge walked back into the courtroom.

Bill stood up—all 6-feet-3 inches of him. He was an imposing figure without one extra pound of fat on his thin frame.

"What's the problem?" he asked his attorney.

"Nothing. There was just some confusion concerning the terms of the settlement agreement. Once that was cleared up, there was no problem at all. Are you still ready to finish this up today?"

"Yes, of course. Let's get this over with. I'm supposed to be working right now."

"Folks, are you ready to sign the agreement and terminate the marriage today?" Judge Hagan asked.

Both Carol and Bill answered, "Yes" simultaneously.

"Then if you will go ahead and sign and have your attorneys notarize your signatures, I will sign the decree and we can all go home."

Carol signed the paperwork and her attorney notarized her signature. He then walked the paperwork over to Bill. With no hesitation whatsoever, he signed above his name and gave the paperwork to his attorney to notarize his signature.

Once completed, Bill's attorney walked the decree to the bench. The judge then signed it and gave it back to him for filing with the clerk of court.

"Mr. and Mrs. Stone I want to commend you on resolving your issues in this case. You did a good job coming to an agreement concerning all these matters and, in addition, saved the judicial system and your attorney's a considerable amount of time and effort in avoiding having to settle everything for you. Thank you for that. You have a lovely family. Keep those kids out of the middle of any issues that might come up involving the two of you and they should be just fine. Good luck and thanks again."

The judge stood up and left the courtroom leaving only the parties and their attorneys. Bill walked over to Carol who by now was standing up beside her attorney, took her in his arms and hugged her.

"I'm sorry," he said.

She whispered back "It's fine Stony. Thank you for handling the ending like a gentleman and a friend."

Stony, his name to all those who knew him beyond a casual hello, walked back over to his attorney and said, "Are we done here? Can I go back to work?"

"Yes, I'll send you copies of everything once they are all file stamped. Thanks Stony."

And with that, eight years of marriage came to an end.

Stony walked into the precinct with a heavy heart but relieved. He was told by the cop manning the front desk the captain wanted to see him as soon as he walked in.

He walked immediately to his office.

"Hi Stony. Everything over with?"

"Yes. Done. Went well. A little tough but it was necessary."

"Are you going to need some professional advice getting through this?"

"No, no I'm fine. We're both still friends and that helps. The kids seem to understand what's going on, at least to some extent, and I'll see them as often as I can. I think Carol will really be good about that to. No, I'll be fine, but thanks for asking."

"How did everything go in the courtroom? Any problems there? I know you mentioned you had Judge Hagan. Did you get along with him?"

"Yes."

"Good. Glad everything went well Stony. Now get back to work. We had two people murdered on the north side last night. The files are on your desk."

As Stony walked back to his desk, he couldn't help but, at least to some extent, feel nostalgic about the end of the marriage. It was bittersweet for him. On the one hand, he was afraid he had lost the love of his life. On the other, he was afraid if he had had to wake up with her one more morning, he would go insane.

All in all, this was the right thing to do. But putting his life back together was going to take some time. He only hoped at some point in the near future, he would enjoy a return to normalcy, as opposed to the roller coaster existence he had endured in his recent past.

Chapter 20

Rosa sat in her office reviewing paperwork concerning a new case. Some kid had broken into an office building and was actually caught with the goods some four blocks away. He would be in to see her shortly and she knew it was important she thoroughly review this matter before he arrived, but her thoughts continued to reflect on her last contact with John.

She tried to concentrate on this stupid kid and his break in. But the harder she tried, the more difficult it became. She finally laid her pen down, swiveled around in her chair, and stared out her window. It was all she could do to keep him off her mind. She had waited three days for his call, which as of this morning, she had not received. Maybe she should just call him. Would that be the right thing to do? She would wait until tomorrow morning and if she hadn't heard from him, she would make the call. She really wanted to see him, to be with him, and the sooner the better.

She had just swiveled back around, when her secretary, June, buzzed her.

"The judge is on the phone for you."

"Which judge? And did he say why?"

She already knew, or at least she hoped she did, but she wanted confirmation before she picked up the phone.

"*The* judge. You know which one I mean. And no he didn't tell me what he wanted."

There was a smile on the other end of the intercom, of that she was certain.

June had worked for Rosa from day one, and it had become difficult to hide anything from her.

"Fine. Put him through."

"Good morning Judge."

"Rosa, good morning. How goes the battle this morning?"

"I was trying to sort it all out when you called. How are you?"

"Good, good. How about supper tonight? Do you already have plans?"

"Let me check my calendar."

She never even looked. It didn't matter what it reflected. She would cancel everything to spend time with him.

"No, my schedule is fine. Same place? What time?"

"Yes. Same place. And will 7:00 work for you?"

"Yes it will. I'll see you then."

She hung up the phone and said one word

"Yes!"

***

The rest of her day would move by very, very slowly. She remained at the office until it was time to leave and meet him. She arrived at the restaurant a little before 7:00 and spotted him immediately upon walking in. He was seated at the exact table they had had for their previous encounter.

He stood up and took her hand when she arrived. He kissed her gently on the cheek. She giggled as he did. *Giggled.* When the hell was the last time that had happened? Not since the seventh grade.

Their conversation covered many of the same topics they had discussed during their previous encounter, although they did talk some about their childhoods, about their parents and about personal matters, both carefully avoiding work-related issues. He talked about his first marriage and how horrific it had become. She listened and offered no opinion, nor did she make any attempt to second guess him concerning the legal issues he discussed involving termination of the marriage.

After they had both finished eating, there was an uncomfortable pause in the conversation. Rosa was wondering if and when they might meet again.

Finally, John said nervously, "Would you like to spend more of the evening with me? Not here. Alone and somewhere else?"

She looked at him while she continued to think this through. Finally she smiled and said, "Yes, I would."

His obvious concern in anticipation of a negative response turned into a quick smile as he responded, "Great. I would like to take you to my home but there are just too many neighbors that watch what I do and I mean *all* the time. I have a room lined up at a hotel south of here if that works for you. Are you ok with that?"

He had read her correctly. He knew what her response would be before she did.

"Do they know you there?"

"Absolutely not. I've never been there before if that is what you are asking. And I haven't lived all that long in Nashville so I'm sure it's safe, for both of us. Don't worry Rosa. I have as much at risk here as you do. I'm trying to be careful to a fault but I also realize my heart, not my brain, is leading the way. I really believe we'll be safe there."

"How do you want to handle this? Do you want me to go in with you? What do you want to do?"

"Let me go in first. I'll handle the paperwork concerning the room and call you with the room number. You can come up then. I don't think it would be a good idea to walk in together. I'm new to all this so I'm thinking out loud here, but that would seem to be the best way to handle it. What do you think?"

"I agree. I can follow you in my car and meet you there."

They walked out together and made their way their respective vehicles. She followed him until they reached the hotel parking lot. He hadn't gone cheap, that was for sure. The hotel was new and beautiful. She waited for his call. Her stomach was churning. She hadn't done this in quite some time. What if she forgot what to do? Oh sure Rosa, as if you forget what to do! You never forget something like that, do you? But could you? Suppose you could. What if she did? What was she to do then? Shit, the wait was almost more than she could handle. Maybe she should just drive off. Would that be best for both of them?

The call finally came. The room number was 519.

Once again, she considered all her options. For a moment, she thought about just driving home, but only for a moment. She had taken days to think through the pros and cons of this exact situation, and had decided being with him, in this situation, was the thing to do.

End of story.

She got out of her car and made her way through the lobby. The hotel was done in extremely good taste—nothing shabby in the lobby. She walked to the elevator and started to punch number 5. Again, she considered her options for just a moment before proceeding. *Is this really what I want?* she wondered. Now is the time to turn around and run if it's not.

A moment later, the doors closed, she punched 5, and she knew she was committed.

She knocked on the room door and he opened it immediately. She walked into a beautifully appointed room and noticed he had already turned down the bed. He closed the door behind her and immediately took her in his arms, held her close, and kissed her. The lights had been dimmed and he started taking off his clothes while still in her embrace. Nothing mattered anymore. Only him, only this moment, only this room and that bed. She took off her blouse and, he unhooked her bra. She loosened her slacks and let them fall to the floor. He removed her panties, all the while remaining as close to her as possible. They moved quickly to the bed and for the first time since she could remember, she felt that unforgettable, exciting warmth of a man near her.

He moved slowly as did she. She wanted this moment, this very second, to last forever, but she wasn't sure either would last long. They were both already sexually excited, even though they had only just touched. He used his hands until she couldn't wait another second. She pulled him into her and her concerns about forgetting what to do were quickly forgotten as she had her first of many orgasms. She made up for lost time after years of no relationship of any kind.

As they both started to relax, he slowly moved off her and they lay, motionless with no sound but the rapid breathing of both. Neither said a word. Neither needed to. He finally put his arm under her head and pulled her over to him. Side by side they lie together until they both slept.

***

The first hint of a new day came when a small stream of light found its way through an opening between the curtains. Rosa woke with a start and quickly looked at the time. It was slightly after 7:00. She jumped out of bed and quickly ran to the bathroom. She looked like hell. How he approached her this morning, with no makeup, in the nude, without brushing her teeth or combing her hair would be interesting.

He watched as she walked out of the bathroom and toward him.

"You know you are an incredibly beautiful woman. Can you stay for a while? Do you need to leave?"

She leaned down and kissed him. That was exactly what she needed to hear. He was a keeper.

"No. Absolutely not. I need to run home and get ready for work. And so do you Mr. Judge. Besides, we don't need to wear each other out our first time do we? I have to go."

He watched as she dressed. He made no move to leave the bed or to get ready to go to work. He just watched.

She was dressed and ready to walk out the door.

"You going to work today? I suppose, being a judge and all, you have the day off? You know you have the perfect job—one that I hope to have someday."

He smiled.

"Yes, I'll get up and get moving shortly. And yes, I do have to go to work today. By the way, it's not all that cushy a job. There are good and bad moments in this job just as there are in every job. But I do like what I do and yes, I do have to do it today. When can we meet again?"

He got up and walked over to her, taking her in his arms.

"I'm ready about anytime. What about tonight? Here?"

"I'm sorry but I can't tonight. I have something to take care off and I really am busy all weekend. But what about Monday? I'll let you know the room number and then we can meet here—maybe meet at 6:00 and eat afterward. What do you think?"

"That works well for me."

He kissed her.

"You are an incredible woman Rosa. You're everything I have ever wanted in a woman and a wife. You are smart, attractive, a great conversationalist…"

"Whoa, hold on there, Judge. Where did this 'wife' stuff come from? Don't you think it's a little early to be talking marriage? We just met." She smiled as she moved toward the door.

"How long is it supposed to take? Are there guidelines somewhere about all this? I know it's been a while since I went out with any one, but I didn't think they had established any type of guidelines for dating and knowing when you were with the right partner. Did I miss something?"

"Let's talk about that Monday. I have to go. I'll wait for a call from you confirming Monday night. Now, I really must leave." She kissed him.

"It's been wonderful. See you Monday."

She walked toward the door. He gave her an abbreviated wave and she smiled back. She walked out the door of the hotel, being careful as she did to make certain no one she knew might be watching.

Once in her vehicle, she reflected back on the night. He was a gentleman. He was a great lover. He had a good job and clearly cared for her.

She thought she would play the attorney game with herself as she often did. Cross-examination. Question: what more could she want or expect in a future husband? Answer: not one blasted thing.

Chapter 21

Mondays were always a bitch and this one was no exception. Rosa had a full schedule of appointments. She had no time to daydream. She had no time to think back on Friday night. She had no time to consider the future—with him or without him. She had 'little man' walking in her door. She needed to speak to him, to communicate in an orderly fashion while she prepared him for trial. But all she could think of was John. After all, she rationalized, this was her first time in forever. No, no not sex—love. Well, sex too. This was the first time in forever and she was loving every minute of it.

She thought of him all weekend. She didn't want to come to work

All she wanted to do was think of him and whether they were really compatible. It wasn't just the present she was considering, it was their future.

He had been sitting there without saying a word for who knew how long, before she finally figured out he was there.

"I'm so sorry, Mr. McKay. I was daydreaming I guess."

"No problem Rosa. I've been ignored many times before. I'm just now reaching the point where I really don't care."

Only the slight smile on his face gave away the truth—that he, in his own way, was joking with her.

First time for that, Rosa thought.

"Ok, Mr. McKay, I want to again go through the process of a jury trial with you. I want you to be familiar with the various stages of the proceedings so there are no surprises when we are sitting in that courtroom. And, once again, I want to discuss your testimony. I've come to the conclusion you will definitely need to testify. Are you still ok with that?"

"Yes, if there is no other way, I'll testify."

"There is no other way. I can't get the self-defense issue into evidence any other way than through you, so, literally, there is no other way."

The next hour was spent going through each and every aspect of the process he would need to endure in about a week. Rosa informed him of the jury selection process and the weeding out of jurors that may be prejudicial, either toward the State or him. She explained how the State must first present their case and when they rest, she would then be allowed to present his case.

They discussed issues involving direct examination versus cross-examination, and how most all cases were won with preplanned organized testimony. Very few cases were won on cross-examination of the other party's witnesses. She told him she would do what she could when cross-examining the State's witnesses but not to expect much. They would be well schooled by Art and were professionals concerning presenting their testimony to a jury. The strength of their case would lie in his testimony. His self-defense testimony would need to be sincere and heart felt. But most of all, it would need to be believable.

Now, Mr. McKay, when you testify, remain calm and keep your hands folded in your lap. Don't use them to testify. And don't show any more signs of being nervous than you must. Talk to the one asking the questions. I don't like witnesses talking to the jury. Talk to the one that questions you. Do you understand?"

"Yes."

"Don't try to answer questions you don't understand. Ask that the question be clarified before answering. Don't try to answer if you don't understand."

"Oh no, I won't."

"Now, again, I must ask you is there anything in your past, anything at all, that we need to discuss that might paint a negative picture of yourself to the jury?"

"No, not that I can think of. I have no criminal history. I have never been married. I have no illegitimate children. I have never ever done anything to harm a soul."

He looked away. God dammit, he looked away when he said that. That was a nice "tell" Mr. McKay.

"There is no information, nor any issues we haven't discussed that might hurt your case that you can think of?"

"No, nothing."

She couldn't ask again. She had asked as many times and as many ways as she could. He had made it crystal clear there were no issues. If something came up, she would just need to deal with it at the time. They were done for today.

***

She was to meet Amy at noon. She was a little late, but as soon as she walked in the restaurant door, she noticed Amy had been early or right on time, because she already had a booth for them.

"Hi, Rosa, where have you been? I've been trying to reach you for two days."

"I know. I'm sorry, but I've been tied up."

"Not with that asshole judge have you? Tell me you haven't been with him again."

"Maybe, maybe not. Not really any of your business now is it?"

The smile gave her away. She was dying to tell Amy everything about her time with the judge. All Amy needed to do was ask.

"Ok, out with it. What the hell is going on? I want it all lady. Every juicy detail. And I want it now, in story form, without me having to ask continual questions. You know, like I normally do. As if I'm cross-examining you. Just lay it all out on the table starting *now*."

Rosa was more than ready to tell someone all that had happened to her last Friday. Detail after intimate detail came spilling out on the table between them. And when she was finished, there was no doubt about what had happened in that hotel room, nor about how Rosa felt about him. There was no question but what the relationship was far from over, and, in fact, had only just begun.

Amy sat back and listened. She started smiling when the conversation turned to Rosa's explanation of her first multiple orgasm experience and her smile remained until Rosa was finished.

Rosa stopped her story only long enough to order lunch. She didn't order much—she was too excited to stop the conversation and eat. A small dinner salad and an unsweetened ice tea was it. Amy, who had to continually watch what went in her mouth, just doubled the same order. So between bites of lettuce covered with a low cal dressing, the story unwound itself with each word carefully scrutinized by Amy.

"So when do you see him again?"

"I don't know. I think maybe tonight or tomorrow. But I really believe this is it Amy. I really do. He is so kind and good looking. He is smart and tender and…"

"Just fucking stop. I get it. You are in love. Do you know anything else about this guy? I mean anything other than he does a pretty good job of screwing you and he is a judge? Do you know anything else about him at all? I mean do you know *anything* about him? Have you ever researched this guy?"

"I know the Bar Association researched him before he became a judge. I know they are thorough. I know they do their job well. That, for me, is enough. I am good with that and with what he tells me. That's all I need."

"Wouldn't be for me. I would want a hell of a lot more information about his background than relying on that stupid Bar Association investigation and his own statements. But that's just me."

Amy was extremely conservative and careful to a fault. Rosa already knew what approach Amy would take concerning this situation before the conversation started.

"You know, I expected that type of response Amy and I understand where you are coming from. I hope you are wrong. I hope what I know about him is all I need to know. Time will tell which of us was right, but for right now, it feels right and I'm going with that emotion, that feeling, until someone or something tells me I was wrong."

"You know I can do some research on his background. I have my own sources. Do you want me to look into him a little further? I will if you want me to."

"Stop right there Amy. No, don't even consider it. I know you're thinking of my best interests, but let me handle my own relationships and I'll let you do the same with yours. Ok?"

Amy looked at her in silence for a few seconds and finally said, "Absolutely. You're right. I may have overstepped a little. I'm happy for you Rosa. You know I love you more than anyone else on this

Earth. I want you to be happy. And I think, for the first time in a while, you are. Just keep me up to date—you know—on the wedding date and all that. I want to keep my calendar clear."

"Asshole. Of course. You'll be the first to know."

They laughed through the rest of the meal as they always did. And as they walked their separate paths back to work, Rosa wondered if Amy would let it lie. It wasn't in Amy's personality to leave things alone, especially when she thought she was right.

She did need to leave this issue alone though. This was not her issue to play with. Friends interfering in other friends relationships could have disastrous results, and even as close as they were, Amy really needed to stay out of this situation. She needed both Amy and the judge, but at this point, if she had to choose between the two, she had a feeling Amy would not make the final cut.

Chapter 22

The judge had called earlier in the day. Everything was set for tonight. They would meet at the hotel around 6:00. Once they had spent their time alone, they would have supper at the same restaurant where they previously met. The hotel was perfect. The restaurant had wonderful food and was very private. No need to alter either of those venues when they were both, in fact, perfect.

As she drove, she considered her situation. Trial for the "little man" was to commence the following Monday. She was ready. In fact she was overly ready. She had thought through each and every detail of his arrest multiple times. Her opening and closing statements were basically outlined and would only need to be tweaked based on any additional evidence or surprise testimony presented at the time of trial. She really had no witnesses to prepare except her client, and she felt he was as ready to testify as he could be. She had done some very basic research on the Internet trying to find any reference to his name or background. She had uncovered nothing. But she had to admit she didn't look too long or too hard. She had done the research just before she left to meet the judge and her mind wasn't really on her work.

Her conversation with Amy lingered. Amy was very conservative and careful about all things in life. If it had been Amy, she would have researched the judge thoroughly before she met him the first time. She fancied herself as somewhat of an amateur detective anyway. Now, as she thought about it, perhaps she should have had Amy do a limited amount of research on the "little man." Amy would have enjoyed it and would have had time to do it the right way.

She was approaching the parking lot. It was shortly before 6:00 and the lot wasn't that full, but it was, after all, a Monday—probably not the busiest night of the week for any hotel.

The front row of parking spots nearest the hotel were full, but the second row was half empty as were the remaining more distant rows. She pulled in between two vehicles and looked for John's car as she did. It wasn't quite 6:00 and she didn't want to leave her vehicle and wait for him in the hotel. Because his vehicle wasn't in the lot, she felt it was best to stay in the lot and wait for him to park, walk in alone and check in.

He was late. He entered the lot in a rush and actually drove directly behind her down near the end of her row before turning into a parking slot stopping his vehicle and getting out.

As she watched, another vehicle pulled into the lot not far behind John. She continued to watch as that vehicle also traveled behind her and as it did she was able to observe the driver. It was broad daylight and he was less than twenty feet away. He was alone and had a hat on of some kind. But there was no doubt about the identity of the driver. It was her client Tommie Thompson.

What was going on here? Why was he here? She sure as hell couldn't get out of her vehicle with him in the lot or going into that hotel. She knew he hadn't seen her. He didn't look her way, and because of the nature of her "situation" with the judge, she was somewhat slumped down in her seat so no one could see her.

The judge had just exited his vehicle when Thompson drove up behind him and stopped. This didn't make sense. Did they know each other? They couldn't know each other. This was just plain crazy.

Thompson had his passenger window rolled down, and as the judge approached his vehicle, Rosa heard a sharp pop. At almost that same instant, she saw the judge drop to the ground.

As she continued to watch, she saw Thompson move over to the passenger seat, lean out the window and point a gun at the judge now lying on the parking lot pavement. He fired it again and again until the pistol was apparently empty. He then moved back over to the driver's side, put the vehicle in gear, looked around quickly and left the lot.

She couldn't think. What should she do? There was no one else in the lot. No one else had seen what had happened but her. *The judge was dead.* Of that there could be no doubt. Thompson had emptied the pistol into his body and she knew there was nothing she could do about saving him. He was gone.

She had just witnessed a murder—the murder of the judge she was having an affair with and with whom she had probably violated every ethics rule ever written. If she told law enforcement what had happened and what she had observed, they could possibly tie the two of them together as could the Bar Association. She would be disbarred. Would everyone just consider both of them being in the same parking lot, of the same hotel, at the same time, an unusual coincidence? Maybe. Could she take a chance and assume they might consider it a coincidence? No way in hell.

Not only had she witnessed a murder, but she had just seen her own client do it. She was a survivor and she would need to figure this out. But not here. Not in this parking lot. Not now.

She waited a couple of minutes, started her vehicle, and slowly left the lot. She was careful to observe everything around her, but she kept her head down as far as she could to avoid security cameras and other watching eyes. No one had entered the lot since the shooting, but it wouldn't be long.

If she had thought there would have been anything she could have done to save the judge's life, she would have, but there was no doubt in her mind he was dead. And it was now a matter of self-survival.

She drove while trying to think this all through. She finally pulled into a gas station to use the restroom and to think if only for a moment. She walked into the bathroom and immediately got sick. She walked out of the stall and splashed some water on her face. She needed to return home, to close the door behind her, lock it and think.

Once she was back in her vehicle, she tried to put everything out of her mind except driving down the road and observing each and every traffic law there was. She needed to return home without getting in trouble. She couldn't speed, she couldn't make an illegal turn, she couldn't chance an accident even as quickly and as much as she wanted to get home.

Once she arrived home, she shut the door behind her and once again got sick. After leaving the bathroom, she poured herself a mixed drink, but not until she had first swallowed two straight shots of whiskey. She knew that wasn't the best thing for her stomach, but she needed it.

She sat down on her davenport and started to cry. And once she started, she couldn't stop. She knew there would be a non-ending investigation. He was assassinated. There was no other term she could use. He was just plain assassinated. She turned on her TV. It was already on the news. There were cops everywhere. It was a special report. They had no idea who did it. There were no witnesses. No one knew of a motive, although they assumed it was done by someone the judge had ruled against.

She needed to figure out what to do. She needed to leave her heart out of the mix and figure out what to do. How could she do that? How could she remove her emotions from all of this? She loved him. She really loved him. How could she function? And she had a trial starting Monday. She assumed they would continue it, but they might not. She needed to talk to Amy. Maybe talking it out would help her come to a conclusion. But should she put that kind of pressure on Amy? Tell her what happened and then ask her what the hell to do? Was that the correct approach here? How could anyone figure out a correct approach to this? There wasn't one. But she knew one thing. She needed to verbalize the issues. And the only one she could do that with was Amy. She needed her and *now*.

Rosa picked up the phone, speed dialed Amy and got her answering machine. She told her to call her as soon as she could. In the meantime, Rosa shut all the curtains, turned off the TV, turned off all the lights and sat alone in the dark. What the hell had she just done? She had placed herself in a position to lose everything she had worked for her whole life. She vowed not to let that happen without a fight. She would figure this out and work it through. She hadn't gotten this far in life to let it all go without a fight.

Chapter 23

Stony walked in the precinct door with a slight hangover. It had been an interesting but involved evening. He had gone out with friends—at least he thought they were friends. It was his first "real" night out since the hearing. They had moved from bar to bar, and he had ended up needing one of his buddies to drive him home. Even thought he had had too much to drink, he was still sober enough to know he wasn't in any condition to drive.

One of those so-called "buddies" had lined him up with some bimbo from the east side of town. She hung on him all evening. If only her brain had been a tenth the size of her breasts, it might have been an interesting evening.

Unfortunately, all she had to offer were those breasts and they repeatedly ended up in his face. Not enough. Not enough last night, not enough ever. He needed to be with a woman that had at least a shred of intelligence and "Connie" fell a bit short. He tried to enjoy the evening with her, but it was like talking to a wall. And the harder he tried, the more awkward it became, and the more he drank. And the more he drank the closer she moved—a terribly vicious cycle which finally ended with her in a cab and a friend driving him home. She was really drunk and offered more than once to go home with him. That wasn't going to happen—at least not with her.

When he arrived home, he went straight to bed. He didn't pass out, but close.

He had heard nothing about the judge when he arrived at work that morning. In fact, the case had been assigned to another detective, but he had asked to have someone else take over. He knew the judge personally and didn't want to be involved with the case in any way.

Soon after starting his shift, the captain called Stony into his office.

"You up to date on what happened with that judge last night?"

"Yes, at least I am now. I was out of commission last night and just heard about it this morning."

"Have you ever had any personal contact with him? You ever met him or had anything to do with him in any respect other than your case?"

"No. Why?"

"You look like shit. You need to take the day off?"

"No. I'm fine. Now could you just get on with it? What's up?"

"I want you to take the lead on his murder. We apparently have no witnesses. No one seems to know exactly how this all happened. We have found out there was a security camera covering the lot so you will need to take a look at what might have been recorded. But, Stony, as you can imagine this is a high-profile investigation. I've already received a call from the commissioner. You've handled this type of case before and handled them well. But this needs to be solved and quickly. It needs to have priority above everything else you are working on. Go ahead and get started today and if you need to move some of your cases to another detective, just let me know."

"I'll get right on it. You want me to work with anyone or do this on my own?"

"Start this one on your own. We're really stretched right now. I'll have someone work with you if you feel you need it, but start on your own right now. Keep me informed every step of the way Stony."

He walked out the door and made his way over to his own desk deep in thought. Where to start? He figured the best place would be the scene of the murder.

***

A few minutes later, he arrived at the scene, which was still completely cordoned off. There were a limited number of vehicles parked in the far back row of the lot, which he assumed probably belonged to employees, but other than that, the lot was empty.

There was a large stain of blood where the judge had been shot. He had apparently lain on the ground for some time before his body had been moved.

After showing his badge and exchanging the minimum of pleasantries, Stony asked one of the officers with forensics how long he thought the judge had been on the ground before he had been noticed.

"I am thinking maybe ten minutes or so. He was dead within just a few seconds. Shot six times. Whoever did this really, really wanted to make sure the guy was dead. They did a good job of finishing him off."

Stony looked around to ascertain a general idea of the layout.

"You know, it's wide open here. Funny no one saw it happen."

"I know. But apparently no one did—at least no one that has come forward."

"I guess there was a security camera. I think I'll go talk to whoever is manning the front desk and see what he can tell me. Thanks for your time."

Stony walked up the steps to the front doors of the Hotel, and as he walked in, he noticed the large check-in area facing the doors. A tall skinny kid, looked about 18, was manning the check-in station.

"Good morning. My name is Detective Bill Stone and I'm with the Nashville Police Department. Do you have a second?"

"Sure do. Yes, I sure do. No problem there."

The poor kid was nervous as hell. He needed to put him at ease

"I'm not here to question you about anything personal. You have nothing to be nervous about. I just need to ask you a few questions about what happened over in the parking lot."

"I understand. Go ahead."

"Were you on duty last night?"

"Where?"

"Here. Were you on duty here last night?"

It was obvious this kid was so nervous he wasn't going to be of much help.

He was sweating profusely. His hands were fidgeting with anything he could get them on and his eyes darted nervously one way then the other.

"Sure. Oh, no, not last night. Some other times, but not last night."

"Who was?"

"When?"

"No, *who* was on duty last night here, where you are standing. Who was on duty?"

"Last night?"

"*Yes,* last night. Can you just calm down a little? You aren't a suspect. I just need a few basic answers."

"Ok. No problem. Just ask that question again would you."

This was going nowhere fast.

"Ok, let's make it real simple. Do you know if there is a security camera that might cover the parking lot? Do you know whether there is one or not?"

"The lot out front?"

"Is there another one?"

"No."

"Then *yes*. The lot out front."

"I don't know."

"Is the manager here?"

"The manager?"

"Yes. You know, your boss."

"Not now. He will be though, sometime I am sure."

"Did he leave you to run this place by yourself?"

This conversation was clearly headed nowhere. It was obvious he would need to come back some other time and visit with the boss. The kid never even answered Stony's last question. He appeared to be in a trance.

Finally, Stony turned around and walked away. He would return later, after calling first and making sure someone was there that could communicate. When he returned he would check the records and see if the judge had been here before and determine if there was some type of security camera on each floor, if that proved necessary.

But for right now, he would head to the courthouse. He wanted to visit with the clerk's office and check out the court files of cases the judge had just completed along with files of cases that were coming to trial. At the same time, he also wanted to visit with the people in and about the courthouse.

Someone really wanted this guy dead. He was almost certain this was not a random shooting. Someone had targeted this judge, sought him out and, made damn sure he never took another breath. This was personal. Or it was a murder for hire. But whomever it was wanted to make sure he didn't make it to the dawn of a new day—and whoever pulled the trigger had by God made sure that happened.

Chapter 24

She fastened her seat belt and the vehicle started to move. She was able to drive without touching the steering wheel. The vehicle drove itself. It had a will of its own. And it headed straight toward that hotel. There was nothing else but the silence of the drive as the vehicle headed toward its inevitable conclusion. It entered the parking lot. There were no vehicles in the lot but hers. It kept moving forward until it reached the location where he lie motionless on the ground in a pool of dried blood. She got out of her vehicle and stood over him. It was clear he was gone. His eyes were wide open and lifeless. He was grey in color. He was, without question, dead. Then why did he move? His was saying something—what was he trying to tell her?

Rosa sat straight up in bed, sweat running down the side of her face, wide eyed and shaking from one end to the other. It had all been a dream. Sure it had. She was in bed. And now, as she had a chance to think, nothing like that could have happened while she was awake. It had only been a dream. She smiled.

Thank God.

And suddenly, reality—not *all* of it was a dream.

He *was* dead.

She remembered that she had to live with that—and with leaving the scene while he lie on that hard, cold concrete.

She looked at the time. It was past her normal wakeup hour, but she had had a hell of time getting to sleep. She pulled herself out of bed, wondering how long that dream would go on. Was this a singular event or would that same dream continue night after night until she was too old to remember or was dead?

She took her time getting ready for work. When she did arrive she looked over her schedule and noticed McKay and Thompson were scheduled for morning appointments. She would cancel them both. She needed to sit here and figure this out. She needed time to think through her next step.

"Amy on line 1 Rosa."

Her secretary's voice cut through her thoughts.

"Amy. Where have you been? I have been trying to reach you for two days."

"I know. I'm sorry. I had a seminar in Lexington. My phone went dead. I was out of town without a charger. What's going on?"

"Have you seen any news since you got back?"

"No. I got back late last night. What's going on?"

"The judge was murdered. Shot. He's dead."

"You have got to be kidding. Oh. My. God. Were you with him when it happened? What happened?"

"Let me put it this way. I saw it all happen. I know who did it. No one knows I was a witness. For obvious reasons, I can't say anything about meeting him to anyone. I need some help Amy. Or at the least I need to talk this out. We need to meet. What about tonight for supper? Will that work for you? What about my place around 6:00?"

"I need to meet with some people in the Opryland area about 6:30. That won't give me enough time to get there." She hesitated while she tried to process everything Rosa had just told her. "Let's meet at the Santa Fe restaurant near Opryland. It's off the beaten path and normally a little noisy. I think we can find a back booth and not be overheard. About 6:00 then?"

"Yes."

"Rosa what the hell…"

"Not now. See you then."

She hung up. There was no way she was going into any of the details on the phone.

She swiveled around in her chair to think about what information she should give her. If she was asking her for advice, she needed to tell her everything. And that was exactly what she would do.

As she continued to reexamine each and every detail, Gene

J.B. Millhollin

Wakefield walked in her office.

As he walked in, her secretary said, "Rosa, I can't seem to reach Mr. Thompson. I have another number he gave me. He said only to use it if I can't reach him on his cell and if we really needed to contact him. He apparently rented some office space in that old Pizza Hut building that's vacant south of the Interstate on 12th. I've never tried him there. Is this one of those times we really, really need to reach him?"

Rosa shuttered at the thought of talking with him after the events of last night.

"Yes. This is one of those times. Try him there and let me know if you reach him."

"Morning Gene, what's up?"

She just didn't have time for his small talk today. He had given her no forewarning he was coming, so he could just take what limited conversation she offered.

"Not much. I thought I would visit with you about the McKay and Thompson cases. I think both of those were to be tried by Judge Hampton weren't they?"

"Yes, they were."

"Have you heard from court administration yet? Wasn't the McKay case set for next Monday?"

"Yes. I heard from them yesterday. They continued it one week. Judge Jackson has been assigned."

"Do you know anything about him?"

"No. I just know of him. He's pretty straight laced and definitely pro law enforcement."

"Well, the good thing about this situation is that the rulings of Judge Hampton will bind Judge Jackson, so he is going to have to try the case based on those prior rulings. That should be good for you shouldn't it?"

"Yes, Gene, that obviously should work in our favor."

"Do you have any other issues with that particular case or are you ready to try it?"

"No, except for resolving the mental issues I have with the death of Judge Hampton, I am ready to try it."

"What do you mean 'mental issues?'"

"Come on Gene. A judge was just murdered. A judge I've been before a lot lately. He seemed like a good guy. I'm trying to cope with this just like the rest of the legal community. You know what I mean!"

She felt herself starting to become emotional. She knew she needed to tone it down a notch.

"Oh, sure. You're right. I understand. Yes, that was awful. But you're fine with trying McKay's case aren't you? Do we need to assign it to someone else in the firm? Are you ok with handling it or not?"

"Yes Gene, I'll handle it. Don't worry about it. I'll try the case. I started it, I'll finish it. And then, when I win it we are going to talk about me becoming a partner, right?"

"Yes, sure, yes that's what we'll do. You win the case. It's perfectly set up—all you need to do is finish it."

She said nothing. Expecting but receiving no response, he finally turned and walked out.

How cold could anyone be? How uncaring could a person be? A man he knew was just murdered and it was clear he didn't give a shit one way or the other.

"Rosa?"

"Yes, June, what is it?"

"I was able to reach Mr. Thompson. He was in his office building and I told him not to come in today. He rescheduled for next Tuesday at 10:00."

"Thanks June."

Now it was time to discuss these issues with someone. Not just someone, with Amy. She would lay the cards out on the table and receive some feedback from someone she trusted with her life. She had no idea how to handle her situation and still retain some semblance of life as she now knew it. Amy would help sort it all out. She only hoped Amy had a workable solution. Because, to be perfectly honest, at this point in time, she had no fucking idea what to do.

Chapter 25

It had not been a good day for Amy Glass. She had just returned from a three-day seminar in Louisville, during which her phone had gone dead and she hadn't taken her charger. As she started to panic, she brought herself back down to Earth, realizing it really wasn't that necessary that her phone remain operational. Her boss knew where she was and where she was staying. Her family also knew where she was staying. Everyone who was important to her, as concerned work and family, knew where she was and knew how to contact her without using her cell. And she would leave it that way. She would try to enjoy the time away without the pressure of her phone buzzing in her pocket every three minutes, and that's exactly what she did.

But, now the payback. Now she was home. Now the phone was turned back on and the computer was fired up, working at peak performance. There were calls to return and emails to answer in that never-ending cycle of business turmoil that she endured almost seven days a week.

Nothing earth shattering that had occurred while she was gone. There had been nothing to undo or fix that couldn't be handled upon her return.

Except this call from Rosa. That was a shock. The issues needed to be thoroughly discussed with Rosa and, together, they needed to figure out an option that was feasible. She was just walking in the door of the Santa Fe, and as she did, she immediately noticed Rosa slumped down in a small corner booth next to the far wall.

Rosa stood to meet Amy as she approached the table. She started to sob as Amy embraced her. Rosa looked around quickly to see if anyone was watching, but all the patrons seemed to be sitting in their own little booths and in their own little world. No one appeared to care about a couple of girls embracing in the corner, even if one of them was crying.

As they sat down, Amy said, "Just tell me everything from the beginning. From the time you were to meet again, and everything after. Don't hold anything back or put your spin on anything. Just tell it to me like it happened."

And that's exactly what Rosa proceeded to do. It was clear to Amy that Rosa was completely caught up in the situation. She could not be objective as she was with her clients that had their own issues. She was so thoroughly trapped within her own situation she simply could not view the big picture. She was locked into details that just didn't matter and she only touched upon issues that appeared to Amy to be gigantic—issues that Amy would need to pull out of her and discuss in more detail before they could come to a rational conclusion.

Amy ordered some onion rings. And then she ordered a fried pickle. And then she ordered some fries. As Rosa continued to tell her story, Amy would eat. Rosa never touched any of the food set in front of Amy by a never ending line of waiters.

Once her story had been completely revealed and it was time for discussion, Amy said "Are you ready to order? I'm starved."

"Good Lord Amy, you must have already had one of everything they offer in this place. Are you sure you are still hungry?"

"Just keep still. You know I eat when I'm nervous and I'm really, really nervous right now."

The waiter approached.

"I want the biggest steak you have. Give me a small salad with it and a side of mac and cheese. You want anything Rosa?"

"Why don't you just bring it to her in a refillable trough? We could be here a long time. No, I want nothing. Amy, you are going to put on five pounds before you leave this table."

"You let me worry about that. What are you going to do about the situation you have gotten yourself in?"

Rosa, short on patience and obviously tired, snapped back a response.

"*DO?* What am I going to *DO!?* I am going to do nothing right now but hope they catch this guy before I *HAVE* to do something. Amy, I'm in a hell of a lot of trouble here. I've witnessed a murder and left the scene. I've violated the Canons of Ethics in a million ways. I'm doing nothing right now but my job and hoping this all works out without my involvement. That's what I am doing."

Amy never backed down.

"Have you evaluated this whole situation at all Rosa? Have you taken the time to delve into why Thompson might have done this? Obviously either he, or someone paying him, had a specific well-reasoned basis for killing the judge. Have you tried to think that through?"

"Amy, I'm just trying to survive here. That's it. I'm putting one foot in front of the other and even that is a major issue for me right now."

"I think we need to get to the underlying issue here rather than just fixating on your current dilemma. I think there are a few facts we need to know and then, maybe based on what we learn, we can get you out of this without ever indicating your involvement."

Rosa's phone rang and reluctantly she answered. As Rosa listened, they brought Amy's food. The T-bone flopped over the edges of the plate. In addition, they brought a huge bowl of mac and cheese. Hash browns, bread and a small order of green beans with bacon, accompanied the steak. There was an ever enlarging semi-circle of food around Amy which she wasted no time in making disappear. Rosa had nothing in front of her but a glass of iced tea. As the phone conversation continued, Rosa answered in short terse responses, mostly of the 'yes' or 'no' variety. Eventually, her coloring changed to one of stark white. Amy watched as her whole demeanor changed and as it did, Amy just ate a little faster.

She finally terminated the call and sat speechless.

Finally, Amy said, between huge bits of everything, "Ok, are you going to tell me who the hell that was?"

"It was a detective. I think his name was Stone or something like that. He wants to talk to me about the murder."

"What else did he say? Did he feel you were involved? Why did he call you?"

Rosa looked down. Her color had started to return.

"He noticed I had been involved in a couple of recent case with the judge and he was contacting most attorneys who had pending cases with him to see if we had any idea who might have been involved. He was very nice but what the hell am I going to tell him?"

"Do you think we should do our own investigating? Maybe take a look at Mr. Thompson and see if we can figure out anything that might implicate him without getting you involved? What do you think?"

"No. Absolutely not. I'm just hoping this all works itself out. I have to meet with this detective tomorrow afternoon. Maybe I can get more information from him than he does from me."

"When is your next appointment with Thompson?"

"Next Tuesday morning at 10:00 I think."

"How are you going to handle that?"

"For now, as if nothing ever happened. I'll discuss with him the fact we are getting a new judge, but I'm not going any further than that right now."

"You know, I really think you are making a mistake. I think we should use the Internet and our own resources to investigate this guy ourselves. We may be able to get you out of this without revealing your involvement in any respect, but I think we need more information."

"Let's wait this out for a while. Let's see what their investigation turns up. Let's let the cops do their thing for a while and if nothing happens, we can figure out what we want to do then. I think a little patience right now could go a long way in solving the problem."

Amy said nothing. She finished off the mac and cheese. There was no bread left and the T-bone had been picked clean long ago.

"You want some dessert? Clearly the 'one of everything' plan hasn't worked out too well yet. Do you want to try that with the dessert menu too?"

"Nope. I'm full. Let's get out of here. I'll pay."

"That's big of you."

Amy smiled, waived at the waiter, and gave him her card for payment.

"I think you're making a mistake Rosa. I really think you need to be a little more proactive, but I guess it's your life."

"I'm not saying you're wrong. I'm just saying let's wait for a day or two before we start doing our own thing. Let's wait."

"Ok. Whatever you think."

They walked out together and gave each other a hug as they got in their respective vehicles to head home. Amy thought about their conversation all the way home. She concluded there were, in fact, two things of which she was sure: One: the best friend she ever had was in a hell of a mess—a mess she had been forewarned would happen, and two: Rosa may be correct—that they both just needed to wait. But she knew herself all too well, and her own worst trait was patience.

Chapter 26

As he walked to his car he could feel the sweat running down the side of his face. It was one of those days in the South when the heat and the humidity seemed to be locked in some type of sadistic race to see which could climb the highest the quickest.

Right now it was a tie—humidity about 80, temperature about 80. Stony wondered if he should move away—maybe Michigan or Minnesota.

But the other side of the coin was once the sun went down, it was beautiful. Once the summer ran out of steam and resolved into fall and once winter warmed into spring, there was no better weather anywhere. About nine months of the year it was heaven, but those other three months could indeed be hell.

He unlocked his car and opened the door. He stood there a moment while the hot air, at least some of it, exited his vehicle. He got in and turned on the car and air conditioning simultaneously, put the vehicle in gear and headed toward the office of Rosa Norway.

In reviewing the court files the clerk's office had previously provided him, he noticed a couple of files involving Judge Hampton and Miss Norway. They were pending and set for trial shortly. One of the files involved a high-profile case. He had heard plenty about the prostitute and her death at the hands of McKay. He had also heard of Miss Norway. Her reputation had preceded her. He had heard she was tough in court, anti-law enforcement, and difficult to work with. He had never met her, but he had done his homework before he ever left his office, as he had done with all the lawyers he was in the process of interviewing.

He had nothing on his plate but this case. Everything else had been shoved aside so he could concentrate only on the judge's murder. And so far he had not had much success, but it was still early. He figured whoever was behind the crime had a pretty good plan from the beginning, and uncovering who was responsible would take some time and some patience, both of which he had an abundance.

He took the elevator to Rosa's floor and walked into a reception area for what appeared to be a number of individual offices, he assumed housing a number of irritating attorneys. The receptionist informed Miss Norway he was there and he took a seat waiting to be escorted to her office.

About fifteen minutes and a *People* magazine later, the receptionist got up and motioned for him to follow her. They walked down a long hallway to Miss Norway's office. She was turned facing her windows and as he walked in, she swiveled around in her chair and stood to greet him almost simultaneously.

She was tall, and very attractive—not what he expected. But as he thought about it, he quickly concluded not all lawyers were necessarily old, wrinkled, scum sucking dicks. Some of them might be like her—tall, pretty, scum sucking dicks.

"Please Mr. Stone, be seated."

"Thank you. Wow is it ever hot out there."

"Yes it is. Now, how can I help you? I'm really busy today and have a couple of issues that need to be handled as soon as you leave. What do you need from me?"

Clearly, she was either really busy or really nervous.

"Oh ok, sure. I'll get right to the point. I wanted to visit about you and Judge Hampton. I noticed you had a number of matters pending with him. Did you know him well?"

"No. I had those two trials pending with him and that's it. I never met him before these two cases came up and were assigned to him."

"Ok. What did you think about him? Good judge, bad judge? Or did you have any opinion at all?"

"I thought he was fair."

"Did you have any contact with him outside the courtroom?"

"I'm sorry. What does that mean? What do you mean 'contact?'"

An Absence of Ethics

"I mean did you see him socially or have any dealings with him other than these two cases?"

"We, as attorneys, are not permitted to have any significant contact with a judge on a personal level when we are handling pending cases before them. That would violate the Canons of Ethics. That should answer your question."

"Did you ever see anything or hear anything about this judge that you felt might be suspicious or unusual. Did you ever hear anyone make any off color remarks about him in any way?"

"No."

"What about your clients? Did either of them ever appear to have a grudge against this judge for any reason? Would there be anything I should consider about them while doing my investigation?"

"No. Mr. Thompson has not been involved with anything that concerned a ruling from the judge yet, and all the rulings in McKay's case have gone his way. Neither of them should have issues with this judge."

"Both you and the judge are from Nashville and you both are substantially involved in the legal system here in Davidson County, but you have never had any contact outside the courtroom with this judge?"

"As you should know by now, he was just appointed and just moved here from Knoxville, so he really hasn't been here long enough for any of us to really get to know him."

"Do you think he brought issues with him from Knoxville?"

"I would have no way of knowing."

"Are you aware he was recently divorced?"

"I heard that yes."

He needed to try this one more time. She clearly evaded the question the first time it was asked.

"And your contact with him has only been in the courtroom, is that correct?"

"That's where my involvement with the judge has taken place, yes."

She was still skirting the issue. He had no doubt she was truthful as far as her answer took her.

"What do you think happened here Miss Norway? Any ideas?"

"No. I don't have any idea. I assume a former client or someone on the other side of some litigation he might have handled was not happy. But not knowing a lot about his personal history, I have no idea. Sorry."

"Do you know who his friends might be? Have you observed him around other people that aren't in the legal profession? I can't find anyone that seems to know anything about him other than their contact through the legal profession."

"No, I have no idea. I have never seen him with anyone but lawyers."

"Is there anything else you can tell me that you think could be helpful in determining who might have wanted to harm this man—anything at all?"

"No."

"By the way, what happened to that case that was set for trial—that McKay case? Is it to be dismissed or tried—or do you know yet?"

"It's going to be tried and it's been rescheduled."

She stood up.

"Now Officer Stone, if there is nothing else, I really do have a number of matters to attend to yet this morning."

She extended her hand. He rose and shook it.

"Ok, thanks. If you think of anything else can you give me a call? Let me leave you a card."

"Yes. Sure. I can call you."

"I am in the process of meeting with a number of other attorneys and if anything comes up that I feel might look a little suspicious, especially if it involved others in the legal field, would you mind if I contacted you for your thoughts or advise?"

"Why me? Why would you want to contact me?"

"I would only if I felt it really necessary. Would you be willing to visit with me from time to time about any issues that come up that may involve the legal community if I feel the need to discuss them with someone?"

"Well, yes, I guess so. It would depend mostly on the nature of your inquiry, but yes I guess I could visit with you if you wish."

"Great. Thank you. Have a good day and thanks for your time."

"You're welcome Mr. Stone."

She finally smiled at him just as he turned to walk out the door.

He walked to the elevator considering all she had just told him. It was hard to move past her physical attributes. She was a beautiful woman. He already knew all he needed to know about her personally, including the fact that she was an over achiever and single.

But he also knew she wasn't telling the truth.

Or maybe she just wasn't telling *all* the truth. Those two questions involving her contact with the judge were not answered directly enough for his satisfaction. And she looked away and flinched before she answered. There was more to the story than what she was telling him.

He walked out into the bright early-morning summer sun and it almost took his breath away. The temperature had prevailed. He figured it was near 100 degrees and not a cloud in the sky.

He needed to visit a few more attorneys before the day ended, but he would definitely need to visit with her again. First and foremost, he knew she hadn't told him everything. But, in addition, he really just wanted to see her again.

He was single. He had no attachment to anyone of any kind. He liked what he saw—in a man-to-woman context, and he simply wanted to be around her again. He only hoped, in the end, that little jag in the road, the one where she wasn't quite telling him all the truth, didn't end up in conflict with the man/woman issue.

Chapter 27

Gene Wakefield had reached the end of his rope. But, the gambler in him remained forever optimistic. What other course did he have other than the one he was taking? Unfortunately, his options had become extremely limited.

As he was sitting in his small office at home contemplating his fate along with contemplating whether to bet on the Yankees or the Dodgers, his wife of 30 years came bouncing in his office door. After that many years, it almost sickened him to see that much "perk" in one body. Her exuberance for life conflicted with all the pressure he was trying to cope with in his own life.

As usual, she was carrying on a conversation with him before she even entered his office door. When she arrived at his door, she would expect him to have heard every word, in spite of the fact that she knew he couldn't hear very well anymore. And, of course, she mumbled her way through half of her sentences.

"So what do you think honey?"

"Sorry, sweetheart, you know I can't hear you when you mumble your way through a question addressed to me from a room halfway across the house. Now, what's the question?"

"Have you figured out financing yet for the boy's college? We have talked and talked about it Gene, you know we have. And you keep telling me that you will get it figured out but you know, Gene, the first payment isn't far away and I'm worried. Should I be worried Gene? Just tell me, should I be?"

"No, no don't you worry about it Margie. I'll get it figured out shortly. I have a few options that I need to pursue, but I'll get it figured out. Now just go back to doing what you were doing before you came in here and let me work on that, will you?"

"Ok, sweetheart. I know you'll get it figured out. You always do."

She smiled that Betty Croker smile, leaned over, and kissed him on the top of his balding head and then went back to knitting some type of cover for one of his golf clubs.

She was right. He *did* need to figure this out—and quickly. He knew there was that issue along with many issues that he needed to somehow conclude within the near future.

His plan of accumulating extra income had fallen flat on its face. But, there was another plan in the making. He hadn't been made aware of the details yet. He was still waiting. He had an idea what was to be proposed, but he also knew it wasn't going to work. If their proposal was what he thought it was going to be, the plan just plain and simple wouldn't work. But he would wait until he received the word from "above," so to speak.

In the meantime, because of the nature of the plan and the individuals he found himself dealing with, he purchased a pistol. He hadn't told Margie and he was sure he would never need it, but he had it tucked neatly into the glove box of his vehicle—just in case.

The most significant financial issue right now was their home. He had borrowed and borrowed until there was no more equity. Of course, Margie had no idea. He told her nothing about finances nor was that an issue he left open for discussion with her. She knew nothing about money. All she knew and understood was a negative or positive mark in front of their bank balance. Life remained "on track" as long as there remained a positive balance and she had checks or her bankcard. If the balance became a negative one or if she lost her bank card, which she had on at least five different occasions, or she ran out of checks, it was crises time in their household and he would need to "fix it honey." Up until now, he had always accommodated her. But times had changed and he was, for the first time in his sixty years, worried about how they would survive.

The office bank account was his biggest slush fund, but he had removed so much out of it this quarter he was afraid he had perhaps gone too far. He would go back to the account again in the morning. He would have to. He couldn't make his mortgage payment. He didn't have enough to even put groceries on the table. His regular paycheck from the firm was a couple of weeks away. He would do what he had to do.

On top of it all, he wanted to retire. He really wanted to completely remove himself from the practice of law. Young attorneys like that Norway were invading the firm. He didn't understand their way of doing things. The world had changed significantly since he entered the practice and he hadn't adjusted. But how could he retire with all those funds missing? He needed to be there to cover his own ass and hide the shortages or defend his position if the shortages were uncovered. He knew he could protect himself as long as he remained in the office. He figured he had taken well over a hundred grand since it had all started.

His cell buzzed. It was them—the people he hoped would save him. The conversation was one sided and to the point. They wanted to meet. They set a time and place of which he was familiar and he said he would be there. The call ended. They never said much. They never expected a response other than one that indicated you would comply with whatever it was they requested. Short and sweet.

He would take his pistol to the meeting. He most likely wouldn't need it, but he would take it tucked into the back of his pants. He barely knew how to use it, and his hands shook so badly when he went to the range to practice that he usually missed the target completely. He prayed he never needed to hit something that mattered.

How far he had come. How much his life had changed. He had been corrupted. He knew it and he knew it as it was happening. But he couldn't turn it around. He couldn't then and he couldn't now. Too much water under the bridge. He knew he had a gambling problem but no one else was going to know. And he sure as hell wasn't going to seek treatment.

Now, before it was too late and the games had started, who would it be—the Yankees or the Dodgers? He still had a small chance of wiggling his way out of this mess. But he needed to start winning, and it needed to begin now with the Yankees or the Dodgers. Which one would it be? Hits, RBI's, ERA's, injuries?

Oh what the heck, he thought, I'll just flip a coin and hope luck will handle the rest. He had five minutes. He flipped it and it came up heads. That worked out well. He had wanted the Yankees in the first place.

He had just acquired a new credit card and with it, he could again start making bets online. The credit card company only gave him $300 credit, but he figured this time that was all he would need. With this new "system" he would turn $300 into $300,000. He made his bet and felt that rush of adrenalin that he always felt once the decision had been made and before the game began.

First batter up for the Yankees struck out. Still eight and two-thirds innings to go. Oh my God...the possibilities!

Chapter 28

The day could surely only get better—there was no way in hell it could get any worse. In one week, Amy had gained back much of her weight it had taken her two months to lose. In addition, houses—at least the ones she had for sale—weren't selling. Owners had the prices jacked up way too high, and discussions with those owners about a slight reduction in the price ended, in most instances, in an argument, not a resolution.

But the number one issue that consumed her every hour of the day was how to resolve Rosa's problem. It was clear to her that Rosa was not thinking in a rational manner. She was too deeply involved in her own dilemma to think objectively and rationally. Amy's idea of research and then resolution was much better. Rosa wasn't going to admit that though—after all, she was a lawyer.

Normally Rosa's solutions and the thought process she used in arriving at a solution was always the best. Amy had come to that conclusion long ago. But in this case, Amy had the best solution and she damn well knew it. Rosa was too close to the problem to arrive at a logical, objective solution.

She decided she would pursue a solution by herself. She was going rogue! She would figure out who this Thompson was and what was behind the judge's murder on her own. If Rosa wouldn't save herself, she would do it for her.

She figured her first move would have to be the Internet, as she really had no other source for information. She researched the real estate tax database and determined Thompson owned no real estate in Davidson County. Rosa had mentioned he lived north of Nashville, but he apparently owned no real estate because he was paying no real estate taxes. So that resolved that issue.

Next, she started using every search engine she knew to pull up anything she could find on Tommie Thompson. Actually, without more identifying information, pulling up that name was quite easy—there were a billion Tommie Thompsons all across the country. She remembered, however, that Rosa had mentioned this one was from New York, so she tried to limit her search to the State of New York.

There were still more than she could count, but one of them was particularly interesting. One Tom Thompson had been associated with mob crime and had been charged with assault and attempted murder, but all the charges had been dismissed. He didn't appear to have a criminal record that she could find, but if this was the guy, he was nothing to mess with.

It was Monday night and she hadn't heard from Rosa since last week. She knew Rosa had been tied up preparing for trial, and she had also been incredibly busy all weekend with assholes that wanted to look at homes, talk seriously about buying homes, but then walk their ass to their vehicle without as much as a "thanks for your time."

She was half way through a bottle of wine when it came to her—she needed to see this guy up close and personal. She needed to find out what Thompson was all about, and the best way to do that was to see him, observe him, and follow him if need be. That would quickly and accurately shed at least a little light on whom this guy really was. She remembered Rosa had said she had an appointment with him at 10:00 tomorrow morning. She would take matters into her own hands and save her friend on her own starting at 10:00.

***

She found a parking space quickly, which was a surprise. Normally, she drove around for an hour in this part of town trying to find a place to park near her destination.

She waited until 9:15 and then left her vehicle, walking quickly toward Rosa's office building. She took the elevator to the firm's floor and stepped off at precisely 9:30. Near the elevator was a directory of offices for that floor. She stood looking at it and waited, appearing to all who noticed her that she was using the directory to look up a particular office.

A number of people exited both of the elevators and a few walked into the firm's office. She knew Rosa like the back of her hand. If she had an appointment at 10:00, that's when her door opened. Clients saw her exactly when their appointment was scheduled—-not a minute before and not a minute after.

So, a minute before 10:00 she walked into the firm's reception area. There were a number of people waiting in the area but there were chairs still available. She walked up to June and said "Is Rosa available?"

"Not right now Amy. She has someone waiting and actually has appointments the rest of the morning."

Her intercom buzzed.

"June send Mr. Thompson in please."

"Mr. Thompson you can go on in now."

A tall, balding man with a decided limp rose from his chair and started down the hallway toward Rosa's door. So that was the infamous Mr. Thompson, the murderer that had created so many issues in Rosa's life. He didn't look so tough, especially with that bum leg. She figured if worse came to worse, she could surely outrun him.

She looked back down at June.

"Just tell her I stopped by to say hello."

Amy smiled at June, turned around, and walked out the door. She took the first available elevator to the ground floor and made her way to her vehicle. Now she would patiently wait. No, she would wait. Patience was not a friend of hers.

***

She had waited for about forty-five minutes when she saw him exit the building. He walked slowly and deliberately, dragging his leg as he went. His car was about a block away and Amy watched him get in and drive down the street. When he was no more than a couple of blocks away, she pulled out and started to follow.

They made their way to 12th Street and turned south. She stayed about two blocks behind him. Surprisingly, today traffic was not heavy on this street, which was unusual. She really wanted to make sure he didn't see her following him. Knowing what she did about him that could turn into a disaster for one of them and probably not him.

He finally pulled into a parking space in front of a building that had been used to house a Pizza Hut. Apparently, the business had failed or had changed locations because it was completely empty.

Thompson got out of his vehicle and used his key to open the front door and walk inside just as she was driving by the front of the building. She drove on past but then found a spot to park about half way down the next block. Again, she would try to exercise patience and wait to see what developed.

***

Three hours later, Amy was still sitting in her car, and nothing had happened. It was nearly 2:30. No one had gone in and no one had left. She needed to change her approach. She needed to know who or what was in that building.

She left her vehicle and walked up the street toward Thompson's building. It was located in the middle of a number of other office buildings, most of which were occupied. But, near the middle of the block was an alley that ran the length of the backside of the buildings from street to street. The alley also ran along the backside of Thompson's building. She could see the back of his building from the street. There appeared to be a door and a small window on the alley side, and there was no one around—at least not in the alley.

She started up the ally, all the while looking in both directions. As she approached the building, she could see the window was uncovered. She would be able to look directly inside. She approached the window from the side and took a deep breath before moving to a point she could see who or what occupied the building.

She looked in. There was no one there. In fact, there was very little inside. This was a mistake. There was nothing to see.

She turned around to leave, and as she did she looked directly down the wrong end of the barrel of a snub nosed pistol. She fell back against the building as she sucked in her breath in fear.

"You make a sound any louder than you just made and I'll blow your head off right here. Who the fuck do you think you're dealing with bitch, some country Nashville hick? Walk through the door. It's unlocked."

Chapter 29

Stony had gone to the courthouse and had reviewed most of the files that involved Judge Hampton. There really weren't all that many, as he hadn't been a judge very long. All of the cases were criminal matters but none of them involved serious issues. There were a number of drug cases, as he had expected, but most of them involved possession or delivery and none of them involved gang activity. There was no information in any of the files indicating a defendant or his attorney was upset with the judge personally or had an axe to grind concerning the handling of their case and absolutely nothing that shed any light on the crime.

He had then gone to see each individual attorney that had been in court with the judge since he had been appointed. In many cases, the public defender's office had been appointed to represent defendants so one trip to their office took care of a substantial number of the cases.

He went to each office in the courthouse and sat down with each officer in charge of his or her respective office. He talked to them about anything they might have seen or heard that involved Judge Hampton. Most of them had never heard of him and none of them had heard or seen anything that helped.

He had even gone to see his ex-wife in Knoxville, and while he was there, he had also gone to see all the members of the judge's law firm along with the chief judge of that district. They all said the same thing. There was no indication of any issues involving Hampton that would generate this type of violence. Nothing that Hampton had touched appeared to have generated the type of problem that could have been resolved by murdering him.

The major issue that seemed to be consistent in terms of discussion was how broke he was when he left Knoxville. Apparently, his former wife had left him completely destitute. He clearly had nothing when he left Knoxville after the divorce. But, being broke in and of itself certainly didn't get you killed.

He traveled back to Nashville with nothing more to go on than he had when he left.

There was only that video of the parking lot, but it was of poor quality and restricted in scope. He had had an opportunity to view it while at the hotel and when the manager was available. He had looked at it briefly and could barely make out anything. Not only was the quality bad, but the video was confined to the middle of the parking lot and neither end was well in view. The judge had parked at the west end of the lot. He could generally make out what happened, but there was absolutely no way the shooter's face could be seen. He had taken a copy of the video to the Nashville crime lab to have it enhanced, but they were not optimistic.

It had been more than a week and nothing had surfaced. His captain was becoming somewhat anxious and had called him in to discuss the direction the investigation was headed. Stony could tell he was uptight about the situation, and he was sure he was getting pressure from outside sources. But there was nothing he could do about it. He was working as hard as he could and turning up nothing.

He had gone to the county attorney's office yesterday and met with the county attorney and Art Walling. Neither of them could shed any light on what happened, but while he was there he had the county attorney's office acquire a subpoena for the judge's phone records. After he left, he served the subpoena on the phone company and waited while they accumulated the records. Back at the office, he and another officer had poured through all those records until midnight. They found nothing out of the ordinary, the same old story he had heard from day one.

Stony then faxed a subpoena to Visa, which was the only credit card the judge had in his billfold. They faxed the records back within hours and he had had a chance to review them just this morning. There was something unusual on the bill that caught his eye almost immediately. There had been a charge to this same hotel not three days before the judge's murder. That caught his attention.

Obviously, the judge was meeting someone at this hotel. He assumed it was a woman, and he assumed whatever had happened had been good because he had made another reservation a very short time after the first.

"Hey Stony, the crime lab is on line one for you."

"Ok, thanks."

"Hi Stony, Joanne, in the lab. I have that disc ready for you. It's still not very good, but the quality is a little better. If you want to come down, I'll run it for you."

"Be right there Joanne. And thanks for finishing that so quickly."

Stony left the precinct office and drove to the lab. Upon arriving, he was quickly escorted through the building to Joanne's office where she had already set up the disc for viewing.

"I really appreciate this Joanne. Thanks for getting this done so quickly."

"Not a problem. I knew it had priority. You ready?"

"Yes. Start it up."

The quality of the video was much improved. But the facts never changed. The events that he had watched unfold so many times remained constant. What he saw before he saw again. Nothing different except the quality was somewhat enhanced.

"Not much there other than the murder. The setup is just not designed to do what you need it to do Stony. Sorry."

"Not a problem Joanne. It is what it is. Can you make me a copy?"

"Already have."

She handed him his copy, he thanked her, and walked out.

Once back in his office, he sat at his desk considering which direction he should move now. Out of all the people he had interviewed, only one caught his attention. That woman attorney, what's her name—Rosa something. She had clearly been stretching the truth. He would need to visit with her again and try to pin her down—no touchy feely interview this time.

He walked back to the conference room and put the disc in his computer. He wanted to run it one more time alone with no distractions of any kind.

He watched it one more time. Nothing—absolutely nothing. He

let the disc run. All prior times he had shut it off right after the perp had left the lot. That was it. Nothing other than the murder was relevant and when the judge was lying on the ground and the perp had left the lot, clearly there was nothing left to see.

But this time, almost three minutes after the shooting, he saw it. He saw a car back up and leave the lot. No one had entered the vehicle after the judge had entered the lot. So whoever was in the vehicle was in there when the judge was shot.

He stopped the disc. He backed it up and ran it again. The vehicle was on the east edge of the lot and on the very edge of view. He could not make out the driver. He could barely make out the type of vehicle and the license plate was visible, but not to the extent he could read all of it. He could read the last three letters but that was it.

He had never bothered to continue to run the disc to any extent after the murder. He sat and thought about his next move. He grabbed the disc out of the computer and headed out the door for the crime lab. Is it possible they could enhance that plate? Could they give him the one piece of information that could break this case wide open? As he walked to his car, one question haunted him. Why hadn't the individual come forward? Obviously, there was an issue, or this case would have been solved immediately that day.

One thing at a time. First off, let's see if the lab can get a plate number. If and when he got the number, he would move on to the next step and try to determine if the owner was driving that day and if so, why in hell they didn't come forward. There was a reason. He just needed a name and he would be ready to break this case wide open.

Chapter 30

She literally could not move a muscle. It was Thompson. Somehow he had gotten behind her. How had he done that? There was no way he could have outflanked her. But then again, she might not be as good at this as she thought.

"Get your ass in that door."

She was unable to move. She wanted to, but she couldn't.

"I'm not going to tell you again. I'll shoot you right here and now if you don't walk through that door."

She finally gathered enough air to say, "Ok, ok I'm going. You scared me. I just need to get my legs under me."

She turned the doorknob and opened the back door into a virtually empty room. The whole building was one big room and the only items there were a small desk, a couple of chairs, and a file cabinet. There was a small lamp on the desk beside some carefully stacked paperwork. Other than that, there was nothing indicating this room was even occupied. The front windows allowed enough light to see your way around, but the further toward the back you were, the less the light filtered through. The back wall remained in total darkness.

"Put your hands behind your back."

She again stared at him.

"Not a question bitch. Not a question."

She put her hands behind her back. He immediately cuffed her. Was this guy a cop? No way. He wouldn't be holding her in the back of this building. He would be taking her "downtown" or somewhere

An Absence of Ethics

other than here.

"Sit down."

Using only the faint light from the desk lamp, she stumbled her way to the chair in front of the desk while he made his way to the chair on the other side. She really, really needed something to eat.

He pulled out his cellphone.

"Who knows where you are?"

"No one."

"No one knows you're here?"

She knew she had made a mistake.

"Let me correct that. Just one or two people know where I am. And I told them if I wasn't back in an hour to send the police."

"Really? What's your name?"

Amy started to function. She hesitated just a moment before taking a new approach.

"What the hell am I, a prisoner of war? I demand you let me go. I haven't done anything wrong."

"Name!" He screamed at her.

"Amy Glass!" she screamed back.

"What are you doing here?"

"I just wanted to see if this building was occupied. I might want to rent it, but I wasn't sure if anyone was in here."

"I think you might be the worst poker player of all time. You are a terrible, terrible liar. Now again, why are you here?"

"I just told you. And that really is the truth. Now let me go."

"Do you know Jake McKay or Gene Wakefield?"

"No."

"What about Rosa Norway?"

She squirmed in her chair.

"No. Never heard of her. Now let me go."

"You are absolutely the worst liar of all time.

He hit an automated number on his cellphone.

"We have a problem," he said to someone on the other end. "I caught a woman peering in the back window of the building. Yes, I have her here in front of me. I don't know. I know she knows Norway, but I'm not sure who else she actually knows that's involved. Needless to say she isn't being very cooperative. Ok. I'll try. But what if I can't get anywhere? You know, I'm sitting here on one of the main streets in Nashville. I don't feel good about this situation. What do you want me to do? Ok. You're the boss. Whatever you say."

After he hung up, he leaned forward as far as he could over his desk and looked Amy straight in the eyes.

"Now look. I need to know why you're here. If you tell me and tell me the truth, perhaps we can work something out. But if you continue to lie to me about wanting to rent this place, you and I are going to have a problem. Now, again, why are you here?"

"I told you. I honestly may want to rent this place. I'm thinking of starting up a small restaurant and this building looked ideal from the outside. I just wanted to take a look at the back room."

"I know you know Rosa Norway. Did she send you here?"

"I told you I don't know any Rosa Norway. I told you why I'm here. You have to believe me."

She lowered her head and started to cry.

"Look. I could torture you half to fucking death. I could pull out your fingernails. I could shoot you in both feet. I could cut off both your tits. I could do all those things. But they're messy and I'm just not in the mood. And you might find a way to yell loud enough to draw attention to the building or on and on and on. Whatever! You need to come clean with me or my boss just told me to shoot you. Is that what you want? You want to die today? Is that really what you want? Now, one more time, why are you here?"

She raised the volume of her response a level as she said, "I TOLD you. I can't make it any clearer than I have. Please let me go. I won't tell a soul about what has happened. I just want out of here."

He picked his pistol that had been sitting on the desk and aimed it at Amy, placing one bullet directly between her eyes. There was little sound. The pistol had a silencer screwed neatly into the end of the muzzle and the sound of the discharge was completely muffed.

Amy never left the chair and fell straight back on the floor. She lay there starring straight up at the ceiling as a small trickle of blood started its exit from the middle of her forehead on its journey to the floor beside her.

"You wanted out of here bitch? You just got your wish. Just not alive."

Thompson picked up the phone again and hit redial.

"It's done. She never knew what hit her. No, I have gloves on. There will be nothing to tie her to this building. She told no one she was coming here. I'll get rid or her. I still have no idea why she was looking in the back window, but it appears to me we could have a problem somewhere. I'll keep my ears open and let you know. Yes, yes I know. You don't need to remind me of the reason for all this, I get it. I'll let you know if I hear anything else."

***

Late that night, he backed his vehicle up to the back door of the building. There were no streetlights, and the only light in the alley came from the taillights of the vehicle he was driving. He opened the backdoor of the building and pulled Amy's lifeless body to the back of his vehicle where he hoisted her up and dumped her in the trunk. Rigor Mortis had started to set in and she was difficult to handle but he got the job done.

He drove east of Nashville on Interstate 40. He then took an off ramp onto Highway 840 and another exit leading to an old dirt road that was infrequently used. There he stopped and opened his trunk. He reached down and pulled the remains of Amy Glass from the bottom of the trunk, and in one single move, tossed her body into the bottom of the road ditch.

That was that. He had done his job. He felt no guilt. He felt no remorse. He had a job to do and he did it…unfortunately the death of Amy Glass was the end product of his 'success.'

Chapter 31

He knew and had worked with a number of people in the Department of Motor Vehicles. At this point, he needed to talk to somebody that knew what they were doing and see what they could do to help him determine who belonged to the plate on that vehicle. Maybe Jim Lyons could help him tie this all down.

"Jim, Stony. How are things in the vehicle business?"

"Hi Stony. Crazy as always. How can I help you?"

Stony expected that type of response. Jim always got right down to business and his short, terse response was not unusual—there were never enough hours in the day for the employees that worked in the Department of Motor Vehicles.

"Jim, I was able to read a partial plate number off a vehicle that could have somehow been involved in a crime that I am investigating. I have the last three sequential numbers but I can't read the first portion of the plate. It's obscured in the video I have been reviewing. If I gave you the last three numbers can you run those and give me a list of all the people in Davidson County that have those last three digits on their plate? Do you had the ability to do that or not?"

"Yes, we do Stony. And yes, I can run it through the computer and give you the names. Are you just going to go through each owner then?"

"Yes. I can't see who the driver is so that will continue to be an issue. But I think through the process of elimination, I can at least, to some degree, tie down who might have been at that location when this crime occurred. How long do you need?"

"Give me the rest of the day. Why don't I give you a call sometime later this afternoon? Is that soon enough?"

Stony laughed.

"What do you think?"

"Let me put it this way. I *will* call you later this afternoon. I hope that's soon enough."

"That's fine Jim. Thanks."

Shortly after 4:00 pm, he received the call he had been waiting for.

"Stony, I have that list you need."

"How many are on it?"

"You know how many vehicles there are registered in Davidson County?"

"Just give me the number on the list Jim."

"Vehicles registered in this county number tens of thousands Stony. And the same last three digits on the plate covers a hell of a lot of plates. You have your work cut out for you. There are almost 5,000 plates with those three digits."

"Are you shitting me? Ok, whatever. I'll be right over to pick it up. Thanks Jim."

He had been excited about the discovery on the tape, but now this. It would take him forever to run down each individual. He would need to look through the list, ask for additional manpower help, and then check each owner. Not fun, but at this point, entirely necessary.

After arriving at the Motor Vehicle Department, he was able to pick up the list from the front desk. As he drove back to the precinct he figured he would scan through it first and then visit with the captain requesting at least one other officer to help him and two more would certainly be appreciated.

The list contained about 30 to a page and was more than 160 pages long. He started scanning through some of the first few pages looking quickly at the names to see if anyone popped out at him. Just as a hunch he turned the pages to the middle of the list—where the list contained the names starting with the letter N. Low and behold, on page 91, right down near the bottom, he found a name he hoped wouldn't be on the list but thought it might be: *ROSA NORWAY.*

He really wasn't surprised.

The fact that she was one of about 5,000 owners on the list did not, in and of itself, put her in that lot at that time, but she would be the one he keyed on until he was sure it wasn't her. This was just too much of a coincidence to overlook.

He went back to the office where he had set up the video and replayed it again. There was absolutely no way he could tell who the driver was. He couldn't even make out if it was a male or female. One issue that continued to bother him, was if the individual in that vehicle had actually been part of all this, wouldn't they have followed the shooter's vehicle out of the lot? Why did this driver wait until everything was over, the shooter was long gone, and then drive out the opposite end of the lot?

So many issues, so little time. But he knew where he needed to go next and that would happen tomorrow morning.

***

At exactly 9:00 the next morning, he walked up to the front desk. "I need to see Rosa Norway."

June had just sat down and started listening to the prior day's dictation.

"She's busy, sir. Can I set you up with a time later today or tomorrow?"

He pulled out his badge.

"That wasn't a question. I need to see her now."

June immediately picked up the phone, mumbled something to Rosa and then said, "Sir, she is really busy getting ready for trial. Is there any way you could wait until tomorrow?"

"No."

June conveyed that one word sentence to Rosa and then looked up at Detective Stone, gave him a serious frown and said, "Go on in. You know your way."

Stony walked down the hall to Rosa's office where she didn't even bother to get up.

"Mr. Stone I am really, really busy getting ready for trial. Can't this wait?"

"No, it can't. I'm not sure I asked you the other day, but where were you the night the judge was murdered? Like say from 5:00 on through the time he was shot?"

Rosa thought for a moment. Then, without further hesitation, said, "I was here."

"Alone?"

"Yes, working on this case and another that is coming up for trial shortly. Why?"

"Do you have anyone that can provide you with an alibi during that time frame?"

Rosa again took her time and collected her thoughts.

"Well, about the time he was actually shot, I was with my friend Amy. We were at her home having a drink. She can vouch for me. I was here after hours getting ready for that trial and then at Amy's for most of the evening."

"You sure of that?"

"Yes, why what is this all about?"

"I know your car was in that parking lot when he was shot. I know that for a fact. Now, again, where were you when he was murdered?"

She felt her face start to turn a light shade of red.

"I told you. Here and with Amy. You saw me in that lot? Is that what you are saying?"

"That's not what I said. I said your car was in that lot. We have a partial plate number and I know it was your car. Are you telling me you weren't there?"

It was time to lie, and Rosa knew it.

"I wasn't there. And my car wasn't either. I was with Amy. You want to call her I'll give you her number. But not now. I'm busy. Now if you don't mind…"

She knew if he had enough to arrest her or take her in for questioning he would. He obviously didn't have enough evidence for either.

"Give me her number and I'll call her right now. From here."

"She isn't in town and I'm not bothering her with this until she returns. Now, are we done here?"

Finally, after what seemed an eternity, he said "Yes, we are done here. For today. But I guarantee you, I'll be back. I know you were in that lot. I know you know more than you are telling me. Just answer one more question. Were you seeing the judge on a personal basis outside that courtroom?"

"Asked and answered Officer Stone. Now please leave."

Stony got up and walked to the door. As he did, he turned around and said, "I'll be back. You can rest assured—we are far from done here."

He walked out her office door and slowly made his way back to his vehicle deep in thought. He had tried to pressure her and it had almost worked. He almost had her, he could feel it. But what did she know? She obviously didn't shoot the judge. Did she have it done? That didn't make sense either. He would ride her for Amy's phone number the rest of the week until she gave it to him. In the meantime, he would start investigating some of the other plate numbers, but he wouldn't work too hard at it. He knew who was in the lot. And she knew he knew who was there. He would be unmerciful with his pressure on her until she told him the truth—something which he felt she had probably circumvented both times he had talked to her.

Chapter 32

Tommie Thompson, again, found himself in a familiar spot—waiting in his underwear by his phone. He had been in this same spot way too many times. This would be his last job. He was not going out on the road again. And if they fought him on this, he would disappear. Now, if they provided him with an opportunity close to home that might be different. But he was just getting to fucking old for this shit.

And one aspect of this particular job, for the first time in his long, storied career, had affected him. At the time, it was a simple decision that needed to be made, the result of which didn't bother him. But since then, with little else to think about, he had time to consider his victim. This girl, apparently named Amy, hadn't deserved to die. Her murder concerned him. She had done nothing wrong. She had harmed no one. She was only in the way. And you just couldn't do that with these people. You just couldn't get in the way.

It had only been a couple of days, but he normally forgot about his work a few minutes after completion. This one was different. He had a daughter—somewhere. And she would be about Amy's age. Was he getting soft in his old age?

As he continued to rationalize her murder, he concluded what he had done couldn't be undone. He knew that and he knew her murder was the appropriate approach concerning resolution of the problem. But her murder still bothered him.

The phone rang. They were late.

"It's me."

The raspy old voice on the other end said, "So you had to murder her huh?"

"Yes, I told you I took care of her."

"Did you try everything you could or did you just fucking shoot her?"

"She wouldn't tell me anything. I tried a couple of things with her but she wasn't going to talk. And we were right there on a busy street. So yes, I terminated her. I felt that was the only thing I could do."

"So you disposed of the body I assume?"

"Yes, I dumped her body along a ditch road south of Mount Juliet. There was absolutely nothing that could tie me in to her. I handled it like I have handled all the others. I did everything the same way I always do. There shouldn't be a problem."

"What the fuck happened? How did she find you?"

"I have no idea. I don't know how she found the building. I've had no contact with anyone in this town other than McKay. I really believe she was on her own and she very well may have just been looking in the back window because she wanted to rent the building and for no other reason. Her car was parked about a block away. I took her keys out of her purse and the key chain identified her car. Later that night I drove it up town and parked it in a residential area. I left it there, walked downtown, and had a taxi take me back to the building. There is absolutely no way I can be tied to any of this."

"We are discussing sending someone out there to help you. Do you need someone to come out and help? We could send Jimmy if you need someone."

"No, it's not necessary. I'll finish what I started."

"Obviously you have fucked this thing up Tommie. Someone knows something they shouldn't know or she wouldn't have found your office and been looking in the back window. Somehow you have screwed this up."

"Hey you SOB, how long have I been doing this? I know what I'm doing. I know there is no reason to be alarmed. And if something does come up, believe me, I'll let you know if I need some help."

"Calm the fuck down you ignorant fuck. You don't talk to *ME* like that. You get yourself under control before I send someone else out there to have a little talk with you, and I assume you know what I mean. "

Tommie hesitated and took a deep breath before responding.

"Sorry boss. You're not really an SOB. I got a little carried away when you implied I didn't know what I was doing. Won't happen again."

"Better not, Tommie, better not. Have you set up a meeting with Jake yet?"

"Yes, he'll be here shortly. We'll have a visit about what's been going on. You know I don't like this guy. I don't like anything about him. Sorry but he's weak, he can't handle anything. He's not my type. But I'll talk to him and make sure everything is still going ok. Maybe he can shed some light on this woman I had to off."

"You aren't telling me anything about him I don't already know. Now, you sure things are ok out there? You sure you have everything under control?"

"Again, boss, everything is fine. I'll call you when I am done talking to Jake."

"Don't screw this up Tommie. You call immediately if there are problems, you understand me?"

"Yes, I'll call you back if there are problems. Otherwise, I'll talk to you next week."

He hung up. What a bunch of shit. He did make a small mistake calling his boss an SOB, but he figured he had been called worse before. No harm no foul.

Just then there was a knock at his door.

"That you Jake? Come on in. It's open."

Jake McKay slowly opened the door and walked in, looking around as he did. He started to smile when he saw his host seated in his underwear.

"Hi Tommie. Long time no see. How you been anyways?"

Tommie got up and walked over to Jake extending his hand.

"Good Jake, doing good. You look good."

Tommie noticed Jake looking at his bum leg.

"Looks like you had a little problem there Tommie."

"Sure did. Nothing I couldn't handle though. I can tell you I ended up a lot better than the guy that did this."

Jake laughed.

"Say, this is a nice place you have. Not much furniture, but I'm sure it's adequate for you."

"It's fine. Sit down Jake.   How are things?"

Jake took a seat in the only chair available.

"Good, good. Been better but things are good. What are you doing out here Tommie? Is there some reason you are in Nashville."

"Nothing very serious. The Family knew you were in a little trouble and wanted me to see if there was anything I could do to help. Now, unfortunately, I have a problem of my own with this fucking drunk driving charge. But, initially I came out to see if we could help you with your case. How's all that coming along? Any chance of resolving it?"

"Really? You came out here because of me? You didn't really need to come all the way out here for that purpose. I can handle my own problems Tommie and the Family should know that. Now, I will admit I am glad to see you. I don't have anybody out here to talk to…no family, hardly a friend, so it is nice to see a shirttail relative and have someone to discuss the case with. I don't think there's a chance of resolving it. It sounds to me like we are going to have to go to trial. I'm not looking forward to it, but it is what it is I guess. My lawyer tells me I'm going to have to testify. I really don't want to, but I will if I must. I really didn't do anything wrong Tommie, I really didn't."

"You know I ended up with that same lawyer for my case. Are you happy with her? I haven't got a feel for her yet. How is she getting along? Is she going to be all right?"

"I think so. She's won every battle she has fought for me. As I say, I really don't want to testify, but if I have to I have to. Are you coming to the trial Tommie? I would like you there if you can be. You would be the only support, the only family, I have there."

"Yes, I'll be there. I have a question. Are you familiar with a young girl by the name of Amy? I don't really know her last name and guess it doesn't matter so much, but have you met someone by that name while you have been here. Young girl, little pudgy, lot of fucking perkiness about her. I've met up with her a couple of times in Rosa's office. Ever met anyone like that while you've been in town?"

"Yes. At least that sounds like Rosa's friend Amy. She's been waiting for Rosa in the reception area a few times when I've been with Rosa. In fact, Rosa introduced me to her one day. Why?"

"No reason. I had heard Rosa mention her name one time and had seen her in the reception area. I was just wondering if she was a cop or an investigator or something like that."

"No, she sells real estate. Nice girl. I really liked her when I met her. How is everyone in the family Tommie? I miss Dad and the brothers."

"As a matter of fact, I just talked to them. They are good and give you their regards."

"Thank you for coming to help me Tommie. And tell Dad and the boys thanks when you talk to them, although I really am not sure I need any help other than moral support. I couldn't be happier with Rosa. Of course, I'll be glad when this is all over, but other than this problem, life is good here. I have to tell you though, I am *NOT* going to prison Tommie. You know I couldn't handle that. I'm willing to do anything not to go there. That's why I was so disappointed the State wouldn't try to settle this."

As Tommie sat in his chair spread eagle and contemplating Jakes answer, he reached down and scratched himself.

"I know about your prison issues Jake. But I just wanted to make sure you were comfortable with everything and felt confident you were going to come out ok when this is all over."

"She continues to assure me we are in a good position. I'm thinking that means we will win and no prison time. At least I'm hoping that's what she means."

"The Family doesn't want you in prison either Jake. That's why I'm here. To help if I can."

The conversation soon reduced itself to more trivial issues. They talked about living in the Nashville area and about old times and old friends. Nothing special—just two acquaintances passing time.

Jake left soon after they reached the point in the conversation where they had exhausted the discussion about family and old friends and literally had nothing else in common to discuss, leaving Thompson deep in thought about how this all might conclude.

One thing was certain. He was glad to hear Amy was a friend of Rosa and not a private dick or a cop. He still had issues with why she was there, but the major issue he was having ended with proof of the fact she wasn't a cop of some kind.

Jake's fear of jail or prison was common knowledge in the Family. He had never been incarcerated before, but the issue of how Jake would have trouble surviving in prison had been discussed within the Family many times. That was one of the reasons he had been ordered to Nashville, to determine what the actual situation might be with Jake and how his "mess" with the law would be resolved.

The resolution of that problem was an issue for the Family—an issue that needed to be concluded successfully. And his sole purpose in Nashville was to make sure it DID conclude successfully.

Chapter 33

Rosa sat in stunned silence. What the hell just happened here? She went from concern to panic in one five-minute session. She needed to process the conversation before she dealt with any of the twenty plus legal issues lying on her desk.

He thinks it was her vehicle in the lot. He thinks she was in it. He thinks she was having a relationship with the judge outside the courtroom. He thinks she may have seen something *if* it was her car and *if* she was in it. But, the truth of the matter was he didn't have shit. If he had, he would have hauled her ass downtown. It's just that simple.

But the clincher concerning this whole issue will be when Amy tells him they were together when the judge was murdered. That will solve all of her problems except how to make sure, after these trials, and particularly the one with Thompson, the authorities are alerted that Thompson was the murderer.

Thank God she never got out of her car after she saw the judge gunned down.

Now to run down Amy before anyone else did. Amy would lie for her. They had lied for each other before. Their untruths always involved small issues, but nevertheless they were always there for each other, no matter what, and Amy would be there for her this time.

"June see if you can contact Amy will you?"

"Sure Rosa. That shouldn't be a problem. She always has her phone."

"I guess. Unless she's in Louisville."

June laughed and Rosa could hear her pushing the buttons to call Amy.

She tried to keep her mind on her work but it was impossible. She needed time. She needed to dispose of these two trials and then figure out what to do. She needed Amy to confirm she was with her that night and perhaps that would get that Stone cop off her back for at least a while.

"Rosa, she didn't answer."

"That's unusual for her. Try her at work will you?"

"Sure."

That was a little strange. However, Rosa had to smile when she remembered Amy's explaining why she had no cellphone in Louisville.

A few minutes later, June said, "Rosa she hasn't been at work for a couple of days. They haven't seen her. They were going to wait one additional day and then contact her folks."

"Thanks June. I'll see what I can do to run her down. Hard telling what's going on this time."

It was close to 5:00. She decided to leave early and drive to Amy's apartment. She had a key, as did Amy for her townhouse.

***

She arrived at Amy's apartment building near 6:00 and unlocked her apartment door. Everything looked normal. There was a shoe here, a bra there, some loose paperwork on the table. Nothing out of the ordinary—but no Amy.

She looked around once more then walked out of the apartment and back to her vehicle. This was not like Amy at all. She would continue to call her through the evening and hopefully reach her before Stone did, in the event he eventually figured out who she was and called her.

Rosa was unable to contact her the rest of the evening. She spent another restless night worrying now about Amy as well as herself. She continued to try to reach her on the way to work but with no success.

Once at the office, she realized the best thing she could do was forget about Amy, lose herself in her work and let matters take care of themselves. She had no idea where Amy was, but she figured she would have some wild tale to tell her when she did surface. Until then

An Absence of Ethics

she was wasting her time trying to figure out her whereabouts.

She decided to work on cross-examination of the State's witnesses in the McKay case. There was really so little to cross them on. The cause of death would be an expert opinion from the medical examiner's office. Certainly not much she could do there. The officer's observations would be an issue, but they saw what they saw. She had checked and cross-checked her facts concerning all the officers that were there and there were little, if any, discrepancies in their statements. The key would be McKay's testimony, and no matter how many ways she looked at how this case playing out, it always came down to that same bottom line. He would make or break his own case.

Shortly after noon, June came barreling through her door.

"Turn on your TV. Rosa turn on your TV to Channel 4 news right now!"

Rosa had a small television in the corner of her office, but she never used it. She had only wanted it there in case of extreme weather or extreme national emergency.

She turned on Channel 4 as they were concluding a live report.

"...once again, police have tentatively identified the remains of a woman found south of Mount Juliet. Her name is Amy Glass. She was a realtor in Nashville. They are going to perform an autopsy, but her identity is apparently not an issue. And from what we understand, cause of death isn't either. She apparently was shot. But an autopsy will be performed and the results will be made public at a later date..."

Rosa heard no more. June continued to look at her but said nothing.

"June, please leave me alone."

"Let me stay with you Rosa...let's talk about this..."

"Please, get out," she said softly.

June knew better than to argue. She turned around and left the room, shutting the door securely behind her.

Rosa knew her life slowly but surely was falling apart. How could this have happened? Who could have done this? Amy didn't have an enemy in the world. And now, just coincidently when all of this was happening to her, her best friend ends up murdered? Not possible and not a coincidence. What would she do without her? How could she go on without her?

She started to cry. She couldn't think and she certainly couldn't make it through the rest of the day in this office.

She got up and closed all the files on her desk. She walked out her door and felt the eyes of June along with other attorneys and support staff huddled around the reception area, staring at her.

"Is there anything we can do Rosa?" June asked.

"No, no thank you. I'm going home. Don't contact me for anything work related June. If something comes up concerning Amy give me a call, but don't call concerning anything pertaining to work."

"I understand. We're all so sorry Rosa."

"I know. Thank you."

She drove home in a fog. She only made it because she knew the way and was able to mechanically drive the route. When she arrived home, she pulled out a beer from the refrigerator and sank down on the couch. She turned off her phone and turned on the television hoping there would be more information about Amy's death.

The only shows on TV were soap operas. After she finished her beer, she went and got another…and another…and another, until finally she passed out. She never even undressed.

She dreamed. She dreamed of past friends and bodies in a parking lot.

She woke up with a start around 7:00 the next morning. She called in sick and asked that one of the other members of the firm see her appointments scheduled for today. She needed to prepare for trial, but not today. Today she would spend the day remembering her friend Amy and nothing else.

Chapter 34

The next few days were a blur. She lost all sense of time or accomplishment. She did what she needed to do and nothing more. Amy's autopsy results had come back. She had died as a result of a single gunshot wound to the head. She had not suffered. They had no idea where it had happened or who had done it. Her car had turned up on a street near downtown Nashville, which was inconsistent with the location of her body.

As could have been expected, her parents were devastated. Rosa spent some of her days and all of her evenings with them prior to the funeral. They, along with so many others that knew Amy, could not come to grips with the manner of her death. So violent, so inconsistent with the way she lived her life. No one could even venture a guess at a motive.

The cop had called her once and asked her if the Amy that they had found south of Mount Juliet happened to be her Amy. She had told him it was. He offered his condolences and just in passing, said he would be in touch after the funeral. Just what she needed—another visit from him.

The funeral was a thing of beauty. She was cared for by so many and would be missed by all. She touched everyone with whom she came in contact.

Rosa couldn't help but notice the cop was at the funeral. What did he have to gain by being there? Certainly it didn't take an Einstein to figure out she had nothing to do with Amy's murder. After all, Amy was her alibi.

And all the while this was going on, Rosa knew McKay's trial was now only a few days away, but she found it difficult to even open the file.

There would be no continuance. It had been continued once and this event would not be enough of an event for it to be continued again. She never even filed a motion asking that it be continued. It would have been wasted effort. She just needed to find the time to get back to work and mentally prepare herself for trial.

The funeral was over by the middle of the afternoon. It was Wednesday and the trial was set to begin on Monday. Her office was close enough to the church where the funeral was held that she had walked. It was a rainy, overcast day in Nashville. Slightly unusual for this time of year, but consistent with how she felt. As she walked, she tried to stay focused on trial preparation and not the death of her best friend, but it was difficult to do. She knew McKay would be in for one last push on Friday, and she needed to put the hammer down. She would attempt to cross-examine him as the county attorney might, in one last ditch effort to prepare him for testifying. If he wasn't ready on Monday, it wouldn't be because of a lack of preparation.

It was late afternoon. She was so ready to go home, to kick back, have another beer, and think of nothing. How she did miss meeting Amy after work. She knew that pain would never end. She would just have to deal with it.

June was getting ready to leave. Rosa's office door was open and she was mindlessly watching June shut everything down and walk to the elevator. She heard the elevator doors open and wondered who was coming to the office so late in the day. Then she saw him—the cop. Shit. She couldn't handle him. Not today. She shut her door.

She heard June's footsteps as she walked toward her office.

"Rosa, that cop is here. He will *not* take no for an answer. He wants to see you. He said for just a moment. He said he would talk to you out here."

"Ok. I'll be right out. Go ahead and go home June. I'll be fine."

"Are you sure? I can stay if you want me to."

"No, go ahead and leave. I'll see you in the morning."

June walked out and left the door open for Rosa.

Rosa walked down the hall and as she approached Detective Stone she said, "How can I help you Mr. Stone?"

"First of all, just call me Stony. Everyone else does. Are you getting ready to leave?"

"Yes. It's been a long day."

"Do you normally stop for a drink or something before you head home?"

"Yes, but I don't know that I will today. Like I said, it's been a really long, emotional day."

"You normally go to that little bar downstairs?"

"Yes. Why?"

"Would you do me a favor and have one drink with me. Right now. Just for a few minutes. I promise I won't grill you about the judge. I would like to get off on a better foot with you. Just shoot the breeze. Or I could ask you to stay here for a while, and again we can be cop and suspect if you wish. Your choice."

So many thoughts raced through her mind in such a short time. She couldn't handle the cop/suspect thing. She just couldn't.

"Ok. Fine. Let me close out what I've been doing. I'll be a minute."

"Great. I'll wait here."

Stony pulled out the same *People* magazine he had now read twice and started leafing through it one more time while Rosa closed out files and shut her computer down.

She walked out into the reception area and he stood as she approached. Together they walked into the elevator and together they found a table in the small crowded bar on the first floor of her office building. They said nothing to each other until after they had both ordered a beer.

"How are you getting along Rosa? Obviously, you and Amy were really close."

"How do you know that Officer Stone?" she said defensively.

He chose his words carefully.

"Ok, let's just change the flow of this conversation right now. Let me lay my cards out on the table. Here's what I know. I know you are a good person. I know you have a stellar reputation. I know you didn't do this. I know you know some things you aren't telling me. I've figured out by now you apparently have a good reason for not telling me. I just figure when you are ready to tell me, you will. I like you. I like everything I've seen about you. I know you're in a fix or you wouldn't be holding back on me. I'm here to help you if I can. I have no doubt you are not involved in anything illegal. I'm going to carry on with my investigation but when you are ready to talk about all this, let me know. For now, can we just talk about you…about your past…about your future? And maybe while we are at it, you may learn a little about me, whether you want to or not. And by the way, again, call me Stony."

He smiled and awaited her response.

She thought for a second. What did she have to lose by following his approach? Absolutely nothing.

"Agreed. As long as we can proceed on that basis, let's have a drink and just talk…not about Amy. I can't talk about her or I'll cry the whole time we are here. But just talk one on one. I'm game for that. And my friend I would have done that with a week ago is no longer amongst the living. So yes, let's just do that."

Three beers, a few hours later, and after small talking each other to near oblivion, Rosa said she needed to go home. He walked her to her vehicle. He told her he enjoyed the evening more than any other he had had in a long time. As she drove home, she concluded he was a good guy. And this time, true to his word, he didn't grill her as he had before. He might be someone she needed before long and she was really glad he seemed to be on her side. She would remain cautious. But for her, certainly any kind of friend looked good right now.

Chapter 35

She sat and waited patiently for "little man." McKay was to be in her office at 10:00 and she would again discuss the jury selection process. She would also start preparing him for cross. She didn't have much time allotted for him today, and she would just have to go as far as she could during his scheduled time, cleaning up what wasn't covered today the next time they met.

But for now, prior to the start of a busy day, she sat in silence. The city was starting to awaken. It wasn't quite 8:00 and the activity in the street below was just getting a good start. She thought of Amy. She remembered those many mornings when Amy would call her on the way to work. She would talk about her evening, what she had done, who she had been with if it wasn't with her. Life without Amy was not going to be an easy task. Replacing her would be impossible. No one would ever take her place. Friends come and friends go, but their relationship was special.

And what about this Stony? She had finally gotten used to calling him that. Maybe a little too familiar for someone who in the end, if he thought she was involved in this crime in any respect, would arrest her and take her to jail. But this guy seemed genuine. He seemed like the type of guy who told it like it was. Someone you could depend upon. Someone that wouldn't tell you one thing and do another. She liked him. And she so badly wanted to tell someone about this whole situation. Someone she could trust and who could help her resolve all this once and for all.

She reflected back on her life prior to the judge. How simple it had been. But how much everything had changed since she met him. How she so wished she could just go back and this time make the correct decision instead of traveling the road she had traveled.

Her office door opened and June walked in.

"Morning Rosa. You have a busy morning. Have you had a chance to check your schedule yet?"

"I have. I need to review a few files this morning before McKay gets here but I've already pulled them. Hold my calls until I'm finished with him. I'll try to return all of them this afternoon."

"Ok. You need a cup of coffee? I would be glad to get you one if you do."

"No. I'm fine. Would you see if you can get Art Walling on the phone? I better visit with him before McKay gets here."

"Sure will. I'll do it right now and let you know if he is available."

She walked out leaving Rosa, once again, to her own thoughts. But her quiet reflection was quickly interrupted by June's voice.

"Art's on line 1."

Rosa needed to confirm, for the last time, that Art would not agree to any type of plea bargain.

"Art, how are you?"

"Busy. How can I help you?"

Rosa noticed no indication of a stutter. He was feeling pretty good about himself this morning.

"I have McKay coming in this morning and I thought we could visit a second about his trial. Do we have any chance at resolving his situation Art, or are we done?"

"It can be easily resolved Rosa. Plead him. I won't push for prison because he apparently has no criminal history, but it wouldn't surprise me if that's where he ends up. This was not a pretty crime scene and you know Judge Jackson. He can be pretty tough."

"Of course, and that's exactly why I can't take that chance. Are you saying there is no way we can compromise this case. Perhaps plead to a charge that isn't a felony and agree, subject to the Judge's approval, on a sentence other than prison?"

"No. We have a good case and there's too much publicity concerning the crime. I can't go there Rosa. Not with this guy."

"Ok. Guess we will just let the chips fall where they may. See you

An Absence of Ethics

Monday."

"Fine."

He hung up.

He was way too upbeat. Way too sure of himself. That wasn't like Art.

She clearly couldn't sit and wonder what was going on with Art. She needed to prepare her own case. It was time to review the files she needed to look over and prepare for McKay. She could only work with what McKay provided her. Hopefully he wasn't withholding anything from her. If he was, in the end the only one that would suffer would be him.

She had reviewed only a portion of the files that needed to be reviewed before the morning ended when June interrupted the process by opening her door and announcing, "Mr. McKay is here Rosa."

How quickly time had slipped away. The rest of the files she wanted to review before McKay got there would need to wait.

"Send him in."

He opened her door and took a chair.

"Good morning Rosa."

"Good morning Jake. The first thing I want to discuss with you this morning is making sure you understand this jury selection process. I know we've discussed it before, but I just want to make sure you understand how important it is. The twelve people we ultimately come up with will be the twelve people that decide your fate. So it's important we do our best to select the right people."

"So how do you know if they are the right ones?"

"As I mentioned, both sides have a right to query all potential jurors in an effort to determine if they can be fair. If there is a question about whether or not one or more of the jurors can be impartial, both sides have an opportunity to strike that juror. To determine whether they can be fair we ask questions of each potential juror to find out what they know or don't know about the case, about you, about this whole process. Now, I gave you a list of the potential jurors. Did you go through it?"

"Yes. I don't know any of those people."

"That's fine. I just wanted to make sure. I've had a chance to review answers to certain questions all potential jurors must provide at the time they are selected as jurors and I didn't find anything that would pose much of a problem. But the important part of this begins when we start questioning each individual juror. This is going to take time. Don't become concerned about how long this takes. It's really important that this be done in an orderly fashion and it's just going to take as long as it takes."

"When can I tell my side? Do I have to wait until that jury selection process is over?"

"Yes. And even after that, the judge will give the jury a few instructions about how to conduct themselves and there will be opening statements, although we have a right to reserve that until we present our case, which I might do. So you will need to be patient but you will get your chance, believe me."

"Who's going to be on this jury? We don't know yet do we?"

"No, but I am inclined to look at women more than men. I think they will be quick to condemn any woman who was there in that room with you in the first place, which may be just a slight edge for us. And in the jury selection business, you need to take any edge you can get. It's a science. There are people who are professionals in helping select jurors. I don't believe we need one here but that's how important it is."

"So when I testify, what should I say? I mean, is it all right to say she was giving me a blow job and she bit me? Is that something I should say?"

"Ok, Jake we have gone through your testimony once and we will obviously need to do it again. You can explain what was going on in terms other than that. I already told you that. But this morning, let's talk about cross-examination. When I am done asking you questions, the prosecutor will be given the opportunity to ask you questions. Now when that happens, just answer his questions. Don't argue with him. Tell him the truth. And if you don't understand a question, just ask him to rephrase it until you do understand the question. Do you understand?"

"No."

"What don't you understand?"

"Why should he get a chance to ask questions? Everything we have to say will be said in response to your questions. Why does he get a chance to ask questions?"

"That's the way this works Jake. And the questions he asks won't be easy. But, you *MUST* answer them. You'll have no choice. That's the problem with testifying. You don't get the opportunity to answer only your attorney's questions. You are subject to cross-examination, and you'll need to answer his too."

"But I don't want to answer his questions. Is there any way around that?"

"No. Not if you want that jury to hear your side of the story. And since there is no one left to tell your story but you, you must testify for us to have a chance in this case."

"What kind of questions can he ask? Can he ask questions about the past or about my family? Because if he can, I may not answer them."

"Why not Jake? Why wouldn't you answer them?"

He hesitated before responding.

"I might not have an answer. I may not know what he is asking."

"Then just tell him that. Now the next time we meet, day after tomorrow, I'll go through some of the specific questions he might ask and we'll be ready to try the case. Are you ok with the process?"

He looked away and thought for a moment before he responded.

"I guess, if there is no other way."

"There isn't. We can't reinvent the process Jake. It is what it is and we have to work within the system."

He said nothing.

His time was up. After once again defining his role in the process, he left. But long after he had walked out the door, his conversation bothered her. What was it he wasn't telling her? It apparently had nothing to do with the facts of this incident. Everything he told her was substantiated by the physical evidence and statements made by the officers at the scene. She thought about it long into the night. She had one more crack at him before trial. She only hoped he would, at some point, tell her the rest of the story. Because there was no doubt in her mind that he had not told her all she needed to know. And without that extra thread of information, she was worried that no matter who those jurors were, she could very well end up on the wrong side of the verdict.

Chapter 36

Art had just hung up the phone after another conversation with Rosa concerning the McKay case. She was certainly anxious to settle. She had made that clear during a number of continuing calls wanting to know if he was ready to resolve the case by plea bargain.

Again and again he had reiterated his position. He would settle for nothing less than a plea to the original charge. In the beginning, he had felt the charge of murder was much more appropriate, but, after a thorough investigation, he ultimately settled for manslaughter—the proof for murder just didn't exist.

He was not normally that hard to get along with, but this case had taken on a life of its own, independent of other cases involving Rosa or anyone else for that matter.

The judge had ruled in Rosa's favor on every issue concerning McKay. It had reached the point of becoming ridiculous and he could tell by his involvement with the officers handling the case that they were put out by the direction the case had taken. Of course, their position in most cases was that they were right in all they did—that a conviction should come without a fight. Each and every defendant should plead guilty because they, in fact, were guilty. All criminal cases should conclude in a matter of hours, not weeks—again because law enforcement was right and the accused were wrong—regardless of the facts of the case.

He had personally reviewed the jury list and had gone through the list with each of his officers. He wanted to make sure there were no potential jurors on the list that might create a problem because of prior dealings with the prosecutor's office or any of the officers involved in the case.

None of the officers seemed to have an issue with any of the prospective jurors. He had handled the questioning of potential jurors so many times he could do it in his sleep. In that respect, there was no need for additional preparation. His approach would be to look for men who were respectful of woman and would condemn another man who handled a woman in any manner but appropriately. He would try to strike as prospective jurors, as many women as he could.

He had met with each officer on two occasions and they were more than ready to testify. Of course, his hands had been tied to some extent by the rulings of Judge Hampton, but he still figured he had enough to convict. He knew Rosa had a problem. There was no one to explain away what happened unless the defendant testified. And if he testified then he would be subjected to cross. Defense attorneys hated having their defendants crossed. That potentially presented a scenario for all types of issues. And one of those issues would indeed, before this defendant was done testifying, be a problem for Rosa.

His intern, Mike Johns, walked in his office with a handful of paperwork.

"You've been busy. What's all that?"

"Copies of all of my research. I've looked all over the net trying to come up with additional information on this guy McKay. His history ends when he moves to Nashville, but up until then there is plenty to read about."

"Is this in addition to what you have already provided me?"

"Yes. In most cases it's the actual newspaper accounts of the facts I was able to uncover on the net. I wanted you to have the factual account in front of you when you needed it."

"Ok. I should have time to look everything over before the trial starts. Have you uncovered any additional information other than what we actually talked about the other day?"

"No. Hopefully you have enough with what I've provided."

As he completed that sentence, Art's boss walked in the room.

"Enough of what 'that's already been provided?'"

"Mike has found considerable information concerning McKay's background. He has a long history of involvement with the mob before he moved to Nashville. This should provide plenty of interesting questions for cross if she calls him, which she will."

"Great. You really think she will call him?"

"She has to. There is no one else to tell his story but him. And without it they *WILL* convict. No doubt about that."

"Art, is there anything else you need me to do for you?"

"No. Great job Mike. Thanks."

As soon as he had left, Art said, "Cal you need to give him a raise and make sure we keep him. The kid is really good at what he does and I don't have much doubt that he would make an excellent permanent addition to our office."

"Could be. Now let's talk about the case. Are you ready to go? Is there anything I can do or provide you that would assist in prosecuting this case?"

"No. I think we are fine. The cross of McKay should be fun. I'm looking forward to it. The case in chief, our case with our witnesses, is set and should present no problem whatsoever. It's the cross of the defendant that will make or break a conviction."

Cal stood up to leave.

"Cal before you go, can you shut the door for a second. I really need to discuss something with you and I don't need the office 'ears' to hear this."

"Sure." He walked over and shut the door.

"You and I have both felt there was something crazy about this case—something that didn't quite meet the eye. And I really believe we were correct in our assessment. But the conclusion I have reached is that the relationship between Rosa and Judge Hampton was not as we think it was or should have been. That's the only thing left. I've ruled out almost every other scenario. I'm convinced they had some type of relationship and that their personal involvement has resulted in the judge ruling the way he has."

Cal walked over and opened the door, turned to Art and said, "You're nuts. Don't even go there. We're not going to get caught up in that kind of shit. File a complaint with the Bar. Do whatever you want on your own time, but don't do it on mine. If you want to look into that issue after the trial, go ahead, but don't dare do it on my time. Besides that, you seem to have this case under control, and obviously it will never present itself again because the judge is dead. What the hell's the difference if she was screwing him or not?"

"But dammit, right is right and wrong is wrong. I've had to work my ass off on a case that should have been pled out long ago, because I believe she personally influenced this judge. No sir! This is wrong and if I have to spend my time and effort getting to the bottom of this I will."

"Well that's exactly what you are going to need to do Art. You aren't going to do it on my time. Now I have other slightly more important issues to handle this morning." he said sarcastically. "Good luck. Get a conviction on this case Art."

Art respected Cal's opinion and his logic. He was correct in that the judge was dead and this type of situation would never occur again. But all his life people had plotted against him. All his life he had had to contend with people watching him, people following him, people wanting him to fail. Because of that, he had always needed to be forever defensive and watchful no matter what he did or what he was doing. He was never able to put his guard down. It had been a long battle and never once had he tried to strike back—to be aggressive and stop those that were out to get him—to stop him from enjoying life as he should.

This time would be different. He was putting his foot down. This time the problem involved his life's profession. If she gets away with it this time, what is to stop her from some type of involvement with other judges again and again and again? It was time to strike back. He had little doubt at this point, Rosa had somehow, someway influenced the judge and that was why the judge ruled in her favor. His best guess was they were sleeping together.

As soon as this trial was over, he would file a complaint with the bar and let *them* do the investigating. Put *her* on the hot seat. He didn't give a shit what his boss said. He would investigate after work each day. He would see this to the end no matter which way it went.

Before it was over, Miss Rosa Norway would come to understand you didn't mess with Art Walling. And maybe then others would take heed. Maybe then they would *all* understand you didn't mess with Art Walling. It was time he set the record straight. Too bad it had to all be at Rosa's expense, but that's the way it goes.

She shouldn't have been doing the judge in the first place. And Art Walling would be more than glad to point that out to her once the investigation had concluded.

Chapter 37

Sunday morning, and, as was always the case when he was knee deep in an investigation, he was working. Stony could never let go until it was solved, or until there wasn't a shred of evidence left to review, one way or the other. This case was no exception.

He had gone through each and every name on the list. He had called a number of the names and had, through some method or another, eliminated about 50 percent of the owners already. It, unfortunately, was a half-hearted effort. He knew Rosa was in that parking lot. But she had denied it and he owed it to himself and to the investigation to at least make some effort to determine if someone else might have been there that day.

He had taken a few moments to think back on his time with Rosa. He had enjoyed every second with her. She was a quality individual and he wanted to spend more time with her. He had a hard time keeping her out of his mind. But the cop in him continued to raise its ugly head. He knew there was more to the story than she was telling him. He knew it would eventually all come out and he just hoped it did not in any respect adversely affect her.

He wondered about her involvement with the judge. Then again, were they involved at all? He suspected the judge was involved with a woman—and that he had apparently met her at that hotel twice in one week. He certainly didn't go by himself. Could he have been with another man? Perhaps. He was definitely with someone and their identity at this stage of the proceedings, he felt, was vital to the case.

He wondered about hall security cameras in the hotel. If they had them, at least he could identify whom the judge might have been with on that one occasion a week earlier. Not that that would necessarily define the murderer, but it might help.

He stopped what he was doing and called the manager. After identifying himself, he asked if there were security cameras in the halls of the hotel. The manager told him they were cameras on each floor for the protection of the guests, but he was reluctant to allow anyone to review the video, concerned about the privacy issue involving each guest who luckily hadn't been murdered. After considerable discussion, during which the manager made it clear he would not release the disc without a search warrant, he finally agreed to view the disc himself until he came to the moment the judge walked down the hall and some other individual walked into the room. He would allow Stony to look at that particular segment without a warrant. But he would not allow any other viewing without a warrant.

That was acceptable to Stony. The manager said he would watch the disc and call Stony later today after he had viewed it and had something for him.

***

About two hours later, he got the call. The manager had found what he was looking for. He wanted Stony to come and view what he had observed. Stony said he would be there in about thirty minutes. He dropped everything and drove to the hotel.

The manager was ready when he arrived, and Stony sat down beside him to watch what he had uncovered.

"Ok, now this is when the judge entered the hallway and you can see he is alone. He walks into the room by himself. But now, let me fast forward fifteen minutes."

Stony watched as he ran the disc forward and low and behold, no surprise—a little disappointment maybe—but certainly no surprise. Rosa walked down the hallway and directly into the judge's room.

He figured she was the one that met him, but he needed it confirmed. No wonder she was so reluctant. She was a potential suspect, a witness, and she was violating the sacred Rules of Ethics. She could be disbarred. No wonder she didn't want to say anything. She would have to now. He knew, and he would tell her he knew. She would need to tell him what information she had or he would place her under arrest for withholding evidence. He surely hoped it never came to that, but that would be up to her. He needed to meet her again. And this time the meeting needed to be productive—

***

Once he returned to the station, he waited to collect his thoughts, and then called her.

"Rosa, Stony. You busy right now?"

"No, other than I'm trying to prepare for trial. The McKay trial starts in the morning. I brought my files home. I didn't want to spend the evening in that damn office, again."

"I can understand that. Unfortunately, that's where I am right now—still working in my office. I need to meet with you. Are you available for a few minutes now?"

"No, no I can't do it now. I have to get ready for this trial. We pick a jury first thing in the morning."

"I really do need to get together and go through some new evidence with you. How do you want to handle this?"

"What new evidence is that?"

"I'm not going to discuss it on the phone. I just need to get together with you. When is a better time?"

"A better time for me would be after this trial is over. But I'm supposing that's not soon enough?"

"Not even close. What about tomorrow? I know the trial won't be over, but if you aren't prepared by the time it starts, you aren't ever going to be."

"Not going to argue with you on that. Ok, let me get through the first day. What about late tomorrow afternoon, after court recesses for the day?"

"I have no doubt you will be going to your office after court recesses, why don't I just meet you at your first floor bar? Say maybe 6:00?"

"Fine."

"I can tell there's plenty of excitement in your voice about meeting" he said sarcastically. "I'm sorry Rosa, but this needs to be done."

"I understand. I'll see you then."

She terminated the call without waiting for a response.

He looked at the phone after she hung up and finally just terminated the call from his end.

This had become unpleasant for him. His feelings for her were starting to get in the way of the investigation. He didn't want her to be involved. But he knew in the long run he needed to do what was best—best for him, best for the department. He needed to figure out what her role might be in all this and tomorrow night she would need to tell him what she knew or he was going to haul her ass in.

He would hate to see her in handcuffs, at least in this context, but if that was the way it had to be, so be it. She needed to stop hindering this investigation and start helping or their relationship was about to turn south.

Big talk—he only hoped when he was sitting across the table from her tomorrow night, looking into those beautiful blue eyes, he could refrain from turning into a bumbling idiot and remain focused on his responsibility as a cop.

Chapter 38

Finally, the wait was over. This was Jake's day—this was the day he could hopefully put the incident completely behind him. She could tell he was nervous but nothing over the top, and nothing she hadn't seen many times before. A jury trial brought out the nerves in everyone, client *and* attorney.

They took the elevator to the second floor where the courtroom was located and found a small conference room where they could discuss the case without interference.

"What now?" Jake asked as he sat down in a chair near the end of the conference table.

"We wait. As I mentioned, I'll need to meet with the Judge and the prosecutor prior to commencement of selection of the jury. There is no need for you to be with me. You can stay right here. The judge is going to want to know the parties' thoughts about resolving the issues and whether there are any pretrial problems we need to discuss. I'll waive your presence if that is acceptable with you. There is really nothing you need to do or say and it would be much more comfortable for you to remain here."

"Are there more decisions for me to make? I'm getting really tired of all this."

"No, at least not for now. But we will just have to wait and see what comes up. This is literally a minute-to-minute process, but for now, you can sit here and relax."

They both sat in silence, neither relaxed. He was lost in the tension of the moment and she was lost in a last minute mental review of her opening argument.

A few moments later she said, "It's time for me to see the judge. You'll be ok in here won't you? You need a glass of water or anything?"

"No, I'm fine. I'll sit here until you get back. Good luck. Get all this resolved if you can, please."

"I'll try. It'll probably be twenty to thirty minutes before I get back here and if it still can't be settled, we'll be ready to walk in the courtroom and get started. I'll see you soon."

She got up and gave him a reassuring pat on the back as she walked by.

Art was already there when she walked into chambers. He was joking with the judge. Always that "good ole boy" issue with the men. She had had to face it a thousand times and she could tell today would be no exception.

She sat down in front of the judge's desk next to Art. The jokes stopped as she took her seat.

"Ok, you two. Do we have any chance of settling this case before we start today? Have all the options for settlement been explored?"

Art said, "First of all, I see the defendant isn't here. Rosa are you waiving his presence?"

"I am."

Judge Jackson looked at his court reporter reporting the hearing and said, "Make sure you show the defendant's attorney waived his presence. Now, what about settlement Art"?

"Judge, we have gone through every option the State felt might be appropriate and apparently this case cannot be resolved.

Rosa said, "Now, let's see. Art's proposal and his *ONLY* proposal to resolve this was for my client to plead to the charge as filed. That's it. And we rejected it. That's the only proposal he has ever made. He's offered no compromise at all. We have made other offers to plead to other charges as long as my client doesn't go to prison, but they've all been rejected."

"Is that correct Art?"

"Pretty much Judge. He pleads, we are done. No other options from the State on this case."

"Well, it sounds like we need to just get this over with then folks. Are there any last-minute pretrial motions from either of you?"

Both she and Art shook their heads no.

"I assume, as is normally the case, you both want witnesses sequestered until they testify, is that correct?"

Both attorneys nodded affirmatively.

"What are you both thinking in terms of the length of time this trial might take? I'll need to ask the jury panel if any of them have time issues."

Art spoke up.

"Judge I can't think this will take more than a couple of days. We don't have all that many witnesses and to the best of my knowledge, Rosa only has her client."

"That's correct Judge. And he will take some time on the stand, as you can imagine. But I agree. Unless something unusual happens, I think a couple of days will handle it."

"You both know we are all bound by Judge Hampton's prior rulings, so I expect you to remember that—don't put on any evidence of any kind that would violate his rulings. I'm not saying I would have ruled the way he did on either motion, but we are bound by those rulings."

"Judge I don't believe *ANY* other judge would have ruled the way he did. But I'll take that up later, after this trial is over with."

The hair stood up on the back of Rosa's neck.

"What do you mean by that Art?"

"Never mind. Let's just stay focused on what we have in front of us right now. Judge, the State is ready to proceed."

"Rosa?"

"Ready Judge."

Both attorneys got up and walked out of the Judge's chambers together.

As they walked down the hallway, Rosa said, "What the hell was that remark about Judge Hampton's rulings all about?"

"Rosa, you know as well as I do those rulings were wrong. Both of them. And I personally don't believe either ruling had anything to do with the law. There was another reason he ruled the way he did. And I'm going to find out what it was. We'll take it up after this trial is over."

He walked into the courtroom and she stood there with her mouth open. She recovered quickly but wondered as she walked into the conference room, if anything else could possibly go wrong. Now the prosecutor's office was on her ass. McKay was waiting for her in exactly the same position he was when she left the room.

"Come on Jake. It's time to go. We have no deal. We're going to need to try the case."

He reluctantly got up and walked toward the door. Together they walked down the hall and into the courtroom. Every seat was filled. There must have been 200 people in the room. Most were prospective jurors waiting for their name to be called. Art was at his usual position at the prosecutor's table, and Rosa along with her client made their way to the table designated for defendants and their attorneys.

Rosa quickly scanned the room. The only thing she noticed other than prospective jurors was Stony sitting in the far corner of the room and Mr. Thompson sitting near the front of the room. Stony must have wanted to make sure his prime suspect didn't get too far without him knowing about it. But Thompson? That was a puzzle. What the hell was he doing there?

She turned to McKay and said, "Why is Mr. Thompson here? What interest would he have in your trial?"

McKay looked at her in silence for a moment and finally said, "Oh, we know each other from years past. He had heard I had a problem and just wanted to see what happened. No other reason. He has a general interest in how these trials proceed and in what might happen in my case—that's all."

This shit just keeps getting more interesting by the moment, she thought. How do they know each other? Thompson is a murderer. How could these two possibly be friends? She knew she didn't have time to worry about it now. This trial needed her full concentration. She would take it up with both of them after the trial was over.

The judge entered the courtroom and took his place behind the bench, and the circus was underway.

During the next six hours, name after name was called to come forward, take a seat in the juror's box, and be questioned by each side. A few potential jurors were dismissed because of health or other personal reasons. Some of them were dismissed because they had heard about the facts of the case and had already formed an opinion about the guilt or innocence of the defendant. But the majority of the jury panel had not heard enough about the case to have formed an opinion.

After each side had been allowed to strike eight potential jurors for whatever reason they wished, the parties were left with twelve people who would sit on this panel. The twelve consisted of eight women and four men. It couldn't have been a better result as far as Rosa was concerned.

Finally, the first day was over and opening arguments would take place first thing in the morning. It was only after Rosa had sent McKay home for the day and she had a chance to relax for a moment that she remembered her appointment with Stony. She wondered if this nightmare would ever end. She thought about Art's remarks and wondered what he would do after the trial was over.

She really wished she could kick back, relax, have a beer in her office and review everything for tomorrow. Hopefully this meeting with Stony would end quickly, although she did have to admit she was somewhat enjoying her time with him. Hopefully, when this was all over, she could spend some time with him and not have to watch every little thing she said, as she would indeed have to do again tonight.

Chapter 39

Frank Hancock could not get excited about Economics 101. What a waste of time. Of course, his conclusion concerning this class was somewhat consistent with his conclusion concerning the rest of the classes he was taking this year. They were all a waste of time. Whether it was math, English, history, or this shit course he was sitting in right now, he knew he would never use any of it when he got out of college—especially if he became a cop and hopefully one day a detective.

He had made it through the first three years of college at Tennessee but only by the skin of his teeth. His grades were poor but they were passing, and that was really all that mattered to him.

Concentration and focusing on what he was doing at that very moment was a major problem. It had plagued him in high school and had now carried over into college. He just had an issue focusing. Somehow he got by and he knew he had a problem, but what the hell was he going to do about it? Quit? Quit everything because he just couldn't focus? Nope, he couldn't quit and he couldn't go back, so he forged ahead, knowing it was an issue and trying to overcome it as best he could.

"Mr. Hancock, what do you say? What is your answer?"

He looked at Professor Brockmore and said nothing.

"What's the answer, Mr. Hancock?"

"You know, I couldn't quite hear the question sir. Could you repeat that one more time?"

The class was large—nearly 200 people. He could hear ripples of laughter throughout the room.

Professor Brockmore looked at him in disgust and then moved on to another student for the answer to what he considered a no brainer.

This class was a 'pass-fail' class so he didn't need a good grade, he just needed to pass. And he needed to concentrate. Luckily for him, today, in another twenty minutes he would be out of here.

After the class had ended Professor Brockmore called to him as he was just about to walk out the door.

"Mr. Hancock, do you have a moment?"

Did he have a choice? Did he want to pass?

"Yes sir, Professor Brockmore, I sure do. Is there a problem?"

"Certainly I don't have one but apparently *you* do. It appears to me you are having an issue keeping up Mr. Hancock. I have no doubt this is all pretty boring to you, but is there some way you could stay with me here in class? I realize it's only a pass/fail course for you, but you still need to keep your head in the game. Is that too much to ask?"

"No sir, it sure isn't. I'll do what I can from now on to do just that sir, just that."

The professor scratched his head, turned around, and walked away. Apparently, that was the end of that conversation. He would try harder but the result was always the same. He remained unattached to his surroundings. He would work at it though, he really would.

***

What he had done wasn't really that bad. Granted, it shouldn't have happened. He had been a cop now for more than ten years—since he left college. Ten years he had been a beat cop, and by now he should have been making good headway toward detective. But here he was. Sitting at a desk.

He thought back. Being a cop was all he had ever wanted to do. His only goal through college had been to get that degree in criminal justice and become involved in law enforcement. And he was lucky enough right out of college to find the job he wanted. Not in Knoxville, but, as it turned out, in Nashville. He loved the job and the guys he worked with. And it all started out so well. He enjoyed every moment as a beat cop. But he also knew he had to keep his eye on the ball and always stay in the game. And he had—at least most of the time.

But it really depended on what the game was. If he was physically involved in something then he never missed a beat. But when his responsibilities slowed down and there was little, if any, physical activity, he was in trouble. And he knew it. But once again, he couldn't do anything about it. His wife had commented on it. His captain had commented on it. They could comment all they wanted but it didn't change the problem.

He figured he probably deserved what he got this time.

He had been on a stakeout in his vehicle watching a house. The department was aware there were problems at that location. Too many undesirables had been seen going in and out of the house. His captain was sure the couple that lived there was dealing. And the stakeout went well until about 10:00.

It was slow, so he had turned on the radio, and because of the lack of any activity, eventually he drifted off to sleep. He awoke a few moments later to the sound of shots fired in the home. He quickly exited his vehicle and climbed the steps to the house, but by then, whoever had fired the shots had gone out the back door and both husband and wife were dead.

They did a half-assed internal investigation trying to figure out why he had not seen who entered the house and shot the two occupants. He had given them a lame excuse about picking up some of the garbage off the floor of his car the very moment the shooter entered the house.

In the end, the shootings helped the department out because there were two less drug dealers they needed to attend to. But, everyone knew Frank had, again, failed to keep his head in the game. He was demoted to a desk job. He knew he was probably lucky that he still had a job so he couldn't fight the demotion. But he also knew he couldn't stand sitting at this desk much longer. He would need to move on to some other type of employment if they intended on leaving him here doing nothing but paperwork. That wasn't happening—not now, not ever.

***

The Department had put up with him about as long as they could, but his continual problems with concentration and his lapse of attention finally did him in. At least that was their story. There had been numerous issues through the years and he had finally given up on the Department about the same time they gave up on him.

That ended the dream. And at 50, after almost 30 years as a cop, he had no idea what he would do. He did have some pension income and his wife, Wanda, had a good job. They had no children so that expense was a nonfactor. Income was not necessarily a problem, but he needed to do something.

He had heard about a job in security with the judicial system. It sounded like something he could handle, so he applied.

That had been 15 years ago. He had been hired and eventually assigned to only courtroom duty. Everyone he worked with liked him and they all knew he meant well. But they also knew he needed to be placed in a position where he didn't need to be completely committed all the time. He had lapses. He had a problem, again, with concentration that had surfaced upon numerous occasions, so they placed him where he could find himself in the least trouble when he was not keeping his head in the game.

Court was an everyday, ongoing event in the Davidson County Courthouse. Frank needed to be in the courtroom every day. And every day, physically, he was there. He was the only one in the room allowed to be armed, and luckily he had never, in 15 years, had to draw his weapon.

He had his own chair situated behind the state prosecutor's table, and it was there he would be every day of the week from 9:00 to 4:00. Everyone knew Frank. But everyone who worked inside the walls of that courtroom knew he had this issue—this problem with living in the moment. Many times a judge would ask him a question and then have to repeat it because Frank just wasn't with it.

There were occasions when a civil matter, mostly between a husband and wife, would become heated—when the parties would lock horns and the husband would try to intimidate by walking over toward the wife's chair. Frank never hesitated to intervene, and there was never an issue about his bravery.

But he hoped he never needed to testify, because he wasn't sure he could come up with an answer to the question in time to remember what the question might have been.

And now he listened as they picked a jury. Something about some poor idiot who had murdered a prostitute or something like that. Boring as hell.

There were more important issues right now. There were questions in his life that needed an answer as soon as possible. He wondered what he would do later today. He wondered what life would have been like if they had had children. And he wondered if it was finally time to retire.

He would successfully answer each question his mind generated as he sat quietly behind the prosecutors table, but as quickly as he determined the answer, he would just as quickly forget what the initial question might have been. Every day was the same for Frank—a never ending battle to remain focused.

Chapter 40

Rosa needed to review all of her notes for tomorrow before she went anywhere. She was to meet Stony at 6:30 so she still had a little time. At least jury selection was out of the way. Tomorrow they would start with the judge's admonition to the jury, telling them what they could and could not do during the time they were jurors. That wouldn't take long. And then each attorney would give their opening statement, pointing out the issues they considered important and telling the jury what they might expect the evidence to show. It was not testimony—-it was not evidence. It was simply a statement of what they might expect from each of their respective cases. Exercising her option, she had decided she would present her opening immediately after the State presented their opening instead of waiting until the State rested.

Her opening never lasted long. She outlined what she thought the State would establish and then made sure the jury understood there were two sides to every story. They simply should not and could not judge the defendant's guilt or innocence until they had heard all the evidence. She had questioned each and every one of the individual jurors during the selection process and had made each of them promise they would not come to a conclusion concerning the case until all the evidence had been submitted.

She again reviewed all her notes concerning cross-examination of the State's witnesses. She was as ready as she would ever be. There would be no surprises with any of them. She anticipated they would take most of the day and that the State would rest late in the afternoon, leaving her to call McKay to the stand the next morning.

As she was finishing up her review, Wakefield walked in her door. It was late enough that she hadn't thought anyone was still in the office.

"Why are you still here?" she asked.

He sat down. She couldn't help but once again notice he looked like he had aged 100 years in just the past few months, and his physical demeanor was different. He looked and acted like a beat dog.

"Oh, I had a few things to tidy up around here before I went home. I saw your lights on and I thought I would check in to see how McKay's case was going. Anything new? How did today go?"

"Fine. It went fine. We have a good jury. At least it's composed the way I wanted and it doesn't appear we ended up with anyone too radical."

"Is there no way to resolve it?"

"Nope. I tried again this morning. Art isn't budging. That's why we picked a jury. He wants a plea to the charge as filed and nothing less."

"So is McKay ready to go?"

"Yes. Today was strange though. One of my other clients, Tommie Thompson, was there with him. I didn't even know they knew each other. I don't know what their connection might be, and it surprised me he was there."

"Probably just moral support. I wouldn't worry about it. You still feeling confident about the case?"

"Yes. Based on Jake's testimony, if he doesn't blow it, I really think our chances are good. His testimony creates reasonable doubt and I think it creates enough reasonable doubt to get him off."

As Wakefield got up to leave, Rosa noticed his pants didn't even fit. They hung on him like they were originally purchased for a man five sizes bigger.

"Ok then. Good luck tomorrow," he said as he walked out.

"Thanks Gene."

After he left, she noticed it was 6:35. *SHIT*. She was already late. That should leave him nice and pissed off before they even got started.

She quickly placed all her paperwork carefully back in her court file and closed it until tomorrow morning. She could do no more. She was ready to finish this off one way or the other.

She arrived about ten minutes late and he was waiting. He stood as she approached the table.

He smiled at her as she approached and said, "I realize this has nothing to do with cop and suspect, but you really look great."

"You know, that statement offends me on so many levels. I look good as a woman but I am still a 'suspect.' Makes me wonder. Should I be talking to you at all?"

She smiled as she sat down, but she clearly meant what she said.

"No, we should be fine. I was actually kidding about you still being a suspect. At this point, you really aren't a suspect as far as I am concerned, but we do need to talk."

They both ordered a beer and as soon as they were finished with small talk, he asked "Are there any other facts you can discuss with me concerning the judge's murder or your relationship with him?"

She tried to read him.

"No. Nothing that I feel might be important. Why?"

"Look, Rosa. I'm going to lay my cards out on the table as I have from the beginning. I've seen a video—there are security cameras on each floor of the hotel. And I saw you entering the judge's room in that hotel just a few days before his murder. I know you were there with him. And please understand, that doesn't mean I think that you were in any way involved with his murder. But, it is what it is. You were having a relationship with him prior to his murder and there is no doubt in my mind you were in that car in that parking lot the day he was murdered."

She continued to look at him expecting more. He said nothing.

The pressure of the day, the unexpected revelation by her interrogator, and the terrible experience of Amy's death all hit her simultaneously. She started to cry. She couldn't find a Kleenex. He handed her his handkerchief. Nothing was said for what seemed to her an eternity.

He reached over and grabbed her hand. She didn't resist.

"Look, I know this must all be a complete nightmare to you, but I can help you. Tell me what's going on. Let me help you."

She thought for a moment and finally said, "Yes. I was involved with him. He was also the trial judge concerning the McKay case and another case coming up for trial shortly. I've never, ever violated even one of the Canons of Ethics—until now. I really thought I would make it through without anyone ever knowing. But, now you know and now my whole career is in jeopardy."

"Please, just calm down. You're jumping to an erroneous conclusion. I have no desire to damage your career in any respect. That's your business and none of mine. But solving this murder *IS* my business. You know more than you're telling me. You need to let me help you out of this mess. I know who you are. I know enough about you to know you are a good attorney. You're honest and hardworking. I know you got into something here you shouldn't have. But, I think I can help you get out of this. Tell me what you know."

In those few minutes since he had confronted her with this new shred of evidence, she had had the time she needed to concoct a workable plan.

She hesitated for another minute without saying anything, making sure this was what she wanted to do. She squeezed his hand.

"I do know more than I'm telling you. And for good reason, I haven't told you everything I know, hoping this would all work itself out. It hasn't and I know now without my information it probably won't. I'll make a deal with you. Let me get through McKay's trial, it should be done in a couple of days, and I'll tell you all I know, no matter what it might cost me personally."

He clearly didn't know how to respond. He looked away, the wheels turning about as fast as they could turn.

Finally he said, "How long is this trial going to take?"

"A couple of days max. Please, please give a little more time."

"Is there a possibility whoever is involved might leave this jurisdiction before I nab them?"

"In my opinion, based on my limited knowledge, I believe the one you are looking for will stay put."

He considered his options once again. Finally he said, "Ok. I don't like it, but on the other hand, I trust you and I assume you have a reason for doing it this way. I'll wait until after the trial is finished and then we will have a 'come to Jesus' meeting at which time you promise me you'll tell me all you know about the judge's murder. Is that a fair, but condensed version of what we've agreed to?"

"Yes."

She held his hand until it was time to leave. She had successfully pulled a resolution to the immediate problem out of her ass.

She needed more time. She just hoped that in the next two days information not coming from her would result in solving the judge's murder, because if it didn't, she would be walking a fine line which would probably result in disbarment. She had two days for something outside her control to occur, or the life that she had come to enjoy, for all intents and purposes, would come to a sudden and immediate end.

Chapter 41

Rosa's dream continued every night, and it always ended up the same way. She would be standing over the judge's dead body in that parking lot. Her nights were sleepless. And even when she did sleep, she woke up most of the time feeling like she had just run in a marathon. Her covers would be at the bottom of the bed. Many times she would be sweating. Never did she feel rested. Such was her punishment.

Last night had been no exception and as usual, she was tired before the day even began.

She arrived at the office before 7:00. She again reviewed everything before McKay got there. The State's case would take all day. She had reviewed the expected testimony of the State's witnesses with Jake so there would be no surprise in any of the evidence today.

Once he arrived at her office, the first thing he asked was when he might be able to tell his side of the story. At least this time she was able to definitively say tomorrow morning would be his time.

They walked in the courtroom at about 8:30. Some of the jurors were already there. The courtroom security guard, Frankie, as he had come to be called, had provided them with a cup of coffee and most had already taken there seat in the jury box.

She took McKay to a conference room and they waited, in silence, until almost 9:00 when Rosa finally said, "I really need to visit with the judge for a second before we proceed this morning.

Nothing important, but I want to make sure there are no issues before the State starts putting on evidence. Are you going to be ok here alone?"

There was a knock on the door. Rosa answered it and saw Tommie Thompson standing in the doorway.

"Good morning. Is Jake here yet?"

"Yes, he's here. Why?"

"Because I want to be a part of all this with him, if that's ok with you."

Rosa noted a small amount of sarcasm in his response but said nothing.

"Jake, is it ok with you if he sits with us here? It's up to you."

Jake smiled and said, "Yes Rosa. I can use him for moral support."

Rosa turned, looked at Tommie and said "I guess you can come on in."

Both of them acted like they hadn't seen each other in years. She just couldn't quite figure this relationship out. But she didn't have time to think about it. She left them alone and walked to the Judge's Chambers.

Of course, Art was already there laughing about something with the judge. She informed both of them she was ready to proceed. The judge indicated that according to Frankie all the jurors were present and in the box, so if they were ready perhaps they would start a little early. That was acceptable to both attorneys and the judge gave them five minutes before he walked in the courtroom.

Rosa walked back to the conference room, opened the door, nodded to McKay, and together the three of them walked into the courtroom.

The State's evidence proceeded as expected. The medical examiner testified that, in his professional opinion and based on a reasonable degree of medical certainty, the prostitute had died as a result of a head injury. He could not say how it had happened nor could he determine, with any degree of certainty, what caused it. Rosa's cross-examination of him confirmed he didn't know if she had died as a result of a fall or as a result of an altercation, which was what Rosa expected him to say.

The two law enforcement officers testified as Rosa had anticipated. None of McKay's statements came into the record. They testified only to what they observed when they entered the room.

There was only one other witness for the State. She was one of the individuals standing in the hallway outside Jakes door when Jake opened it, standing there only in his underwear and covered in blood. She testified she had just left her own room when she heard a woman scream. She didn't know what to do, so she waited a few moments gathering up courage, before she walked over to the door and knocked. McKay opened the door, covered in blood. She could see the woman lying on the floor, not moving, and shortly after that law enforcement arrived.

Cross-examination by Rosa was as usual, short and sweet. There was little she could do except as she had already done with each witness—ask the witness if she had any idea what had happened in the room, to which she answered as they all did—she didn't know.

At the conclusion of her testimony, the State rested.

It was almost 4:00 by that time and as a result, the judge released the jury panel for the evening.

After they had left the room, the judge asked Rosa if she wanted to make a record concerning any of the issues prior to the commencement of her case, to which Rosa stated she did. He told her to proceed.

"Judge, based on the evidence that has been submitted by the State, we would ask for a Judgment of Acquittal under Rule 29 of the Tennessee Rules of Criminal Procedure. Clearly, the State has failed to establish its case. They have failed to carry their burden of proof. There is absolutely no evidence of a crime here. They have failed in each and every respect to establish my client did anything wrong. A woman died. Mr. McKay was in the room. That's it. That's all they have established. This case, in the interest of justice, should be dismissed."

"Mr. Walling, your response."

"Well, Judge, we have established a death did occur while the defendant was present. There was a scream from that room at the time it occurred. The defendant had blood all over him immediately after it happened. We believe that's enough to let the jury determine whether the defendant caused her death—and that's at least enough to get the case to the jury."

The judge reviewed his notes for a few minutes.

"The defendant's motion is overruled," he said.

Rosa immediately stood.

"Would the court care to explain? Clearly there is insufficient evidence at this point in time to convict. Could the court explain its reasoning?"

"Apparently my conclusion isn't enough for you, so let me clarify," the judge replied sarcastically. "First of all, let's go back to the two rulings Judge Hampton made in this case—rulings which have, at least to some degree, tied my hands. In my opinion, they were ridiculous. The statements should have never been excluded. I believe any jury would convict this defendant if those excluded statements had been allowed at the time of trial, which they should have been. So I feel a small amount of justice needs to be injected into these proceedings and that's what I'm doing. In addition, the defendant was in the room with the victim when she died. A scream is heard and the defendant shows up at the door with blood all over him. Let him explain that away if he wishes. I just feel, if no more evidence is introduced, the jury could find him guilty of the charge as filed. That's my ruling and that's the way it's going to be. Anything further?"

Rosa said, "No Judge. I guess that's it."

"Good. Now let's go home, have a stiff drink, and get a good night's sleep. See you all in the morning."

He got up and left the courtroom, along with Art and Frankie leaving only Thompson, McKay, and Rosa.

Thompson got up and started pacing. Finally he said, "You know that is bullshit. There is absolutely no evidence he did anything wrong. That ruling was fucking bullshit."

Rosa watched his demeanor. His face was red and his eyes were bugging out of his head. She wasn't sure how to handle the situation or him.

"Ok, Mr. Thompson, I agree, but that is his ruling and we're going to have to live with it."

She stood to go.

Thompson looked at her with a stare like she had never seen from anyone before. He said, "What the hell are you going to do about it?"

It took her a second to gather up enough courage to respond.

"We have no choice, Mr. Thompson, but to live with his ruling. That's the way it works. Now let's go."

She started out of the courtroom but neither Thompson nor

McKay moved a muscle.

Again she said, with slightly more authority "Let's go."

They both reluctantly moved toward the door. As Thompson walked by, he said, "Maybe we have to live with it, but it sure as shit doesn't mean we have to like it. This legal system is fucked up."

She ignored his statement and never even looked in his direction.

"Jake, let's meet at my office tomorrow morning to go over your testimony one more time. Maybe about 7:00? Does that work for you?"

"Yes, that's fine. I'll see you then."

Thompson was half way down the hallway, clearly done with the conversation.

Rosa thought about his demeanor and attitude long after she left the courtroom. She had decided this was it for him. Immediately after this trial, she would file a motion to withdraw. Once it was granted, she would tell Stony what happened. She had decided that was the only way this was all going to end. She just hoped Thompson didn't somehow alter the flow of this case. The ruling the judge made wasn't correct. However, with Jake's testimony tomorrow, if it was presented as she expected, they still had a good chance of winning.

She was finished with Thompson. Hopefully, she was making the correct decision in deferring her withdrawal until after this trial was over.

Chapter 42

"Hey man you need some help? In all my life, I have never seen a worse shot than you"

Gene Wakefield had decided it was time to learn how to use his pistol. He hardly knew how to load it, let alone shoot it. It had taken him a half hour just to put shells in the thing. Once that had been accomplished, he had tried to hit the bull's-eye, but still had had trouble even hitting the target.

"Oh really? You think I'm the worst you have ever seen? I hit that thing once. That's not bad."

"Oh shit no. You've only fired fifty times. Nope, you're right. One hit out of fifty is just great. You're one shot out of fifty from achieving perfection—perfect at never ever hitting the target at all. Some kind of perfection man. You ever had a lesson?"

"No."

"Well, let me tell you man, I've been around guns all my life and you are without a doubt the worst shot I have ever seen. You make my 90-year-old grandma who has Parkinson's disease look like Annie Oakley. You need to take lessons. I would love to be the guy that breaks into your house."

"Real funny...*man*. Thanks for your help."

He was the only one shooting. His "man" friend had just finished up. It was early in the day and he wanted to get this over with and return to the office. He figured the McKay case would wind up sometime today, and he wanted to be there if the jury came back, or

An Absence of Ethics

in the unlikely event the case was summarily dismissed by the judge before it was submitted to the jury.

He knew he was a bad shot. He couldn't hold the gun still. He hated guns. He hated that noise. It identified with violence. He hated everything the weapon stood for. But he also was smart enough to know that now, the way things were in his life, he needed it. He needed it for his own protection. And having it meant learning how to use it. What the hell—he was improving. The last time he missed the target all 50 times. He had now improved to 1 in 50. He knew he would never be any good at it, but he needed to at least know what to expect when it went off and how it would feel in his hands just in case he absolutely had no other choice but to fire it.

One good thing about shooting at the range was that here he could at least find some peace away from the issues of the day, of which were many.

He returned the weapon to the sanctity of the glove box, hoping he never had to remove it again, then slid in behind the wheel and headed toward his office.

How could this happen? When he started gambling it was so much fun—so easy. And profitable. Where had he gone so wrong?

He couldn't eat. He couldn't sleep. He couldn't think about anything except getting even. And he was so far down, he knew even in the haze he seemed to find himself each and every day, getting even was now impossible. At this point, it had become a matter of survival.

Bill collectors hounded him day and night. He couldn't get away from them. He tried to protect his wife from their incessant phone calls, but that was becoming harder and harder to do. He had protected her from the tough side of life every day he had been married to her, but it was becoming increasing difficult to shield her. And she was starting to ask questions. For the first time in their marriage, she was asking questions about finances, about when they might retire and where they might live when they do retire. Questions, which, at least for now, had no answers.

And then there was the ever-present issue of the kids' college tuition. If the situation continued as is, the kids would need to borrow as much as they could and both of them would need to find jobs. There were no other options available.

He knew how he looked. He didn't need to be told again. He had lost at least 50 pounds. Life was a living nightmare.

The office bank account was a disaster. He knew if anyone took the time to look through the records and then through the account, he would be through. And even if he won back the money to replenish the account, he figured, once the books were audited, which they were once a year, the theft would be uncovered. Then he would certainly become unemployed. He just hoped they would allow him to replace it, if he hadn't already been able to, and forget about any criminal charges. A criminal investigation wouldn't look good for the firm and if he replaced the funds, none of the partners would be out anything. Hopefully, that wasn't just wishful thinking.

Once all his credit cards had been maxed, he could no longer bet online. So he had contacted a local bookie. He had represented him in a number of different legal issues and knew he could be trusted to pay off when he owed. However, it too wasn't working out quite like he had hoped. He was in to him some $25,000 and the bookie wanted his money. He had started calling and pushing for payment about a month ago and now had reached the point where he was showing up at the office.

He had told the other attorneys who noticed the bookie in the waiting room that he was helping the man on some personal matters and that explanation had satisfied them for the time. But it wouldn't last long, and the last time the bookie had presented himself at his office, he had threatened him. He had told him he needed his money or he would find some other way to collect it.

Gene Wakefield was at the end of his rope. He was absolutely desperate for a solution. There was only one way out. The chance of winning back enough to pay everyone off was over. He was in way too deep. But, if the present plan worked out, he might have enough to pay the office back and pay off the bookie, but that was it. He would need to find other methods to pay off the rest of his debt.

The next day or two would most likely determine his financial fate. He was optimistic, but, just in case it all didn't proceed as planned, he needed to know how to use the pistol.

He only hoped if he did need to use it, the target was large. And it needed to be close. And it couldn't be moving. In addition, whoever he was shooting at couldn't shoot back. If any of those factors came into play he would be lucky if he came out alive. But at this point, did it really matter? At this point, death seemed like the easiest option still available.

Chapter 43

They had thoroughly reviewed his testimony and Jake was as ready as he was ever going to be. Direct examination would not be an issue. They had been through every element of his testimony. In addition, all the issues concerning possible objections the State might make during his testimony had also been covered.

He was not a stupid man. She thought he was actually quite intelligent. He was soft spoken and slow to anger. He did not confuse easily, although once he was confused he tended to become frustrated and then she would see a hint of anger come out in his responses. She never pushed him when he reached that point. She hoped it would never come to that on the stand.

They arrived at the courthouse just short of 9:00, and many of the jurors were already in their seats. Frankie had provided coffee and the jurors were speaking softly amongst themselves.

The judge walked in the courtroom and took his position behind the bench. He asked if the parties were ready to proceed. Both indicated they were, and the judge asked the defense to call their first witness, which was Jake.

His direct examination presented no issues. She went through his background, a few personal facts about himself, and then started into the facts of the case. Art hardly opened his mouth, and when he did it was only to make a meaningless objection, more than anything just to make sure the jury knew he was still there. But the one thing that did bother Rosa to some extent was that he didn't stutter, which to her meant he was still confident in the case.

Jake testified she had bit him, which made the male jurors squirm and the female jurors smile, but he testified his subsequent actions were taken only in self-defense. The State, in their case, had confirmed Jake had fresh scratches on his face and arms. Jake testified those were from her, and that he had pushed her away from him fearing, based on her obvious state of mind, that she was going to inflict more than a few scratches before she was done.

All went well and by 11:30, she was finished with direct. The judge took the noon break early and advised the jurors to be seated by 1:00.

She and Jake had sandwiches in the conference room. Frankie had brought them back after Rosa had carefully written down exactly what they wanted him to do. She knew he would never remember unless it was written down.

Once the noon recess ended, Art was ready to cross. After a few questions concerning the basic facts of the case, Art asked, "Now, Mr. McKay, where did you say you moved here from?"

"The New York area."

"And what did you do for a living while you lived there?"

"Different things. Odds and ends. Nothing very complicated. Of course, I haven't lived there for more than ten years."

"And while you lived there, did you ever hear of a family by the name of Reardon?"

Rosa could see Jake starting to move uneasily in his chair.

"Objection. Relevance."

"Now, Miss Norway, you asked him about his background. Surely the State has a right to cross him on the same issue. Overruled. Mr. McKay you may answer."

"Might have. I met a lot of families while I lived there. Why?"

"Mr. McKay just let me ask the questions here."

Art got up and walked toward the witness.

"Are you related to a Reardon family in the New York area?"

"Why?"

"Just answer the question."

After a moment's hesitation, he said, "I have a couple of uncles that are named Reardon."

"And what about your father? Is he a member of that family in some way?"

"I don't understand. What does this all have to do with this case?" Rosa stood up.

"Sidebar."

The Judge motioned both attorneys to come forward.

"Judge, this is improper cross. Where are we going here Art?"

"Rosa, this man's family is all part of a family of people involved in drugs and murder. They are part of the mob. He apparently moved here to get out of it, but he was part of it for a long, long time. And I think the jury should at least be made aware of his prior involvement. They can do as they wish with the information but they should at least be aware."

Rosa could feel her confidence in the case begin to waiver. This was clearly the "other shoe," and it was just starting to drop.

"Judge, this information is not relevant to the case. It could also be highly prejudicial without being the least bit relevant. We would ask that you put an end to this line of questioning immediately."

"Well now, Miss Norway, how do you purpose I do that? You opened up this line of questioning. It is proper cross. You can clean it up on redirect, but if that can't be done, I guess the jurors will just have to decide how prejudicial it all is won't they? Your objection is overruled."

"But Judge, I......"

"Step back. Both of you. Art proceed with your cross."

"So what line of work was your family in Mr. Thompson?"

"What do you mean?"

"Simple. What did they do for a living?"

"Different things."

"And did you work with them when you lived back east?"

"What do you mean 'work with them?'"

"Were you with them on a regular daily basis week after week after week?"

"Well I guess I was."

"Did you have any other employment with any other party during that period of time?"

"No, not that I can recall,"

"Your source of pay—your income—was from them then, is that correct?"

Jake hesitated.

"Yes, I guess"

An Absence of Ethics

Rosa could tell McKay was starting to become frustrated. He was turning a dull shade of red and noticeably starting to fidget in his chair.

"Your Honor, would now be a good time for an afternoon recess?" Rosa needed to get him off the stand and visit with him before this went any further.

"We just started Miss Norway. No we aren't taking a break now. Proceed."

The next few moments were the longest of Rosa's career. Art took him down a long path, during which time all of Jake's family issues were discussed. Art didn't miss a trick. He had done his research well and Jake paid the price. Issues from years long past were discussed even during a time Jake wasn't living in the East. That didn't seem to matter. Rosa would object until she was blue in the face, but the judge sustained nothing.

Art would bring up murder after murder that appeared to implicate the Family and Jake would repeatedly reaffirm he knew nothing about it. Again Art would reiterate he was related to those people and worked with them for many years.

After what seemed like a lifetime to Rosa, they took a break. Art had finished up with his cross and it was now up to Rosa to redirect and try to do some damage control.

They walked into the conference room and shut the door. Thompson immediately began pacing the floor. Jake sat down and stared into space.

"Jake. Jake, look at me. We need to fix this. We are fine. You weren't involved in any of these things were you?"

He said nothing. He just stared into space.

"Jake. You need to get yourself under control here. We are fine. We have another chance to testify and we need to clean this up. Do you understand me?"

He finally looked up and with resignation in his voice, said, "Ok. What do we need to do?"

She knew at that moment, that they were in deep trouble. He appeared clearly, to be a broken man. He spoke in a whisper—his whole demeanor reeked of guilt. Rosa would not ask him point blank if he had been part of this Family—she didn't need to—the answer was obvious.

"We're going to stick to the facts of the case Jake. Nothing more, nothing less."

Thompson stopped pacing.

"He has to deny all that shit. Each and every point he raised has to be denied. What are you going to do here Rosa? This is a fucking mess. How are you going to set the record straight?"

"Tommie, let Rosa handle it as she feels best. She's the lawyer here. What do I need to do Rosa?"

"We're going to deny, in general, you had anything to do with any of those specific acts he mentioned, Jake. I don't want any more emphasis on that particular issue than we already have. I want to keep the juror's minds focused on the facts of this case, not the facts surrounding whatever happened more than ten years ago. So that's exactly what we are going to do. Do you understand? Short and sweet. And I'll try to clean it up a little further in closing."

"Ok Rosa. If that's what you think will work."

At that point, Thompson walked over to within an inch of Rosa's face.

"You *do* know what you are doing don't you Rosa? I mean from what I just heard, I'm wondering if you know a fucking thing. Jake, you need to respond to each one of those events and tell that jury you knew nothing about it. This woman is an idiot."

McKay jumped up and looked at Thompson with rage in his eyes.

"Back off Tommie. How the fuck do you know if she's an idiot? You a lawyer too? She's the one I've put my faith in and that's the way it's going to be. Now either shut up or get your ass out of the room."

Just then, Frankie knocked on the door, opened it and said, "The judge is ready to go."

Rosa nodded. She was shaken, but it was time to become a professional again and as soon as the courtroom door opened, she showed no sign of the altercation that had just occurred in the conference room.

They all three walked back into the courtroom and Rosa couldn't help but notice not one of the jurors would look at them. They were all either looking at each other or around the room but not one set of eyes was on any one of the three.

Rosa finished with her redirect, but the excitement for the day was over. Jake was a beaten man. You could hardly hear his testimony. And when she was done, Art didn't even bother to recross him. He could see the damage had been done and he wasn't about to screw it up by hammering Jake with additional issues. He had made his point and he didn't have to make it again. The case would now be in the hands of the jury. They would need to decide whether to limit the issues to the facts of the case or condemn the defendant for sins of the "Family," and most likely Jake, committed many years prior.

Long after she turned out the lights and turned off the TV, Rosa laid in bed and tossed and turned, unable to sleep. Her closing had been nothing to write home about. She had hammered the jury about sticking to the facts of the case, but she could see it in their eyes. They weren't on board—at least not on her train.

Jury deliberations would start in the morning. She didn't figure it would take them long one way or the other. It wasn't that complicated. She just hoped by the time night fell tomorrow night she was drinking a glass of wine in celebration rather than looking over her shoulder hoping Thompson wasn't right behind her. She wouldn't be able to withdraw from further representation of him soon enough. She only hoped he didn't try to kill someone else before this was all over—specifically her.

Chapter 44

Art walked back to his office with a feeling of compete gratification. He had won the day. Now it would be up to the jury to confirm what he already knew.

It was apparent the moment he started his cross using the information about McKay's mob ties that he had caught Rosa with her pants down—or her panties down—whatever—however that observation was supposed to apply to women. She objected to no avail. She tried to convince the judge to take a recess—he wasn't buying that. She made a half-assed effort to do some damage control on re-direct but, after the damage that he had already inflicted, her efforts were futile. She was screwed and she knew it. It was just a matter of having the jury do their job and do it right.

Speaking of getting screwed, he had an idea that was exactly what happened to Rosa concerning Judge Hampton. Something was very wrong there. The judge had confirmed that today with his approach to the trial. The judge was letting him have his way with everything. There was nothing he could do wrong in that courtroom. The message was clear. The rulings Hampton had made in the McKay case were clearly erroneous. One bad ruling would have been strange, but two bad rulings in the same case involving the same attorney, now that was something else. And he couldn't let it go. Even knowing the office wasn't behind him, he couldn't let it go. As soon as this case was over, he would start an investigation on his own, hopefully with the assistance of the Bar Association. Someone needed to get to the bottom of this and if he needed to lead the way, he would be glad to do so.

The lights were on all over the office as prosecutors continued preparing their cases for trial into the night. The hour of the day meant nothing to the attorneys in this office. Those who weren't willing to work their job on those terms and commit to that degree of dedication were weeded out quickly. Tonight was no exception. He noticed at least three offices with lights on.

He had stopped and picked up a sandwich on the way back to his office. The fact that this case was almost over did not give him the privilege of stopping long enough to catch his breath. He had another trial starting in a few days and Rosa's other case, the one involving Thompson, was only as matter of a week away. He would pull both of those files before he left for the night and review what might yet need to be done before the trials started.

As he finished his sandwich, his boss walked in his office door.

"Hi Cal. What are you still doing here?"

"Being the boss isn't an eight-hour-a-day job Art. You surely know that by now. Someone still has to answer questions and I'm actually trying one of the cases coming up next week, State vs. Clampton. How did it go today?"

"Couldn't have gone better. That new intern is worth his weight in gold. We caught them completely by surprise concerning McKay's old history with that eastern mob. And if I can read the jury at all it won't take long. When I brought all that information up about his family and their ties to them, McKay had absolutely no response. I don't have much doubt about the verdict in this one."

"Great. Maybe when this is over, we can talk about a salary adjustment. Looks like it's been quite a while for you. Hopefully the verdict will come back like it is supposed to and we can discuss the future with you then."

"That sounds wonderful to me."

"What about Rosa? Are you still convinced something was going on involving both she and Judge Hampton?"

"Even more so now. Judge Jackson is all over her ass, and he told us both those rulings by Hampton were improper. I don't think, I *know* something is wrong. And even without this offices assistance, I'm going to look into it."

"We can't back you Art. I know you already know that, but we just don't have the time to deal with it. However, if you do come up with something, bring it to me and I'll take a look at it. I'm not saying we won't take a hard look at something if you want to take your own time and resources to investigate it initially, but we aren't going to become involved until there is some firm, positive evidence something was wrong."

"I understand. I'll take a look and if I do uncover something I'll bring it to you. Perhaps the office can take it from there."

Cal got up to walk out of the room.

"Good luck tomorrow Art. Let me know what happens as soon as you get a verdict."

Art finished up his review of both files and left the office. He noticed someone across the street lurking in the shadows, but the day had been too positive to waste the night worrying about whether some son of a bitch was following him. He would continue to glance at his rear view mirror and make sure he wasn't behind him as he drove home.

***

The next morning as he walked through the courtroom door, the only individual in the room was Frank. It was early and none of the jurors had yet arrived. He was sitting in his chair staring at the floor.

"Morning Frankie. How are you this morning?"

He looked up as Art approached him. Art couldn't help but notice a faraway look in his eyes.

"Oh I'm fine sir, how are you?" Frank stuck out his hand.

Art shook hands with him and replied, "It's going to be a good day Frankie, I can just feel it in the air."

"Good, good sir. I hope so."

"You feeling ok Frank?"

"I guess, yes, I think I'm ok. Unfortunately, I think I'm going to have to quit my job though. Probably time to retire."

"Really? Why is that?"

"Oh, I don't know. I'm having some problems with paying attention. I just don't stay with things like I used to. It's probably time for me to hang it up."

Art headed to the judge's chambers and as he walked away he said, "Well that's a shame Frankie. We'll sure miss you if that's really what you are going to do."

"Thank you sir, thank you. I will sure miss all of you too."

An Absence of Ethics

Art wondered at what point Frank figured out he couldn't keep his head in the game. He wasn't much of a security guard from day one but he was likeable. Basically he had always done his job, just not very well.

"Morning Judge. How are things this morning?"

Judge Jackson was having his first cup of coffee and reviewing the court file.

"Good Art and you?"

"Good Judge. You ready to wrap this up?"

"I sure am. You said both you and Rosa have approved my jury instructions, is that correct?"

"Yes we have. There isn't much there other than the stock instructions. I have no problem with those and Rosa didn't either. I don't believe there is a need for a sealed verdict. Rosa told me they were going to stay in the courtroom until there was a verdict and so am I."

"Ok good. Do you have much doubt about the verdict Art?"

"No, I really don't Judge. I think this jury will find him guilty and I believe that's what should happen, so no I don't have much doubt."

"Neither do I. And by the way, your cross yesterday was well done. I was watching the jurors and it appeared to me they were taking it all in."

"Thank you. Yes, I thought it went well to. Hopefully they won't be out long."

"I doubt they will. Want a cup of coffee? Yell at Frankie and have him get one for you. We can see if he remembers what he is to do from the time you tell him until he gets to the coffeepot in the clerk's office."

They both laughed.

The conversation remained jovial until Rosa joined them. It turned then to a discussion only about the trial and shortly thereafter, both attorneys left the judge's chambers to take their chairs in the courtroom.

The words of praise from his boss the night before and the judge this morning stayed with Art as he took his seat in the courtroom. They were the first words of encouragement he had received from anyone for a long, long time. Maybe he should tell his father how well he was doing. Maybe, for the first time in his life, he would be proud of his son. Maybe.

Chapter 45

Tommie had listened to the cross of Jake and it had taken everything he had to sit still. Clearly Jake was in it up to his neck. It didn't appear he had been adequately prepared for unanticipated cross-examination. He had expressed his opinion in the conference room, but it had been ignored.

Neither Rosa nor Jake would take his advice and as a result, redirect by Rosa was nothing short of a tragedy. It appeared as though Jake had given up, as if the cross by the prosecutor had taken it all out of him. He could only imagine how that must have looked to the jury. Because clearly, it appeared to him, and he was sure to all in the courtroom, that Jake was a beaten man—that what the prosecutor brought up was all accurate and Jake was simply trying to conceal the real truth.

That "real truth" to the prosecutor and in all likelihood to the jury, was that this man, this Jake McKay had reverted back to the old days and whacked this woman in cold blood. If he had been on the jury after all he had heard, he would convict.

After the testimony had ended for the day, he met Jake alone outside the courthouse.

"Jake, that didn't go very well."

"How would I know Tommie? I have never been through anything like this before. I have nothing to base it on. But I know I don't feel good about it—especially about that prick prosecutor. He's the one that's to blame for all this. He wouldn't compromise the charges. And then to top it all off, he brings up all that shit about my prior life. That just doesn't seem fair. But I trust Rosa. She has been good to me and I believe she has my best interests in mind. She has no control over that prosecutor. If it wasn't for him, I wouldn't have had to go through this."

"Stay strong. The jury will most likely come back tomorrow and they may convict. But if they do, I don't want you doing anything rash before talking to me about it. Ok?"

"What do you mean Tommie?"

"Just don't start making any kind of deal with the State until we think through your position, and certainly don't do anything without first discussing it with me. Of course, if they come back not guilty, then we don't have to worry anyway. But if the verdict is guilty, promise me you will not discuss any type of deal with them before we talk about it."

"Ok. I won't. But Tommie, you know I can't go to prison. I could never do that. I can't handle that Tommie and you know that."

"I know that Jake—we *ALL* know that. But stay strong until we discuss a plan, ok?"

"Ok, I will."

***

Later that night, Tommie was in his usual position—in his underwear waiting for the phone to ring. He couldn't help but reflect back on Jake's remarks. The one thing that stood out was his unwavering devotion to his lawyer. Jake seemed completely taken by her, but Tommie wasn't so sure. He felt she could have done a much better job on redirect than she did. She refuted nothing. She only emphasized the facts of this case and denied none of Jakes prior history. That to him was a huge mistake. Maybe a better approach would have been to…

"Yes sir, I am here."

"I understand the trial is not going to well. What the fuck happened?"

"No sir, things did not go all that well. Somehow the prosecutor came in possession of a considerable amount of old information concerning the Family, and he used it against him. The judge allowed it all and the prosecutor never missed a beat. He knew what he was doing and he got all of it in front of the jury. I was watching them and they were taking it all in."

"Has all the evidence been submitted? Is the trial portion of it actually over?"

"Yes, it's over as far as the evidence is concerned. It'll be turned over to the jury tomorrow morning. Then it will be up to them."

"So there is nothing else that we can do, or that anyone can do, concerning the actual trial."

"No, there's nothing more that can be done. It's up to them. And we'll just have to respond based on the verdict. If it comes back guilty, then we'll need to wait until sentencing and see what happens. I'm keeping a close watch on it all."

"What do you think this jury will do? Talk to me in percentages Tommie. Is there no chance of getting him off?"

"We still have a small chance of acquittal, but after today, I would say it's slim—under 20%."

"What do you think the judge will do to him if he is convicted?"

"I would say he'll probably be sentenced to prison. This judge doesn't like Jake. That's apparent. And he also appears to listen to this prosecutor. I really think if he's convicted, Jake will end up in prison."

"Well then we will have a major problem, Tommie, a major problem."

"I know. I understand and I agree. There is no doubt in my mind that if he is sentenced to prison, we'll have a problem. But that is still a ways away yet. They may not even convict him. I'll stay in touch and keep you informed."

"How much time will it take you to get out if you have to leave town immediately?"

"I'm ready to leave here in the blink of an eye. All my personal possessions are packed except for what I need from day to day. If I need to get out of here my car is ready to go."

"Keep me informed. Do you understand?"

"Sure. Now, I just want to make sure everything is still as we discussed. Whatever happens, I'm to use my own judgment as to what to do, correct?"

He hesitated for a moment before his short response, "Yes."

"Ok. I don't want any of you guys second guessing me. I'll do what I think needs to be done at that time and based on the circumstances. And you are good with that right?"

Again a hesitation preceded his response. Finally "yes."

"Ok. I'll let you know what happens."
Tommie terminated the call.

He knew no matter what decision he made, they would second-guess him. But he would do what he thought was right at the time. That was all he could do. There was a very good chance he would have no time for a consensus of opinion. He figured if anything needed to be done to handle this situation, he would need to act quickly. And he wasn't going to take time for the Family to get together and come to a fucking conclusion on what he should or shouldn't do. He would make the decision on the spot and they would just have to live with it.

Chapter 46

Stony had about exhausted all of his normal investigatory methods trying to run down additional leads, all to no avail. He had talked to friends and friends of friends until there was no one left to talk to. No one knew anything.

He had checked the registry at the hotel after securing a search warrant and had talked too many of the guests that were there the day of the murder. No one saw or knew anything. He had also researched the list of license plate numbers to the extent it was humanly possible, but once again to no avail.

There was virtually nowhere else to look. Every rock had been turned over. He had come to the conclusion that he would need to wait until this trial was over, and then grill Rosa for all she knew. He had sat through the trial and had witnessed the ugly turn of events. Cross-examination of McKay was a thing of beauty for the prosecution. And once it had ended, Rosa had little response. Clearly, McKay's testimony on cross had caught her totally by surprise. And even on redirect, she had provided little if any testimony to offset the damage that had already been done.

He had thought through their last conversation a number of times since then. If he had been dealing with a male lawyer, the deal would have never been made, of that he was certain. But a female in distress, crying and carrying on as she did, had affected his ability to make a rational decision and she had benefited from his obvious lack of judgment.

He would wait. It was only one more day. But once the verdict was rendered and McKay was sentenced or set free then it was all over and he would show no mercy. He needed to solve this crime. And hopefully she had at least a small amount of information to assist in its resolution.

He had stopped over to see her after the completion of the evidence but prior to the verdict. Her secretary had tried to send him on his way, but he wasn't having it. He finally got in to see her, however the conversation was virtually nonexistent. She was visibly distraught about the course the trial had taken. He tried to visit with her about it, but she was consumed with what had already taken place in the courtroom and what she was afraid was about to take place. She had no time to discuss anything else.

He reminded her of her promise. She quickly informed him she remembered and she would do as she said she would do. He told her he would be there for the verdict and once it was over, maybe they could meet in her office and discuss what she knew about the judge. She was fine with that and that's how it was left.

This time there would be no mercy. This time he had no choice. He thought when he made the deal with her, that by now he might have perhaps acquired additional evidence without her help, which might solve this case, but he had nothing new. So it all came down to her. And this time his feelings for her personally could not stand in the way, and wouldn't.

Another issue had come up that was a concern for Stony and it had nothing to do with Rosa's situation. He had been called in to talk to the captain about "job-related issues."

As he walked in the captain's office door, the captain never even verbally acknowledged him—he just nodded for him to take a chair.

"Stony, how busy are you?"

"About as busy as I can be Cap. Why?"

"You know the city cut our budget right?"

"I heard that yes. Of course, I don't have any idea how that might impact all of us, but I assume there will be some repercussions from the loss of dollars."

"We're trying to figure it out now, but it does look like there are going to be cuts. We're already overworked. I'm not really sure yet how that might impact our workload—the officers that remain here I mean."

"Are officers going to be terminated?"

"Yes. And that's one reason I wanted to visit with you. Are you at the limit with how much you can handle right now?"

"Yes. I'm here day and night and most weekends. I don't think I can squeeze another second out of the day. My case load is at an all-time high. Why do you ask?"

"Because I think the officers that are left after this is all sorted out are going to have a caseload that is over the top, and I wanted your reaction to that. Are you going to be able to handle it?"

"Hell, how would I know Cap, until I know how many cases I'm going to be expected to work. Do you have any idea how large the load is going to be?"

"I am thinking probably about 30 percent more than you have now."

"I don't think I can handle that many more. I could try I guess but that will mean me working literally day and night. And it will result in not being able to do justice to any of the cases I already have. I'll be moving from case to case without being able to really concentrate on any of them. I don't know if I can do that. Is that going to be how it is? Are all of us that stay going to have to pick up that kind of load?"

"That's how it looks right now."

"I don't know if I want any part of that. I'm going to have to think about that Cap."

"That's why I had you in here Stony. You are one of our best officers. I wanted to at least forewarn you that this may be where we are headed so you could think it through before you had to make a decision. Think about it and let me know what you may want to do. It will probably all come to a head sometime next week so let me know what you want to do."

"Ok. Thanks for the forewarning Cap."

"This was none of my doing Stony. But, as long as you have been here, you deserve the opportunity to figure out what you want to do before having it dumped in your lap with 24 hours to decide. Just let me know sometime next week."

Stony walked out scratching his head. This was not a good turn of events. He could not do justice to that type of work load—no one could.

He needed to make a few calls. He had a few friends in the

security business that might be able to find him a good job at a decent salary. He didn't want to leave the cop business. However, he also didn't want to let down all those people that relied upon him to solve crimes committed against themselves and their families.

But this wasn't at the top of his list right now. He needed to finish off the investigation concerning the judge's homicide and Rosa's involvement. Then he would figure out whether he would stay with the force or move on to something new.

Chapter 47

Rosa had to handle a few issues at the office that needed her immediate attention. She hurried down the street to the office so she could return to the courtroom and await the verdict. The judge knew she would be gone for a short time and had agreed to hold the verdict if the jury came in before she got back.

And as luck would have it, Stony walked into her office while she was there. Of course, he wouldn't take no for an answer. He had to talk to her. She would have told him anything to get him out of her office so she could finish up and return to the courtroom. Once he left and she had handled those matters that needed to be handled, she walked back to the courthouse.

She would continue to try and put him off hoping something happened that would resolve the Judge's murder without her involvement. Stony had agreed to wait until this case had concluded and she would hold him to that. They hadn't discussed sentencing if McKay was found guilty, but the case wasn't technically over until the defendant was sentenced, and she would use that as her last ace in the hole if he was convicted. But that was it. That was the end of her excuses. She would need to come clean at that time. She knew he was all business and she had been very lucky to have even been able to hold him off this long.

She had just sat down when Frankie came in and told her the judge wanted to see both attorneys.

They both walked into the judge's chambers.

"The jury has come to a verdict. Are you both ready?" the judge asked.

Both attorneys nodded yes.

Rosa walked back to her chair. Unfortunately, she was pretty sure she knew what this meant. They hadn't been out but a couple of hours. That normally meant a guilty verdict.

She sat down, turned to McKay and said, "The jury has reached a verdict. Now once it is read, regardless of what it might be, you must stand silent until they leave the room. Then we will figure out what our next step might be without them here. Do you both understand? You must stand silent no matter what happens."

Frankie brought the jury in and as they passed by Rosa, she again noticed no one looked at her or at her client. Not a good sign.

Once they were seated, the judge said, "Mr. Foreman, it is my understanding you have arrived at a verdict. Is that correct?"

"Yes, Your Honor we have."

"It's unanimous?"

"Yes sir, it is."

"Please give the verdict to the officer and he will hand it to the clerk to read. Please stand Mr. McKay."

The foreman handed it to Frankie who then passed it on to the clerk. She opened the verdict and read it out loud.

The only word Rosa heard was "guilty."

She turned to look at McKay. He stood quietly with his head bowed. Thompson glared at her and she could tell he was ready to explode.

The judge asked Rosa if she wanted the jury polled. Rosa explained to McKay that the judge could ask each and every juror if that was, in fact, their individual verdict. McKay never looked up at her but shook his head no.

Rosa looked up at the judge and said, "No, Your Honor. That won't be necessary."

The jury was released. Rosa and McKay sat back down. The judge then looked at Rosa.

"What do you want to do about sentencing? I'll order a presentence investigation and normally that would take about six weeks to prepare. But we are overwhelmed right now, and I can't guarantee it will be ready in less than three months. Sorry, but that's how much of a backlog we have. How is your schedule Rosa?"

She turned to McKay and said "Are you going to be in the area during that time frame so we can finish this up?"

McKay looked up, turned to her and said, "I don't want to wait three months. I want this over now."

"Sentencing can be done sooner, but you will need to waive the PSI. And if you do, there is no telling what the judge might do. If he doesn't have all your background information in front of him and no recommendation from the writer of the report as to sentencing, he will be free to do exactly as he wishes. Are you willing to take that chance?"

"I told you I want this over now and that's what I meant."

Rosa stood.

"Your Honor, I believe we are willing to waive the PSI and proceed to sentencing immediately."

"Under these circumstances, we are permitted to waive it but I need to hear it from the defendant. Mr. McKay is that what you wish to do?"

"Yes."

"You understand that means sentencing will be completely up to me? There will be no background information for me to use—no recommendation from anyone. Are you willing to live with that?"

"Yes. I want it waived and to proceed as soon as we can."

"Fine. I can't do it today but I can tomorrow at 10:00 if that will work for everyone."

Art said, "That will work for me Judge."

"That's fine with us also." Rosa responded.

"Ok, then that's when it will be. Now, let's talk about disposition pending sentencing. Does the State have a problem with releasing the defendant pending sentencing under the same conditions as he had in affect prior to trial?"

Art immediately said, "We sure do Judge. He has now been convicted of manslaughter and we believe he should, without question, be incarcerated pending sentencing."

"Judge this man has been out on bond for quite some time," Rosa said. "During that time, he has done nothing wrong. He has gone nowhere and been a model citizen since this happened. The charge was not an upper level felony. We believe he should be released under the same conditions he had pending trial."

"I tend to agree with Rosa," the judge said. "And sentencing is tomorrow Art, not six months down the road. I'm going to release him pending sentencing."

"But, JJJJUdge that's nnnott…"

"Just wait Art. That's my ruling. Now Mr. McKay, you understand the conditions you had for your release are still in effect. And you are to be here tomorrow at 10:00 for sentencing. Do you have any questions about that?"

"No Judge."

"Then that will be the order."

The judge left the bench and walked out of the courtroom.

Rosa looked at both McKay and Thompson.

"Let's walk back to the conference room and talk."

When they arrived, Thompson shut the door behind them and then whirled around to confront Rosa.

"I told you this fucking thing would go this way. You have to be the worst lawyer I have ever seen. That prosecutor had his way with you. You were his bitch."

He started walking toward her. Jake stepped between the two of them. "Tommie calm down. She is a good attorney. She is my friend. Leave her alone. It wasn't her. It was the prosecutor and that judge friend of his. This isn't her fault."

Thompson stopped in his tracks. He glared at the two of them one last time, then turned and left the room, slamming the door as he did.

"I'm sorry he acted the way he did Rosa. He just gets really worked up. Now, is there anything I can do to get ready for tomorrow?"

Rosa was shaking. She took a second to compose herself.

"Yes. Be ready to make a simple statement to the court about how sorry you are this all happened, and probably a statement about your issues with going to prison. It needs to be from the heart and sincere. You write something up and we can discuss it before the hearing. Is Tommie going to be here too?"

"I suppose he will be. Rosa, you know I just can't do jail time. I just can't."

"You better tell Mr. Thompson to stay under control tomorrow or they will arrest him on the spot. Along with your statement, I'll speak for you at the sentencing too Jake. I really don't know what this judge will do. Let's keep our fingers crossed and hope for the best. I need to return to the office so call me if you want to discuss sentencing any further."

She leaned in and hugged him.

"Thank you, Rosa, for all your help."

"I'll see you in the morning around 8:00."

They both walked out of the conference room and Rosa walked back to her office. She had known after Art's cross of Jake this trial was headed in the wrong direction. But after all she had seen and heard, McKay wasn't as much a worry as Thompson. She worried about his reaction if McKay was sent to prison.

Obviously, these two had a solid connection. Thompson was clearly out of control. She knew Stony would be there for the sentencing and this was the first time since they met that she was actually looking forward to having him in the same room with her.

Chapter 48

Rosa watched the sun rise, but not by choice. She was extremely worried how today would play out and sleep was impossible. She not only had the uncertainty of the sentencing of McKay but she had the unpredictable issue of the volatility of both her client and his one-legged friend.

She sat alone waiting for McKay to arrive, worried that he would bring Thompson with him. She had already dictated her motion to withdraw from further representation of Thompson, but she was concerned about whether, as close to trial as they now were, the court would allow her to withdraw. However, she would have to face that problem later. She had too many other issues on her mind to think about that now.

McKay arrived alone at 7:30. She went through his statement with him and to some extent, revised the wording. It was short and sweet, and she had no doubt it would be delivered from the heart when it was time. He again reiterated, for the twentieth time, that he would have a problem if he was sent to prison. And for the twentieth time, Rosa acknowledged the issue and told him they would just have to let the chips fall and go from there. She had not discussed an appeal yet. To be perfectly honest, it did not appear to her there were grounds for appeal. Judge Jackson's rulings may have been borderline, but it did not appear to her they resulted in sufficient error to justify overturning the verdict and ordering a new trial.

They left for the courthouse shortly before 9:30. When they

walked into the courtroom, Frankie was waiting. Stony was near the back and Thompson had taken up his customary seat behind Frankie and the prosecutor's table. Thompson appeared surprisingly calm.

As she set her paperwork down on the defense table, Frankie said, "Rosa this is my last day on the job. I'm retiring. I just want you to know it's been a pleasure working with you."

"Frankie, I didn't know you were quitting. Well, it's also been a pleasure for me. Good luck in your retirement. Enjoy."

He simply nodded. She had often wondered if he had dementia or Alzheimer's. Perhaps they would hire someone now that they could send to get two cups of coffee without first writing it down. Even this morning, he appeared in a fog. Good thing he was done.

Art arrived shortly after Rosa and took his seat, both of them waiting for the judge to enter the room and start the last act of this show.

They didn't have to wait long. Rosa figured the judge and Art were having coffee together, because not two minutes after Art arrived, the Judge walked in the courtroom.

"Everyone ready to proceed?"

Both attorneys nodded affirmatively.

"Mr. McKay, before we go any further I'm going to give you the opportunity to tell the court your thoughts on what your sentence should be and why. Do you have anything to say?"

Jake stood.

"Judge, I never intended for any of this to happen. It happened the way I testified. I didn't intentionally kill this woman. It was self-defense and her death was an accident. I've never been charged or convicted of anything in my life. I've lived a good life and stayed out of trouble. I don't think the verdict was fair. But that's over. I've been convicted and that is that. I've always had an issue with enclosed spaces. I don't think I could handle time in jail—any time. I would ask the court, because this is my first offense of any kind, to consider probation. I could handle that. And I can guarantee the court I would never ever violate the terms of probation. I haven't violated any of the pretrial release conditions and I wouldn't violate any probation conditions. I'm just asking the court to place me on probation. I promise I won't let you down."

He sat down and bowed his head. Heartfelt and humble. Just the way Rosa wanted it.

"Thank you Mr. McKay. Anything to add Rosa?"

Rosa stood and addressed the court.

"Not too much Your Honor. My client has been a model of consistency on pretrial release. He has never been in trouble with the law, as the court knows. I would suggest that he would not be the type of individual that should be sentenced to prison and would in fact be a great prospect for probation. Thank you."

"Thank you Rosa. What about you Art. Any thoughts?"

"Yes, Your Honor. The State feels without doubt, this man should be incarcerated. He murdered this woman. That may not be what he was convicted of, but that's what he did, no more no less. He should go to prison. The State feels there should be absolutely no leniency given here whatsoever. Many have gone to prison for much less. There is only one place for someone like him. He needs to be locked up for as long as the statute allows. Thank you, Your Honor."

"Ok, thank you. I have reviewed the file, listened to all the testimony, listened to all the comments and am ready to sentence the defendant. I'm at a small disadvantage in that I haven't been provided with a presentence investigation, but I think I know enough about the facts and the defendant to rule. Mr. McKay please stand."

McKay, Rosa and Art all stood at once.

"Based on all the evidence submitted in this case, including the information basically admitted on cross-examination concerning the defendant's past, the court truly believes society would be best served by incarceration. This was, in the court's opinion, a murder. You, sir, were not charged with murder, but you should have been. You ended this woman's life. Your history indicates you most likely were involved most of your life in violence and illegal activities. I can find no reason for one ounce of compassion or leniency in sentencing you. I commend you for following all the rules while on pretrial release, but that doesn't affect what your punishment should be for what you have done. It is the judgment and sentence of this court that you be sentenced to a term of not less than three and no more than six years in the Tennessee penal system. Your reception point will be Knoxville. You are entitled to appeal this judgment and sentence Mr. McKay. You have thirty days to perfect your appeal and if you have other questions in that respect, you can talk with your attorney. Any questions?"

Rosa looked at Art. He was grinning from ear to ear.

"The State has none. Thank you, Your Honor."

"Your Honor, might the defendant have a few days to get his affairs in order before he goes in?"

"I don't think that would be a good idea Rosa. In fact, Frankie, I want you to take the defendant into custody immediately please."

Rosa turned to look at Frankie. He was looking down. He hadn't heard a word the judge said.

"Frankie!"

Frankie looked up and stood.

"Yes, Your Honor?"

"I want you to take this man into custody. Get him ready to send off to prison. Do you understand?"

"Sure."

Rosa turned to look at her client and heard Frankie start toward them. But suddenly, there were sounds that weren't consistent with Frankie's movements. A scuffle. Rosa turned and all she could see was Thompson standing behind Frankie with his left arm and hand around Frankie's neck and his right hand removing his pistol from its holster. She stood up as did Art and the judge.

Once Thompson had removed the weapon from the holster, he slammed it against the back of Frankie's head. Frankie dropped to the floor, out like a light. He then immediately pointed the gun at Rosa and swiveled around to look at Stoney.

"You want her dead just move one muscle cop."

Chapter 49

He knew this would happen. He just fucking knew this would happen. He had a bad feeling they would convict. And then what? What was the plan then? He actually hadn't planned on the cops taking McKay straight from the courthouse. From everything McKay said, Rosa had told him she really felt they would release him for a time to put his affairs in order. He figured, if that was the case, both he and Jake could make their move then. But that fucking prosecutor and his judge friend made sure that didn't happen. So it was time to act. He needed to act now—before they took McKay and before this whole situation became uncontrollable.

He had been watching Frankie the cop since the trial started, if "cop" was what you could call him. He appeared to be somewhere else most of the time. Frankie definitely wasn't with it, which is what he was banking on when he got up and grabbed his weapon from behind. He caught everyone completely by surprise, which is exactly what he had planned. The cop never knew what hit him.

That left only the guy in the back as an unknown variable. He had seen his weapon. He knew he was a cop or private security. His profession was really not an issue. He was not an enemy—he was just in the way. Of those that were left—the prosecutor, the judge and Rosa—none of them would present a major issue. The court reporter had left the room once sentencing was pronounced.

"Want her dead?"

"Now just calm down. Can we talk…?"

"Simple question. Answer it now."

"No, no. I don't want her dead."

"Throw your weapon out on the floor along with your phone."

He turned to the judge.

"Get your ass down here and if you make a move to touch that hidden alarm, I'll shoot her and make sure you never make it out the door. Do you understand?"

The judge looked at him, frozen, unable to utter a word. But he raised his hands above his head and got up, walking slowly to the front of the bench.

Stony knew he had no choice. He threw his revolver and his phone out in the middle of the aisle separating both rows of seats in the courtroom.

Thompson turned to McKay.

"Go get his revolver and stomp on the phone until it's useless."

Jake looked at Tommie and said, "Good Lord Tommie, do you know what you're doing?"

"You wanna go to prison?"

"No, but..."

"Go get his weapon and make that phone into a piece of shit!"

Jake walked up the aisle and picked up the weapon. He then walked over to the phone and stomped it a couple of times with his heel, rendering it completely useless.

He looked at Stony and said, "I'm sorry. Really looked like a nice phone."

Stony replied, "Sure whatever. Thanks for nothing."

Jake walked back to where Thompson was standing.

Thompson looked at Rosa.

"Give me your phone."

He did the same thing to her phone that Jake had done to Stony's phone also rendering it completely useless.

The judge was standing in front of the bench. The look on his face made it clear he could not fathom what was happening.

Thompson said to Jake, who had worn a suit for sentencing, "Take off your suit jacket."

"Why Tommie, are you cold?"

"For Christ's sake Jake, take it off and give it to me!"

Jake complied.

Tommie wrapped it around the pistol so as to muffle the sound, looked quickly at the judge, and pulled the trigger twice. He was far enough away he was concerned he might miss him the first time he fired—and he did. But the second bullet found its mark and the judge fell to the floor.

He then turned his attention to Art.

"You know if you would have compromised and settled this case we wouldn't be here. You and your judge friend that you obviously had in your back pocket—if it hadn't been for the two of you, this would have ended long ago and no one would have been hurt."

'BBBut I waas juuust doing my jobbb. Ittt wasssnt personal Mr. TTTThompson. RRReally it wasn't."

The fear in Art's eyes said it all. He stood there, hands in the air, scared half to death.

Thomson never hesitated. He shot him twice in the head before Art could stammer out another word.

"That wasn't personal either. Just like you Art—just a matter of business."   Tommie was certain, as much blood as was lying on the floor, Frankie was already dead.

He looked back at Stony.

"Come on up here, Cop."

Rosa, who was crying, said, "Please don't hurt him. He hasn't done anything. He hasn't been involved in any of this."

"Sit down over there. Both of you."

Both Rosa and Stony sat in the front row of seats.

Thompson was standing beside Jake. There was a deathly silence in the room, which Thompson knew would soon change drastically.

"What do I do with them Jake? Your call. There are cameras everywhere, so it doesn't fucking matter whether these two can identify who did this or not. My picture will be everywhere without assistance from either of them. What do you want me to do with them?"

"Holy shit, Tommie, don't hurt either of them. They have done nothing to us. Rosa did what she thought was right. Don't hurt them. You have done enough already. Leave them alone."

Tommie thought for a moment.

"Ok...I'm not going to hurt either of you. You both stay the fuck here. Do *NOT* leave this room or I swear to God, you both will pay, along with your families. Jake likes you Rosa. And I'm going to leave you alone because of that. And I normally don't kill cops unless I absolutely have to. Consider this a lucky day for both of you. We're getting out of here. Don't follow us. Stay here until we are well gone, or I swear you'll both pay the price."

Both Rosa and Stony nodded affirmatively.

Jake and Tommie started backing their way out of the courtroom at an increasing speed. Thompson had Stony's weapon and had also picked up Frankie's pistol. He was waiving both around as he talked.

The whole incident hadn't taken but a matter of minutes. They quickly moved through the doors of the courtroom into the hallway. From there it was but a few feet to the elevator which, luckily, was waiting for them.

The elevator quickly found its way to the first floor where, as of yet, no one knew anything about the carnage on the second floor. Tommie had stuffed both revolvers inside his pants under his jacket, and there was no metal detector to worry about on the way out.

They moved quickly through the front doors and down the steps of the courthouse, neither saying a word. Thompson had parked his vehicle across the street and within seconds they were traveling toward South Nashville.

He had taken the more traveled of the available routes, and on this particular morning, it was packed with traffic in both directions. *NOT* what he wanted to see. He knew he had little time and this complicated the matter that much more.

But he also knew he had to get to his office—the old Pizza Hut building—and it had to be soon.

"Where are we going Tommie? You know we got to get out of here. We are in one hell of a lot of trouble. You even more than me now."

"Just shut up Jake and let me think. This traffic is unreal. I need to be in my office for about two minutes before we leave town."

What for? Don't you have everything already packed? I can't believe you're still packing your stuff. What the hell do we need to go back there for?"

"Got a loose end Jake. Got one loose end that absolutely must be cleaned up before we leave town. As soon as that's over, we're long gone. Just relax. I'll get this all cleaned up and I'll get us out of town, just like they sent me to do."

"Whose idea was this Tommie? Is this all your idea?"

"Just shut up Jake. Let me drive. There'll be plenty of time to discuss this once I get everything cleaned up. Just sit back and relax. I'll take care of it."

But it was clear, if he couldn't get through the traffic shortly, he would need to again adjust his plan. He was so close to cleaning up this job—if that idiot in front of him would only move a little faster. Maybe he needed to shoot him and move him out of the way—and then again maybe not. Just a little ways further…only a few more blocks and this would all finally be over.

Chapter 50

They sat alone in stone silence. Both waited and watched as Thompson and McKay left the room, each immersed in their own thoughts. Finally, a few seconds after both had left, Stony broke the silence.

"I'll check on the judge. Why don't you see if Art still has a pulse?"

Rosa wiped away the tears and nodded affirmatively.

Stony took no time in reaching the judge's side. He was unconscious, but alive. The bullet struck him on the right side of his torso, but did not appear life threatening. Stony turned him on his back and quickly realized there really wasn't much he could do. He needed an ambulance and an emergency room.

"How is Art?" Stony asked as he ran to her side.

Rosa stood as he approached.

"He's dead."

"I figured he was. He was shot at pointblank range and it was apparent Thompson wanted to make sure he killed him. I need to get out of here and find both of them. I think it's been long enough—they're probably out of the courthouse by now. Do you have their home addresses?"

"I think I have McKay's. I brought Thompson's file with me because I was going to tell him that tomorrow I would file a motion to withraw from further representation of him. He never has given me his home address."

An Absence of Ethics

She thought for a moment.

"But I think he has a building rented on the south side. And I do have that address. He told me he spent more time there than he did at his home."

"Get it out."

As they spoke, a cop slowly entered the room, pistol drawn.

"Hands up, don't move."

Stony quickly responded, "I'm a detective, officer. We had nothing to do with this. Two have been shot and the shooter took my revolver. You need to call an ambulance right away. That one is dead but the judge is still alive."

The officer just stared at them.

Finally he said "Stony? What the hell are you doing here? I know you. We met a while back on that Blackman murder case."

He lowered his pistol.

"What the hell happened here?"

"One of the defendant's friends shot the judge and Art. They are probably out of the courthouse by now. I need to find them before they get out of town. You need to stay here and secure the area. Give me your revolver."

He immediately handed over his weapon.

Stony looked at Rosa and said, "Do you have that address for his office"?"

"Yes."

"Give it to me. What about McKay's home address?"

"Yes. Do you want it?"

"The shooter appears to be in complete control of this situation. I have a feeling his office would be where they might head first. On the way down there, maybe we can call dispatch and send officers to McKay's home. I'm heading to the office building."

"I'm going with you."

"No fucking way. Now give me that address."

"Stony, I had a part in starting all this. I go or I tear this address into a million pieces. Your choice."

He just stared at her. Finally, he said, "Ok, let's go. Now, I mean this Rosa—*you stay out of the way*. Give me the address."

She handed it over.

"We're going to try to find the two that did this, Officer. Stay with these people at least until the ambulance crew gets here. As I said, the judge is still alive. Come on Rosa, let's go."

They ran from the courtroom and made their way to the elevator. It was still coming up and Stony had a pretty good idea who would be riding it up to their floor. He grabbed his badge and held it up as two officers jumped out of the elevator.

They glanced quickly at the badge and one of them said, "Is the courtroom secure?"

"I think so yes," Stony replied. "There's only one officer there. You might want to see if you can help him."

Both officers raced down the hall to the courtroom door and disappeared into the scene of the bloodbath.

Rosa and Stony got on the elevator and quickly reached the main floor. They both ran out the front door as Stony led the way to his vehicle.

As he started the engine he said, "Do you know where this place is? Do you know what the building looks like or exactly where it's at?"

"All I know is that it used to be a Pizza Hut building. The business moved to a new location, but I assume the outward appearance of the building still continues to look like a Pizza Hut."

"On south 12th, right?"

"Yes."

"I know right where it is. I don't think we'll take 12th down there. It's normally crazy this time of day. Let's go down 10th. That should be much quicker."

"You would know better than me. Whichever is fastest is obviously the way to go."

He turned his siren on. Cars and people scattered like ants. Traffic on 10th was no issue whatsoever. Stony turned his siren off a block before they arrived and parked across the street from the building.

"You stay here. I'm going in."

"I told you I was going and I didn't mean just for a car ride. I'm part of this. I was at least to some degree involved in this from the beginning. You aren't going in alone. Sorry. Now let's go."

"You can't go in there. I don't want to be responsible for you. Stay here."

"I'm going in with you. Now let's go!"

He realized, once again, he could not tell her no.

"You are the most bullheaded woman…"

She had left the vehicle and was walking across the street before he finished his sentence. Stony used the vehicle radio and hurriedly called dispatch asking them to send backup. Dispatch informed him most officers were on the way to the courthouse—that there had been a problem in the courtroom but she would send backup as quickly as she could.

He jumped out of the vehicle, caught up with Rosa, and led the way to the front door. They could see through the front window, but all was dark with the exception of a small light which was burning near the back of a large room. Stony tried the door. It was unlocked.

He opened it after drawing his pistol. She followed him through the door and both were swallowed up by the darkness.

They had walked about ten feet into the building and their eyes were starting to become accustomed to the lack of light when they heard someone say, "Drop the weapon on the floor in front of you and move forward."

Stony knew they could do nothing other than what he told them to do. He could vaguely make out a distant figure next to the darkened wall, but he couldn't take a chance on firing and missing. He had the drop on both of them.

Stony laid the pistol on the floor and they both moved forward into the somewhat lighter area approaching the desk. As they did, Gene Wakefield left the darkness and moved away from the wall far enough that Rosa could make out his features.

"Gene, what are you doing here? What the hell is going on?"

"Rosa you shouldn't have come here."

Even in the darkness and the distance between them, Stony could see Wakefield's hand shaking—the hand with the pistol—the pistol he had pointed directly at the two of them.

"I don't understand. Gene what are you doing here?"

"You made a huge mistake coming here—one of many you have made in the last few weeks—but this one, unfortunately, will cost you your life."

Chapter 51

Gene Wakefield had left his office before the sentencing of McKay. He needed to drive to Thompson's building and be there for their prearranged meeting. The traffic had been horrendous. He had to fight it all the way down 12th Street and had actually thought he might arrive late for the meeting.

When he arrived, the door was locked but he had a key. He walked in, proceeding straight to the back and, once there, turned on the small desk light while he waited. He had grabbed his pistol from the glove box hoping he wouldn't need it, but being realistic enough to know he might.

He waited in the darkness with only his thoughts to keep him company. This meeting had been set up by Thompson and was hopefully to be the end of his contact with him and that whole "Family." For some reason, a little voice in the back of his mind told him he was crazy if he truly thought this would end his involvement with them—that any thoughts along those lines were just optimistic craziness. He could only hope this was it—that it would all end today.

He didn't know which door Thompson would use. He had unlocked both the front and back and stood nervously awaiting his arrival. He really wasn't sure who was coming—whether Thompson would bring McKay with him or come alone. It didn't matter to him as long as he got paid.

He heard someone trying to enter the front door. That had to be Thompson. He stood in the darkness next to the wall, waiting for whoever it was to enter the room before he showed himself.

And then in walked Norway and that cop of hers. What the hell were they doing there? How did they find this place? This could blow this whole deal clean out of the water.

He slowly drew his pistol, and when they were well within the building and walking toward the back through the darkness, he walked out into the faint light given off by the desk lamp and confronted both of them.

The expression of shock registered plainly on both the faces of Wakefield's new guests.

Once the initial shock had worn off and both Stony and Rosa knew who stood in the darkness, Wakefield continued the conversation. "Cop, do you have a weapon?"

"Yes."

"Remove it slowly and slide it across the floor."

Stony removed the weapon from his shoulder holster and kicked it over to Wakefield, wondering how many times in one day he would lose his weapon. He was sure he had already set a record.

Wakefield now was visibly shaking as he held the pistol on both of them.

"What did the judge do to McKay?"

"Have you not heard what happened in the courtroom?" Rosa asked.

"No. I've been here. What do you mean?"

"Thompson grabbed Frankie's gun. He killed him, shot and killed Art, and wounded the Judge. He left with McKay. I knew about this building and we thought they might have come here. Stony was going to try and stop them before they got out of town."

"Oh my God. Art's dead?'

"Yes. Now, what are you doing here?"

He was clearly affected by the direction the conversation had taken. He took a few deep breaths before he spoke.

"Well, now that you are here and knowing neither of you will make it out of here alive, I suppose I can tell you a shortened version of the 'rest of the story.'"

He began before Rosa and Stony could say a word.

"McKay worked for the Family back in Jersey. He severed all contact with them about 10 years ago. They all kept an eye on him after he moved out here. And they all knew if he ever was arrested and had some type of jail term imposed, he would never be able to handle it. He had made that clear through the years. He could never handle any type of confined space. He would go crazy.

"So when he was arrested for manslaughter, the whole Family sat up and took notice. They all felt that if he were sentenced to jail, he would cut some kind of deal to avoid going. And they all felt that a 'deal' would probably involve a thorough discussion of the 'Family operation.' They just couldn't take a chance that would happen. McKay was well respected and a Family member, so they would take no action of any kind if he got off. But if he was convicted and sentenced to prison, they knew for their own preservation they would need to do whatever was necessary to stop that from happening and that's when they contacted me.

"The Family checked with some of their contacts here and determined Rosa should represent him. They felt you were up and coming and more than able to handle his defense. They told me to call him and tell him which attorney to contact and actually employed me to work for them, which I agreed to do. They also had me quietly contact Judge Hampton, since I had determined he was designated to handle McKay's case. I did that knowing his financial situation was a disaster. After some friendly persuading, he agreed to take a little money and make sure McKay got off."

"The judge was being bribed" Rosa asked quietly and in utter disbelief.

"Oh yes, and he was a very willing participant. He was really, really broke. And all went well until he crawled between your legs, you stupid bitch. Once that happened, it all went south quickly. He got saved—he became honest. He told us he was done. He was taking no more money. This all coincidentally happened once you two 'found' each other. Oh course, that would never work, so they had Thompson kill him."

Rosa gasped.

"And then there was the role you were to play. Time after time I asked you if McKay was going to get off and time after time you told me he was. Well, we all saw how that turned out. He was convicted in record time. Well done, Rosa, well done."

There was silence. Wakefield was shaking, clearly emotionally and physically distraught.

"And then there was that idiot girlfriend of yours who thought she was going to get involved in all of this. She was peering in the back window of this building when Thompson caught her. She wouldn't tell him anything and he finally killed her. Just another screw up in an overall plan that continues to go south."

"What now Wakefield?" Stony chimed in. "Are you going to complicate it all even further by killing us? Now come on. Does that really make sense? Let us go and let me do what I need to do to finish this all up. Neither of us will say anything about your involvement. Just let me do my job."

"Sorry, I can't do that cop," Wakefield replied. "I need what they are paying me. That's why I'm here. See, I have a few issues with the law firm's checking accounts. Nothing that you need to know about. Suffice it to say, when Thompson gets here, he is to pay me off and then it will all be over. You two aren't going to get in the way. I'm not going down the road the judge took. You can see where that got him."

"So what's the plan now Gene?" Rosa asked. "Obviously, this has turned into a complete fiasco,"

"I don't know, now that the circumstances have changed. I'll know as soon as they get here I guess. I know whatever the plan is, the two of you aren't part of it. You know Rosa, if you could have just kept your panties on a couple more weeks, none of this would have happened. You and you alone are to blame for all of these events. You can just take that to the grave with you."

"Now wait a minute Wakefield," Stony said. "Surely we can talk this through and all of us get out of here alive. Goddamn it Wakefield, can't we talk it out here. You are surely smart enough to know this is all going to end as badly as it has been going. No one is going to win."

Softly, Wakefield said "This conversation has gone on long enough."

He fired the pistol in the general direction of Stony, hitting him in the right side about mid torso. Stony immediately dropped to his knees and then to the floor. Before Rosa could even comprehend what was happening, he moved the barrel of the pistol in her direction and pulled the trigger. The bullet found its mark and she, too, dropped to the floor.

Even though he felt certain they were both dead or dying, he started walking toward both bodies lying silently on the floor when the backdoor opened and in walked Thompson and McKay.

"What the hell? What is going on in here? Did I just hear gunshots?" asked Thompson.

"Yes," Wakefield replied. "Norway and that cop friend of hers walked in the front door before you got here. They knew too much. So I killed them."

"Are they both dead?" Thompson asked.

"You killed Rosa? You son of a bitch, you killed Rosa?" McKay screamed.

"Yes, I did. They were in the way. I felt we needed to get rid of them. I felt it was our only option."

"Your time for determining what options we may or may not have is over. Thompson pulled his pistol and aimed it directly at Wakefield.

Chapter 52

That was the first time in his life that Wakefield had stared down the wrong end of a pistol. He dropped his weapon immediately and raised his hands above his head.

"Ok, you don't have to pay me. I'll just write it off. No problem here. No problem with me. Just write it off. I'm good with that and you never…"

"Shut up. You know, you have given us nothing but bad advice from day one. We obviously knew about your gambling problem and we knew you needed money, which is why we chose you. You were in a perfect position to handle all this for us. But, unfortunately, you screwed this up about as badly as you've screwed up the rest of your life."

"I did what you asked. I got you good people in the right places. Unfortunately I had no control over these people's sex drives. That was what created the problem. It was nothing I did or didn't do. Now, I'm willing to just move on, unpaid, and forget about this whole thing. Good luck and goodbye."

"Not that easy Wakefield. Just not that easy."

Thompson pulled the trigger twice in rapid succession. Both bullets hit their mark. The problems confronting Gene Wakefield ended once and for all on the floor in that abandoned Pizza Hut.

Thompson knew he needed to leave the building and the area as quickly as he could. He figured law enforcement couldn't be far away.

He turned to McKay and said, "Do you have anything at all in your home that would in any respect implicate me or the Family?"

"No. I brought nothing with me from that old life. I don't own a computer so there's no issue there. There is nothing in that house that would tie me to you or to the Family. Why?"

"Because when you are gone and they are going through that house we don't want to be tied in to you in any way other than what they have already found from years ago on the net, that's why."

"When you say gone, you mean with you right?"

Thompson again leveled his pistol, and again fired twice, dropping McKay to the floor.

"Nope. That's not what I meant at all."

Thompson rushed out the back door closing it behind him. He got in his vehicle which was parked in the alley and drove slowly into the street.

Once he reached the street he could hear sirens approaching the building but the further he drove the more distant the sirens sounded. He approached and entered Interstate 65 on the south side of Nashville heading south toward Birmingham.

As soon as he traveled a few miles and was outside the city limits of Nashville, he used his vehicle phone to make one, necessary, final call.

"It's done."

"It's done? The job is finished?"

"Yes. It's over."

"Is Jake ok?"

"Wakefield is dead. Jake is too."

"Jesus Christ did you have to kill Jake *TOO?*"

"Sorry. It had to be that way. Nothing else I could do. This had to be finished off and I did it the way I thought was best for the Family."

"So, are you out of there without any issues? Do they know you are involved?"

"They know. My picture will be plastered all over the place before long. I'm heading south on I-65 toward Birmingham and then New Orleans. They would have expected me to head east. So I figured I should be able to head south and hide out for a while. I'll stay with our Family there. The heat isn't going to die down quickly and I figure I'll probably need a face job and new ID before I leave there."

There was a long hesitation before a response.

"Do you know how to get paid from there?"

"Yes, I know how to access the account to collect what I'm owed, and I'll do that in the next couple of days."

Again, he waited for a response.

"Did Jake suffer?"

"No, he didn't. It was quick and painless."

"Did you have to kill him? Was it necessary Tommie?"

"Look, I told you I was sorry. I know he was your only son. But we've talked about that. You both gave up that relationship years ago. I'm sorry this all turned out the way it did but I didn't start any of this. You just asked me to finish it, and I did."

"I guess if that's the way it had to end, that's the way it had to end. Be careful. Don't get caught Tommie. You know I can't do much for you if you do. And, of course, you know what happens if you talk."

"I'll be careful. And I won't get caught. Now, I need to get off the phone and drive the car. Traffic is moving at around 80 and there's a lot of it. I'll touch base once I'm settled in New Orleans."

He hung up.

This job probably cost him his future with the family, and he was fine with that. He would retire. He was ready. He figured he could find a way to get to Italy. And there, he could lose himself in great wines, great food, and *NO* family. He had had about enough "family" for one lifetime.

Chapter 53

She had fallen off her pony when she was 10 and fractured her arm—hurt like hell. She had been in a car accident when she was 16—fractured her leg—hurt like hell. She had slammed the closet door shut on her fingers in a small fit of anger about a year ago—hurt like hell. But nothing she had *ever* experienced hurt like this.

The bullet felt red hot and tore its way through soft tissue on the left side of her torso. She had felt it pass all the way through and out her back. She wasn't unconscious, but she knew she needed to appear dead. This was far from over.

She was starting to bleed, and she could feel it was much more than a trickle. She could see Wakefield's outline in the dim light—he was starting to walk toward them. She could only assume it was to make sure they were dead, and if they weren't, he would make sure they were before he was done with them.

But, then she heard voices in the back of the building. She opened her eyes long enough to see Thompson and McKay walk in. She was able to see Wakefield turn around and start walking towards them. Then it all became one big blur of black and she felt nothing.

***

She was in the process of trying to wake up, caught somewhere between groggy and awake. She could feel someone else was with her, and she knew her hand was in someone else's hand. She finally opened her eyes and realized from the antiseptic smell and all that white that she was in a hospital. She was now starting to remember

An Absence of Ethics

and to focus. She turned her head and Stony was sitting in a wheel chair, by her bed, holding her hand. She looked at him with a vacant stare but said nothing.

"Just relax. You didn't have a very good night. You had nightmares all night. You even tried to get out of bed once and they had to hold you down. They said that was somewhat normal. After we went through what we both did, they said sometimes this happens. They've had you sedated and you've been in and out for a couple of days. Do you remember anything?"

"It's all a blur. I remember getting shot but not much else other than maybe waking up once in this hospital. How long have I been here?"

"Going on three days now. How do you feel?"

"Really not too bad. My side hurts, but other than that I feel pretty good. What all happened? Can you fill me in?"

"Sure. After Wakefield shot us, he was moving in our direction to make sure we were dead. But Thompson and McKay came in the back door so instead of finishing us off, he walked back to talk to them. If it hadn't been for them walking in the back door when they did, we would be dead. No doubt about it."

"So I suppose in some strange, roundabout way, we owe our lives to those two. Did you ever lose consciousness?"

"No. I was conscious right up until the cops walked in and the ambulance took us away. They gave me a shot for the pain when they put me in the ambulance and I passed out, but until then I was conscious. Damn glad I called for help before we walked in that building or you and I might have bled to death before they found us."

"How badly are you hurt?"

"Not bad at all. Like your wound, the bullet passed clear through. Good thing that idiot Wakefield was such a bad shot."

"Speaking of Wakefield, did he make it?"

"No, Thompson shot and killed both McKay and Wakefield."

"Oh no, not Jake. He killed Jake. Why?"

"No one seems to know. Apparently to keep him quiet about something, but no one knows for sure."

"So was there enough of a conversation between all of them for you to figure out what this was all about? Or did Thompson just shoot everyone without a word?"

"There was some additional conversation before Thompson

pulled the trigger. Yes Rosa, I heard it all. But fortunately, I was able to tell them what I *wanted* to tell them and leave the rest out. Your secret with the judge is forever safe. It wasn't a relevant factor when it came to the reason the judge was murdered. I'm not really sure what they are going to do about pursuing the whole mess until they find Thompson, though. In my short discussions with the officers, I think they really believe before they can move against the Family they need Thompson as their link."

She squeezed his hand as tears started to roll down her cheeks.

"Thank you."

"Hey. That's what friends are for right?"

"Sorry buddy, but I have a feeling we passed the friendship stage a long time ago. We can discuss that when I get out of here. Did you hear Wakefield's comments about killing Amy? Rotten bastards."

"Yes. And I also passed that on to law enforcement. Her investigation has now been closed."

"What about Art and the Judge? Did either of them make it?"

"Art didn't, but the Judge pulled through. He's going to be in the hospital for a time but he should be fine."

"Was Wakefield telling the truth about the law firm's bank accounts? He made it sound as if he had embezzled money from the firm."

"Yes. They've checked the accounts and he had taken more than a hundred grand. It's all been reported to law enforcement. Of course, his family was devastated. You know he had two kids ready for college? His wife has no idea what she is going to do. A real tragedy for so many people."

"What about Thompson?"

"The guy has completely disappeared. No one knows where he went. Of course, he had never given his personal address out to anyone that we could find. And there is nothing in the old Pizza Hut building that indicates where he was from or lived while he was here. They have law enforcement out looking for him all the way from here to New York, but they have seen nothing of him. And to be honest, I figure he may not be going east. As connected as he seemed to be, I imagine they will bury him somewhere in the Family either in the States or out of the country. I doubt we ever see him again. Of course, if it gets too hot, the Family will probably just bury him anyway, and by that, I mean literally."

An Absence of Ethics

"So this whole episode is really over?"

"Yes. It's really over."

She squeezed his hand—and didn't let go.

"How bad are your wounds—you're sitting up and in a wheelchair so they must feel you aren't too bad."

"No, I'm fine. I've walked around some but they wanted me in the chair when I came down the hall to be with you when you finally woke up. You're, at least physically, in pretty good shape too. We were both really, really lucky. They are talking about releasing both of us in a couple of days, assuming neither of us have any setbacks."

"That brings up an interesting thought. Release us to where? Or, at least me. Release me to go where? I have no doubt the firm is in a complete uproar over all this. And to be perfectly honest, I have no desire to go back, or for that matter, to be associated with a large firm again. I have a little money put away and a few contacts in the legal field. I think I may just end my association with the firm, go out on my own and set up my own practice. I really think I'm ready for that."

"It's funny you should mention the future. I've had time to think things through while I have been here to. The Captain told me, right before this case became so time consuming, that the budget cutbacks were really going to impact our jobs, and specifically mine. He told me my caseload would explode with new cases and he wanted to make sure I was ok with that. Now that I have had some peace and quiet and time to think on it, I guess I'm not. I've given a lot of thought to changing my profession and getting out of law enforcement altogether—maybe into private investigating."

Rosa thought for a moment.

"Really? What do you think about sharing office space? I have no doubt much of my practice will involve domestic disputes of some type. I always have a need for a private investigator. We could refer business to each other."

"Let me think about it. Do you think we could share both a business and personal relationship? I don't want to lose what appears to me to be a budding romance."

"We can sure as hell give it a shot. I'm willing to try if you are."

"Let me think it through and we can figure it out as we go."

He sat with her, held her hand, and talked the rest of the morning, all the while mulling over their potential partnership. He finally told her if they could get through what they had just been through, and could still hold hands, still remain close, they could probably get through anything. And she agreed.

Epilogue

SIX MONTHS LATER
Mt. Juliet, Tennessee

The day was cloudy and gloomy with just a hint of Tennessee mist in the air. Rosa looked through the windshield of her parked car and up at the sign over her doorway.

ROSA NORWAY
Attorney at Law

It was really simple, but it said all she wanted it to say and not one word more.

Below, a smaller sign and with smaller letters, read:

Stone Investigative Services

That too, was more than sufficient.

She had done it. She had quit the firm. She had walked in, dictated letters to all her clients telling them she was quitting the firm advising them that they would need to make new arraignments either with her, or with a different firm. And June followed her. June had been her secretary since Rosa joined the firm and she wasn't letting Rosa leave without her.

Shortly after she left the firm, Stony quit the force. They had both decided the pace of downtown Nashville was more than they were wanted. They had looked for and found a nice sized office building in the town of Mount Juliet, about twenty minutes from downtown Nashville. They signed the lease immediately.

The building had a large reception area and as one proceeded from the entry way through the office area, the first office on the right belonged to Rosa. Across the hallway in a smaller but adequate office, Stony set up shop and June handled clients for both of them.

Their relationship had blossomed and they were "involved." They did almost everything together, both within and outside the office. She had not yet moved in with him, but that was being discussed. She had still not quite come to the conclusion that this relationship, established out of a series of disastrous events, would last forever.

Time would tell. But for now, all was good for the first time in a long time. The issues involving Thompson had not died down. Wakefield's embezzlement had created extensive problems at the firm and many of the lawyers had walked out. She had just been the first. The problem surrounding the loss of Art in the prosecutor's office had lasted about a week. He was quickly replaced and just as quickly forgotten.

She was sorry for Jake. She felt once he had removed himself from the influence of his Family, he had turned into a good man, and she often thought of how wasted a life he had lived.

Business had been good for both Rosa and Stony. They were able to send each other clients on almost a daily basis. Both of them were touted as "very competent" and "knowledgeable" in their areas of expertise.

Today she had arrived late. She had taken care of some personal business, and it was after 10:00 before she walked in the office door. She knew she had no appointments until after the noon hour, so she used the time to her advantage and had just finished up all those little things that remain on your mind as needing to be done, but never quite receive the appropriate attention.

"Morning Rosa." June was taking a phone call while acknowledging her.

"Morning June."

"Stony is already in his office. You received a strange call earlier this morning. He wouldn't say his name but wanted to visit."

"Ok. Don't put him through if he calls again unless he gives you his name."

"No, I won't."

She walked slowly down the hallway and peaked around the doorway of Stony's office. Her wound had healed but still remained painful. She figured it would probably always remain—just a small lifetime reminder of a good reason to let her head and not her heart lead the way.

Stony, who was handling some paperwork, looked up and saw Rosa.

"Well, good morning. You are a little late today Miss Norway." He grinned that big, good-looking grin that had helped attract her to him in the first place.

"Morning to you, Mr. Stone. I had a few things to handle before I got here but…"

"Rosa, that guy's on the phone again. He says his last name is McKay and you are going to want to talk to him."

Rosa's stomach churned. She looked back at Stony.

"Did you hear what June just said? Someone by the name of McKay is on the phone for me. Coincidence?"

"Probably not. Go ahead and take it. I'll be right there."

Rosa walked in her office, turned on the lights, and sat down at her desk.

She slowly picked up the phone and said, "Hello."

"Rosa, my name is George McKay. I was a shirttail relative of Jake McKay. You surely still remember Jake don't you?"

"Yes, I do Mr. McKay. How can I help you?"

"Rosa, Rosa, Rosa. You let us down. We sent Jake to you and you got him killed. We were told you were the best. And we are told you are still the best. But Rosa, you just let us down. We sent poor old Jake to you and now he's dead."

"Regardless of who you say you are, I shouldn't even be discussing this with you. How do I know you are who you say you are?"

"Well, first of all, I am who I say I am. Of that you can be certain. Think about it. Who the hell would be calling you about Jake McKay with this type of information? Oh, yes Rosa, I am who I say I am."

Rosa hesitated for a moment before proceeding.

"Ok, I'm going to assume you knew or had some connection with

Jake. I can tell you, without breaching any issues of confidentiality, that wasn't all my fault. If he had told me everything, I might have been able to file a motion in limine, a motion prior to the start of the trial, and that would have kept all that history out of evidence. That was what convicted him. If he would have been up front with me, he would *NOT* have been convicted and none of this would have happened."

"Moving on, regardless of the intricacies of the practice of law, the end result here is what our Family looks at and it just didn't turn out as we had hoped. But, and this is why I am calling, we are going to give you another chance. We have a guy in Nashville that has been charged with murder. He likes women. He wants a woman attorney. He wants you to represent him."

Rosa laughed.

"As if! Not a chance. I am not going down that road again. The case cost my best friend her life and almost cost me mine too. That is just not happening Mr. McKay. Not now, not never."

Stony's face had long lost its color and he had shut the door, dropping down into one of the four chairs in front of Rosa's desk.

"You don't understand, Rosa. This isn't a request. I'm telling you that you *WILL* represent him. He needs help. He wants you. And this is a chance to redeem yourself. Not many people get a second chance with us. This is yours. His name is Rico Montego. He's in jail, but he is about to bond out. He'll set up an appointment. You will represent him and this time you *WILL* be successful. Now, please understand, this isn't a request. If you decide not to represent Mr. Montego, your life, the life of your associate, Mr. Stone and the lives of your family will be in extreme jeopardy, Rosa. And you can take that to the bank. You need to see him when he walks in your door. You'll be well paid. But you need to handle this. Not many people get a second chance with us. You have one. Put it to good use."

He hung up.

She looked up at Stony visibly shaken.

"What happened? Who was that?"

She hesitated.

"Rosa, who was that?"

"Stony, we have a small problem."

Made in the USA
Charleston, SC
12 July 2014